CAP

GOLD HOCKEY #16

ELISE FABER

CAP

BY ELISE FABER

Newsletter sign-up

This is a work of fiction. Names, places, characters, and events are fictitious in every regard. Any similarities to actual events and persons, living or dead, are purely coincidental. Any trademarks, service marks, product names, or named features are assumed to be the property of their respective owners, and are used only for reference. There is no implied endorsement if any of these terms are used. Except for review purposes, the reproduction of this book in whole or part, electronically or mechanically, constitutes a copyright violation.

GOLD HOCKEY SERIES

ONE

JESS

It was official.

The universe hated her.

That could be the only reason for this man to be seated next to her during a required training session.

Why he wasn't up with the players was beyond her.

Probably because he wanted to torment her.

"Can I borrow a pencil?" he whispered.

She glanced from her notebook—and yes, *two* pencils (because it never hurt to have a spare)—up to one Joshua Webb. He was watching her innocently, but she knew his type—too confident, too self-assured, too suave and a playboy and too goddamned attractive.

He also lived to push her buttons.

Case in point, plunking down next to her when their every interaction ended with an argument.

Distracting her when she needed to pay attention.

She was part of the coaching staff, liked to sit in on team meetings so that she could understand some of the on-ice coaches' strategies.

As a video coach, her job was to catalog video for the players and other coaches to review, to study, to use as a tool to improve. She wasn't advising the guys on their gameplay, but understanding the thought behind it meant that she was better able to anticipate clips to grab that would be helpful during and after the matchups.

Maybe it was overkill to be here.

But...she liked hockey.

Liked learning about it and understanding the team's dynamic. She liked the players—minus Josh and his apparent need to torment her.

"I didn't know that women did this job."

Yup.

He'd uttered those words.

To her.

Didn't know that *women* did her job.

Cute.

She gritted her teeth. Her blood pressure rising with just the memory of that statement and how it had brought her childhood right *fucking* back into the forefront of her mind. Had her hackles prickled? Fuck yeah. Had she responded in a slightly unprofessional way? Also, yeah (mostly because telling a person she worked with to fuck off—and not in a joking locker room way or on the ice kind of way—wasn't the most professional route she could have taken).

But...a woman doing her job?

The fucking misogynistic asshole.

Of course, a devil's advocate might point out that she hadn't seen any further misogyny. Nope. None. Not over the last—*cough* —three years. Which was...beside the point.

She was a Leo.

Which meant that she was a master freaking grudge holder.

He cleared his throat, and her head whipped back in his direction. "What?" she hissed as Calle, one of the team's assistant coaches, kept talking.

A big, calloused hand extended in her direction, palms up, fingers twitching. "The pencil?"

Did she notice the big, broad fingers? Yup.

Did she hate herself a bit for imaging what they might feel like inside her? Also, yup.

A breath that flared her nostrils, frustration filling her every cell. "Fine," she snapped, picking it up.

His hand twitched. "I'll take it without a side of stabbing."

And no lie, she'd thought about jabbing it into the fleshy skin of his palm. That would be so satisfying...for about ten seconds because—

One, she wasn't a fan of blood.

Two, she liked her job and didn't want to get fired.

Three, the thought of actually stabbing someone made her feel more than a bit queasy.

Four, he was a talented hockey player with good hands, and the team needed him if they were going to win the Cup this season.

In. *Out.* Release the frustration. In. *Out.* Focus on the positive.

Great, now she sounded like her sleeping app.

But just like it didn't do shit for helping her sleep, it didn't do fuck all to make that urge to stab him dwindle.

"Please, sweetcheeks."

She narrowed her eyes at him but didn't respond, just took another breath, held on to her temple (and stifled that urge to stab) then handed the pencil over.

Attempted to ignore him and focus on the screen, which in truth was displaying some hockey knowledge that was well above her pay grade *and* understanding. None of which was made easier by the man sitting beside her, his broad thigh coming close to hers, close enough that if she shifted, even the tiniest bit, their legs might touch.

And then she might spontaneously combust.

Because it had been too long.

Because Joshua Webb was *hot*.

Of course, he was also an asshole, albeit a hot one.

And smart on the ice. Talented. Overall, a great pickup by their GM. It had taken a bit for him to find his groove, but Jess knew—this from her limited *womanly* skills (*and* her well-tuned video coach ones)—that this was going to be his season.

He had the work ethic, the determination, and the chemistry with the guys to help the team go all the way.

His assholeness off the ice didn't affect his skill on it.

Unfortunately.

See? Petty, grudge holder for one thousand, thank her very much.

"Thank you," he murmured, sliding the pencil from her grip.

Those calloused fingers brushed along the inside of her wrist.

Just a brush.

A light touch of calloused fingertips over her skin.

But the effect...

Was overwhelming.

That single point of contact turned into a million, sparking through her, lighting her veins on fire, sending fireworks sparking through her nerves, pleasure jumping from cell to cell to *cell*.

Until it landed in her pussy.

And there were straight-up amusement park-grade fireworks in her...motherland.

Jerking her hand back—and it had to be said, squeezing her thighs together—she forced herself to focus on Calle.

On the chalk—PowerPoint—talk.

On her job.

But all she could focus on was the man sitting next to her.

And that was the problem.

Had been the problem.

From the moment they'd had that first argument.

Two

Josh

He leaned against the wall, watching the guys shooting the shit.

So fucking relaxed as they interacted with the fans at the preseason fundraiser for the team's charity, the Miner's Club.

He'd been in the league for enough years to have been to plenty of these events.

But part of him would never get used to it.

To people wanting his autograph, wanting to talk with him. He wasn't...*like* the other guys, wasn't flashy and didn't get stopped on the street to discuss the team's prospects. He did his job as well as he could and tried to contribute to the best of his abilities.

But he wasn't the player discussed on sports blogs or ESPN.

Didn't get selected for the All-Star game and hadn't even been discussed for the national team.

Which was fine.

He just...wished he could be one of *them*.

Brit with her wide smile and her comfort in her own skin,

badass goalie and only female in the league. She'd been selected for the national team three times and had even helped the guys bring home a bronze medal at the last winter games.

Blue, confident as fuck and always ready with a great quote.

None of Josh's own, "Um...we did some good things out there, but need to do better?"

What things?

Do better? Yeah, that was an obvious thing to say after a freaking loss (and probably why he hadn't been pulled after that for an interview for the remainder of last season).

Liam was quiet but always bonded with the kids, getting down on their level and winning over many a mom because he'd made their offspring smile.

Coop, outgoing and confident, the face of a cologne, a brand of jeans, *and* had filled in up in the broadcasting booth when he'd had an injury last season, and been so natural at the process that he already had offers lined up for when he retired.

Then there was Josh.

Quiet and awkward with kids that weren't his nieces and nephews. Not ready with one-liners for the media. Unsteady with the female fans who tied up their jerseys to reveal their stomachs and the men who were convinced that *their* idea for a play was definitely going to work.

Outside.

Looking in.

Better at observing than being.

The locker room was pretty much the one place where he didn't feel uncomfortable in his own skin. He knew how to deal with teasing, how to occasionally dish it back.

Maybe he still felt a bit removed from the guys—partly because in this third year of his contract, he was worried that he wasn't living up to the expectations management had for him, that it might mean a trade was in his future. But mostly it was because Coop and Logan and Liam and Brit and Blue and the others were *legends*.

The players he had looked up to for years.

Wanted to be like when he grew up.

And...just never quite feeling like he was measuring up.

"Hi."

He blinked, gripped his wine glass a little tighter (this event was at a local winery that was donating a big chunk of money to the foundation—which Josh respected, even if he wasn't a huge fan of the overrated grape juice), and glanced down at the woman in front of him.

Her hair was...poofy. That was the only way he could think to describe it. Frizzy brown curls encircling her head, made even crazier by a sparkling gold headband. Her smile was a little goofy. But her eyes...they mirrored what was in his mind so totally that his heart actually skipped a beat.

Uncomfortable. Nervous. Self-conscious. An outsider looking in through a thick plane of glass.

"Hey," he said gently. "I'm Josh."

"I...um...Christina."

Extending a hand, he said, "Nice to meet you."

And silence.

Two anxious people coming together and staring at each other.

Right. He'd done this before, so he needed to make it easier. "What brings you to the event tonight?"

Her head jerked to the side, indicating a burly man with a gray bushy beard who was talking gregariously with Brit. "My dad owns the winery."

"Ah. And he seems...like he got the talkative gene."

A grin, and he watched her relax. "It definitely skipped a generation."

He grinned back. "I know the feeling."

His siblings were outgoing, confident, and he...

Was Josh.

"I really just wanted to say that I like you."

The blurt jerked him to laser focus, watching as her cheeks flared.

"I—*shit*—" She sputtered. "I mean, I like the way I play." Embarrassment in brown eyes, mouth forming an O for a brief moment. "Shit—no—you—" She sighed, shoulders slumping. "I'm really bad at this. I like the way *you* play."

He reached to the side, snagged one of the glasses of wine, and handed it to her. "Pro tip for the nerves," he said, closing her fingers around the stem. "Even if you don't drink, it's nice to have something to do with your hands when you're nervous."

Wide eyes on his. "*You* get nervous?"

He laughed. "Are you kidding? These kinds of events can make the steeliest man quiver with fear."

She giggled. "I can't imagine you quivering."

"Yeah?" His lips twitched. "Well, I definitely quiver before a puck drops. I've got some big shoes to fill here. The Gold are a legacy and I..." He trailed off with a shrug. He wasn't *that*.

"You seem like you've fit in, especially toward the end of last season." She smiled, and it was wide and a little goofy. "Which is what I *meant* to say. I really like the way you've been playing."

"Do you play?"

Pink cheeks again. "Just a little bit in a rec league. I had so much fun watching you guys that I wanted to try it."

"That's really cool," he said and meant it.

"Thanks," she whispered. "And thanks for the pro tip." She smiled again, but there was teasing in her tone now. "Though, considering that my dad owns the winery"—she held up her glass, pointed at the logo etched on the front—"I definitely drink wine."

She was funny when she wasn't nervous.

"So you've got one up on me." He pointed to his untouched glass. "I'm not a fan. Though, I probably shouldn't say that to the daughter of the man who owns the place and who's donated a lot of money for the night."

Her smile was soft, with just a hint of goofy, and he had the distinct thought that she would be beautiful in a couple of years. Young now, but she would totally be drop-dead gorgeous in the future.

"Or maybe I should bribe you into coaching my team," she said lightly, her eyes sparkling with humor.

And mercenary.

The young guys better watch out.

He leaned back against the column, lifted his glass in a toast. "So, you've gone from nervous to blackmail."

She giggled. "I just took your pro tip to heart."

"Well, cheers to that." He lifted his glass, tapped hers. "And, schedule depending, I'd be down to come help out a little...not that I have much coaching experience."

"Really?"

"Yeah, of course," he said, and pulled out his phone. They made quick work of exchanging numbers and then talked a bit more about hockey and the team's prospects. But by the time they really got into a rhythm and he found out that she was in college studying kinesiology with the intent of being a sports therapist, a couple of fans had come up wanting to talk, so he said goodbye and promised to call.

Right as Jess walked by.

Her head jerked, eyes hitting his, filling with disdain.

Fuck, she was pretty, even when she was pissed at him.

Which was...all the time.

Because the first thing he'd said to her had pretty much been him firmly inserting his foot into his mouth.

She lifted an eyebrow, shook her head slightly, and then kept walking, and fuck if he didn't want to go after her, tell her that he wasn't hitting on a woman who was way too young for him, that the *only* woman he wanted was the one throwing shade at him, the one who was perpetually pissed off at him, the one who fought with him every second, the one he fucking dreamt about and—

A breath.

There were fans in front of him.

People looking at him, expecting him to be like the rest of the team, to schmooze and make the donors who'd paid several hundred dollars for a ticket happy.

He had a job to do.

He couldn't worry about what he wanted.

Who he wanted.

THREE

JESS

She glugged down the remainder of her glass of wine—the only one she'd allowed herself that evening because she was the designated driver—and went to find Dani and Ethan.

Dani because her friend had asked for moral support and Jess didn't mind putting on a show, not when it was for the team.

Ethan, because he was one of the Gold's key players and it was necessary for him to be here to make this fundraiser a success (this had come straight from Scarlett, their current lead publicist's mouth). And considering that Scarlett was married to Kayden, another Gold player, the optional event wasn't very optional.

Not that anyone minded.

This was for the kids.

And it was a universal fact for the Gold organization that kids came first.

Bar none.

Simple as that.

And yet, so freaking *not* simple because that often had Jess feeling like she was living in a fantasy world. Kids coming first?

Not in *her* lifetime. She hadn't believed it was anything more than a publicity stunt for a long time when she'd come to the team. But now? After years of seeing the Gold organization and its players volunteering and raising money and taking time out of their day to make kids' lives better?

Jess believed the hype.

It was a big reason why she'd stuck around, why she was so invested in the team and all they did.

The Gold were her family.

More than her own biological parents and siblings had ever been.

She'd work her ass off for them, jump in with babysitting, bring properly healthy meal-plan-abiding food to sick players in her off time, come to charity events like this even though no one wanted to meet her and she mainly ended up being a glorified waitress and taxi driver.

Because they would do the same.

Had done the same.

Brit had brought her chicken soup (and some bread that was definitely not on Nutritionist Rebecca's meal plan—though thankfully, Jess wasn't a player and could snarf any and all junk food she wanted) last time she was sick.

Dani had included her for all the holidays, even though she and Ethan were busy building their own life.

Mandy, the head trainer for the team, had sleuthed Jess's favorite cake and there was always a cupcake and small gift on her desk when her birthday rolled around, no matter how busy the season was.

She'd been to numerous family and team barbeques, pre and post and on-holiday celebrations. Invited to vacations during the summer, had stayed with teammates' parents in Canada and Finland and Germany in the off-season.

One of them, even though her contribution was small.

Belonging when they had no obligation to make her feel that way.

So, suffice to say, she'd launch herself off the Golden Gate if it meant that she was putting the organization at risk.

Which was why she hadn't stabbed Josh the other day or run him over with her truck or just casually *tapped* him with her bike. Even though it was very tempting.

The man brought out the devil in her.

That was the only way she could think to describe it.

Every time she thought she was done being annoyed with what was clearly him misspeaking, he managed to piss her off again.

She glared at him as the girl who looked like he'd hung the moon, squeezed his arm and moved away, another fan coming up to take her place. Josh was animated, presumably charming, based on the laughter and smiles surrounding him.

And yet, a total devil around her.

His gaze slid off the man who was chattering, hit hers, and he winked.

The man *winked.*

Sighing, she deliberately turned away, muttered under her breath, "Get it together, Jess."

"You've got that look, Jess, honey."

Dani.

Calling *her* honey. Before Ethan, that would have never happened. Dani was one of her best friends, but that didn't change the fact that she was cripplingly shy—or *had* been, anyway. Her comfort with interpersonal relationships had grown over the years, not that Jess thought her friend needed to change any part of her—shy, outgoing, or in between.

She was just glad that Dani was happy.

And being called *honey* wasn't too bad either.

Jess...well, she hadn't had a childhood full of puppies and rainbows. Affection had been limited. Abuse...

Present.

It had been present.

Right.

But that wasn't something she was going to think about in this moment, at a fundraiser for kids who would hopefully have something better than she did.

"What look?" she asked innocently.

"The one that says you want to carve Josh into teeny tiny pieces with his skates," Dani said, her lips twitching.

Maybe.

But, alas, Josh was a good player and the team needed him.

She smiled at Dani. "I would never do that to Richie"—the equipment manager—"he's got enough to do."

Dani hid her grin behind her glass of wine. "Got enough to do without cleaning blood off of skates?"

A tap to the tip of her nose. "Ding. Ding. Ding. Give the woman a prize."

Dani took a sip, then tilted her head to the side, studying Jess. "You okay? Like really okay?"

"I am perfectly fine."

Fine.

Fuck. In. Noggin'. Everyday.

That was what *fine* meant in Jess's universe, but that was also a meaning she kept to herself, one that she was really good at keeping to herself. Though, based on the way that Dani's eyes narrowed slightly, Jess thought that her keeping her thoughts to herself days might be limited.

"Hmm."

Brit was walking by, so Jess grabbed her opportunity. Keeping to herself meet distraction meet not having to divulge that her mind kept running against a date. Memories.

A decade since—

"Brit!" she called.

The tall, blond woman halted, came over to their huddle. "Oh, thank God. I know I'm an extrovert, but I need a moment's break from Scar's special brand of small talk."

"How's the baby?"

Brit—tough, badass goalie—melted. "Roxie is *amazing.*" She

and the former captain of the Gold, Stefan Barie, had adopted a little girl not long before. "Growing too fast and acting less like a baby every day." Brit pretended to swipe a tear away. "I can't stand it. Everyone says it goes fast, but it really does. Hell, just the other day, Stefan was talking about putting skates on her."

"She'll probably take to it like a duck to water," Jess said. "God knows all the other Gold kids are great on the ice."

"*Terrors* on the ice, you mean," Brit teased.

Laughter in her throat. "Well, I don't even know how to skate," she said. "So I'd be down for learning how to Bambi on the ice, let alone become a terror."

Brit stopped, set her glass down. "Tell me you're kidding."

"What?" Jess asked, brows drawing together.

"Please don't tell me that you've been with the team for as long as you have and no one has taught you to skate yet."

"Well..." Jess looked around for an exit. "I kind of lied and said I knew how to."

"And then volunteered to size all the kids or family anytime an event called for actual skating so you could avoid admitting it," Dani said sweetly.

See?

Her friend paid attention.

Too much so.

She wrinkled her nose. "Well, no one likes a tattletale."

Dani giggled. "Is that any way to talk to your boss?"

"When your boss outs your skating ability"—a firm nod at Dani before her gaze went back to Brit—"yup, it certainly is."

Brit flashed a grin and pulled out her phone. "Well, luckily for you, you have a team full of good skaters, all of whom can teach you the basics."

"And leave me with a bruised ass," Jess muttered.

"Nah," Brit teased. "I'm good at saving damsels in distress. I wouldn't let you fall." A beat. "Not much anyway."

"Gee, thanks."

Brit flashed a grin then held out her hand. "Phone, please."

"What?"

Dani snagged her cell from her dress pocket, passed it over to Brit, who held it up to Jess's face and swiped, unlocking the screen. "What are you doing?" Jess asked.

"Plugging myself into your calendar." She turned the cell back to herself, pulled her own phone out and set both on the high-top table next to them, apparently comparing schedules. "Ah, there," she said, tapping some more. "Saturday at seven, scheduled in both of our phones. I'll secure the ice time and the skates, you get your butt to the rink bright and early."

Brit tossed her phone back and Jess scrambled to catch it. "Wait, what. No. I—"

"Oh, look," Brit said. "Scar wants me." A finger wave. "I'll see you Saturday."

Then she was wind in the air, weaving her way through the tables, joining Scar and her group.

Jess blinked, turned to Dani. "Did I just end up with a skating lesson from Brit Plantain?"

"You say lesson, I say torture session," Dani quipped.

Another blink. Then a glare in her friend's direction. "I blame you in advance for my bruised ass."

Dani tried to bite back her smile.

Failed.

"Well, at least you'll learn how to skate?" she said innocently.

"No more Hot Tamales," Jess muttered.

A gasp. "Such cruelty."

Jess sighed, but already her amusement was winning out. "Brit Freaking Plantain."

Dani giggled. "You should probably be thrilled that Mandy wasn't involved. Otherwise, you'd end up with sparkles, a skating outfit, and performing a whole routine at Fanny's next competition."

Her fat ass in Lycra and sparkles, stumbling through a routine to Tchaikovsky.

She shuddered.

Then joined Dani in her giggles. "So, you're saying that I should thank you?"

A beatific smile. "Damn straight."

A laugh. A sigh. A shake of her head. And then...love for her friend, for this team, for her makeshift family. "Come on," Jess said, looping her arm through her friend's. "If my bruised ass is on the line, this DD needs another glass of wine."

Jess plunked her head on Dani's shoulder. "Well, the good news for your bruised ass is that I haven't started drinking tonight, so I'll take on DD responsibilities *and* get you another glass of wine."

"So much kindness for my bruised ass."

A pat to Jess's butt that had her busting up. "Well, someone has to look out for it." A beat. "It's a capable ass."

More laughter, so much that it nearly stole her breath. "Capable?"

Dani nodded, her own giggles joining Jess's. "Yup. Capable." She nodded to Ethan. "Now, you're going to march that capable ass over to the bar, get yourself a glass of whatever wine you want, and then you're going to enjoy your night."

"Because my doom is coming on Saturday?"

"Nope." Another squeeze. "Because you deserve to have a good night, honey." A penetrating look. "Even if you won't tell me exactly what's wrong."

"I'm—"

A nudge. "Wine. Jess."

Before she could add that she was fine, Dani had headed back to her man.

Leaving Jess alone.

But with a full heart.

Which was enough. Because it was more than she could have ever hoped for.

FOUR

JOSH

His phone rang just as he was rolling out of bed early on Saturday morning. He was dragging his ass out for a run, knowing that he needed to be ready for the upcoming season.

Top shape.

Top effort.

Making sure to pull his weight.

To step up, fill those shoes.

He hadn't been able to do that with his family, having gone away to play on the road for half the year. When his mom fell and broke her collarbone while their dad was traveling for work, it was his younger brother who'd taken her to the hospital, his sister who'd flown out to Michigan—two young kids in tow—to help her convalesce. Because he'd been in the middle of the playoffs.

Because hockey had taken priority.

Like it typically did.

They'd never resented him for his dream, but he'd felt guilty anyway.

He was the other brother. He should be there to step in, to pick up the slack. To pull his weight.

Instead, he'd moved away, strained the family's finances with ice time and equipment and player fees and travel costs, and he'd missed holidays and his siblings' sporting events (though they'd made an effort to come to his big ones). But in all of his living and breathing for the sport, trying to make it into the league, he'd missed a lot. He hadn't been to the school plays and state soccer tournaments, hadn't seen the art exhibitions or taken prom photos. Graduations were hit or miss, depending on how the season went. Weddings had to be scheduled for the off-season if they wanted him to attend. Babies being born happened on their own schedule, and often that schedule didn't coincide with his.

He'd lived for the sport.

He'd gotten his dream.

But he worried about all his family had sacrificed to get him here.

Did they resent the money spent, the time away, the absences and missed events? Or maybe he wasn't even part of the nuclear family any longer.

Maybe they didn't miss him.

Because he'd had one foot in the family and one foot out for so long that he didn't actually belong.

Like with the team.

His contract being up soon.

Not sure quite where he belonged. He hadn't been around long enough to be part of the backbone, but he wasn't new either, wasn't a rookie.

He was just...Josh.

His phone rang again, and he shot out a hand, snagging it from the charger. It was probably his brother, since he lived on the opposite coast and was a couple of hours ahead, though it could just as easily be his sister, who lived up in Oregon and was in the same time zone, because her two boys were energy personified and if they slept till seven that was a miracle.

"Hello," he said, swiping across the screen and lifting it to his ear before the call went to voicemail.

"Josh."

He frowned at the sound of Brit's voice coming through the speaker. "Brit?"

"The one and only," she teased. Then chuckled, sounding far too awake for this early in the morning. "And God, that was cheesy."

He waited.

But she didn't say anything else.

So, he didn't comment on the cheesiness of that statement, only asked, "Did you need something?"

Which was a stupid question, considering that this probably wasn't a social call.

"Yeah, actually," she said. "Roxie is sick, and I was supposed to give a beginning skating lesson to a friend at seven this morning. But Stefan was up with her all night and he's wiped and I think he's coming down with the bug himself. I don't want to wake him up to watch her when he's exhausted and not feeling well, so I was wondering if you could give my friend a quick lesson. She's a total beginner and just needs to learn some basics."

"Sure, no problem, but—"

"Oh, awesome. Richie left some skates by the door out to the ice and is going to get her inside."

"Right. Okay, I—"

Rustling in the background, followed by a wail that he knew based on his nieces and nephews meant that a full-blown meltdown was coming. "Shoot. Sorry. I need to grab her. You sure you're good with this?"

"I'm fine," he said quickly. "Just take care of your family."

"Thanks, Joshie. I owe you—" The volume of the wail increased. "*One,*" she said over the noise.

A quick goodbye.

The phone clicked off.

Josh rubbed a hand over his face, the stubble from his beard rubbing against his palm. But, when he looked at the clock, he knew he didn't have time to shave.

He needed to get to the rink.

———

A cup of coffee had gone a long way toward waking him up, but as he walked into the practice facility and felt the cold air on his cheeks, he knew that he wouldn't really need it.

This was...home.

The way his skin prickled in the cool rink atmosphere.

The smell of the ice. The way the glass always fogged on cold mornings, shrouding the rink, making it seem like it was in its own world when he skated on it. He saw Richie and waved, the other man calling, "She's laced up and on the ice." He pointed to the bench by the door. "Your skates are there."

"Thanks, man," he called back, making short work of walking to the bench and shoving his feet into his skates.

Laces snug but not tight over the tops of his feet (too tight would cause skate bite, a condition that was uncomfortable, but not dangerous, sending pain from shin to the tops of the feet). He pulled the laces tighter around his ankles, tying the bow off as securely as he could.

Ankle strength and security were key.

Then he walked to the rink, climbed the steps to the door, opened it and stepped onto the ice.

Then...nearly ate shit.

Jess was there.

Looking cute as fuck in a Gold beanie, the black pom-pom dancing on the top of her head as she attempted to skate—or at least, that was what he thought the odd waddle-walk she was doing resembled.

Leggings encased her from ankle to thigh, lovingly cupped an ass he'd admired more than once (*cough,* more times than he could count, truthfully) that he got a nice glimpse of when she jerked on her skates and nearly fell, bending at the waist to save herself.

"I thought you were going to rescue this damsel," she called, righting herself and starting to turn toward him. "You promised my ass wouldn't get bru...*ah*...ised." More waddling, more jerking, and bending.

Then she glanced up.

Saw him.

Her eyes went wide, and she jerked again, but this time in a way that no amount of bending was going to save her.

He moved, digging his edges into the surface, shooting himself across the ice, closing the distance between them... catching her against his body before she went down.

Her lips parted, breath sliding out shakily.

A moment later, her chin came up, and she yanked against his hold.

"Easy, sweetcheeks," he murmured, running his hand down and up her back, keeping her against him. "We don't want that ass to get bruised."

Her mouth slammed shut. "What the fuck are you doing here?" she snapped.

"Roxie is sick," he said. "She didn't want to leave you hanging." And also, now that he was awake and here and really thinking about it, Brit probably had an ulterior motive—namely matchmaking. Which meant that his interest in Jess was probably widely known on the gossip train.

Great.

Though, he supposed he shouldn't be surprised.

It wasn't like he and Jess fought in private.

They bickered in public, and the guys—and Brit—were as nosy as old ladies.

Jess snorted. "Yeah. Right. Roxie might really be sick, but I guarantee that she wasn't planning on coming."

"No?"

"She strong-armed me into this lesson at the wine event."

"Oh?" He'd kept his hand moving up and down her spine, up and down, taking advantage of her allowing him to touch her, getting his fill, knowing it wouldn't last long.

And he wasn't wrong.

Because her eyes narrowed. "You know?" she pressed. "The event where you exchanged numbers with a woman who was practically a *child*."

She flexed against his hold, and he dropped his arms slowly, making sure she was steady.

"I did get a number that night."

A disgusted snort.

"And it wasn't from a child, though Christina is only a sophomore in college."

More disgust.

"Where are you going on your date? Chuck E. Cheese?"

"I do have a fondness for winning tickets." He pushed back a strand of her hair, tucking it behind her ear. "Reminds me of our free time between games at hockey tournaments. We'd always try to find an arcade. For the record, I kick ass at Skee-Ball."

"Wow. I'm so impressed."

He pretended to buff his knuckles on his shoulder. "You should be. I think I still have the top score in my hometown."

Sighing, she shook her head. "I'm going to go."

"Wait." He moved, skating next to her as she did some wobble-walking toward the door.

"Yeah, no. Not happening."

"Christina isn't a child, but she's a young girl." A snort. "But not one I'm interested in. She's the daughter of the man who owns the vineyard and she asked if I could come to coach a game or two for her team in her rec hockey league."

"I don't want to hear—" She stopped, spinning slowly toward him, brows forming a deep V. "Wait. You're going to *coach* rec hockey?"

"Stupid, huh?" He shrugged, gaze drifting down. "I don't even know why I agreed. I don't know the first thing about coaching, especially about coaching young women who are playing for fun. I should probably text her back and say I can't do it, or maybe I can see if Calle has the time to make an appearance."

Silence.

He cleared his throat. "Right. Yeah. Calle is probably busy. I bet Liam would be game. He helps his wife with all those karate classes. He's got experience teaching and would be a better choice."

More silence.

"Or, I guess, Brit owes me for coming, and she's so well-known that they would probably get a kick out of her going..."

"No."

He cleared his throat, glanced up at Jess. "Yeah. You're right. I promised. I need to follow through on that." Something flashed through her eyes, but he just cleared his throat. "Okay, right, so I know this morning hasn't worked out like you expected and I might not be much of a coach, but I think I can manage some basics." He shoved his hands in his pockets. "So, that being said, you're here. I'm here. Do you really want to learn how to skate?"

She leaned back, nostrils flaring as she sucked in a breath.

And nearly toppled ass over tea kettle—because, this just in, weight on the heels of hockey skate blades and a beginner skater didn't mix well.

He caught her again, wrapping his arms tightly around her, steadying her.

And fuck if she didn't feel right against him.

Her head tilted back, lips parting.

And *fuck* if he didn't want to kiss her.

But they'd gone thirty seconds without fighting. He wasn't going to fuck that up.

Thankfully, for once, Jess seemed to be on the same page as him.

"Okay," she whispered.

Why did that make him feel like he could fucking *fly?*

His brain made no sense.

And anyway, he ignored it, got his shit together, and set about teaching this woman who hated him to not end up with a bruised ass.

FIVE

"Yes!" he exclaimed, as she managed to not eat shit as she slowly made her way around the edge of the rink.

He.

Josh.

Her archnemesis.

The yummy man who she wanted to throttle and kiss in equal measure.

And after today, the kiss quotient was slowly ramping up. Gorgeous and sexy, totally kissable before, but also a total devil who made her want to resort to skate slicing and pencil stabbing.

Except, today...

He wasn't stabbable.

He was actually likable.

Coaching rec hockey and nervous about it, thinking that he, as a professional player, wasn't qualified, even as he gave her a skating lesson that could have rivaled the ones that Fanny—the Gold's skating coach—put on.

She'd gone from Bambi to...someone who wasn't in imminent danger of ass bruising in less than ten minutes, and now a half hour later, was skating without him hovering and prepared to break her fall.

By catching her against his heavily muscled body.

Making her forget she hated him.

Danger. Danger.

She kept careful distance between herself and any of the single Gold players because she didn't mix work and pleasure, couldn't risk a relationship with someone where it might turn serious, or where it might create conflict in her one happy place when it ended.

Because she didn't think she could ever open herself up to another relationship, wouldn't fully be able to trust a man.

Not ever again.

And those broken pieces in her, the shards that had been left behind, they couldn't be mended.

Not by a gorgeous hockey player. Not by *anyone*.

She'd fuck it up, break it, break *him*.

And she couldn't risk bringing that ruination into her life, the consequences that it would bring her with her family.

The Gold were all she had.

It was as simple as that.

But maybe, she thought as he whooped on her second loop around, maybe she could hate him a little less.

———

Come Monday morning, Jess walked in to find Brit standing outside the video suite, a shit-eating grin on her face.

"Come to see how your matchmaking went?" Jess asked dryly.

Brit attempted innocence. "Matchmaking? Me?"

Considering Jess had enjoyed playing matchmaker plenty (so long as it didn't involve herself), she didn't buy the innocent act. Not one bit. "Yes," Jess said. "Matchmaking. *You.*"

A sniff. "Roxie was sick. Josh happened to answer the call."

"And how many people did you call before him?"

"That is beside the point."

"Exactly," she muttered. "*None.*"

"Josh is a good guy."

Jess knew that.

"I know that he didn't start off on the best foot with you, and that you guys fight," Brit began. "But don't you think that you two holding your own with each other is a good thing? And he's owned his fuck up, tried to make it right."

Jess knew that, too.

It was just easier and safer to hold on to her grudge.

"Plus, he taught you how to skate."

Jess fixed her friend with a glare. "Really?"

"Well he did, didn't he?"

She took a page out of Brit's book. "That's beside the point."

A flash of a grin. "Touché."

"Is the ass safe?"

Jess smiled despite herself. "It's safe."

Another grin. "Good."

"But no more matchmaking, okay?"

"Okay."

Too quick of an agreement with too innocent of an expression on her friend's face.

"I mean it, Brit. I...can't do anything serious, and," she added quickly when she watched the protest well up on Brit's face. "you know if it involves anyone on the team, it's going to be immediately serious. You guys breed happy endings like rabbits around here. I don't want to be the one to break the streak—"

"You won't—"

"Brit," she whispered. "Please." She held her friend's eyes, shook her head once, firmly. "I can't."

"Okay."

"Thank you."

"You know—" Brit's voice gentled. "If you ever need to talk about it, I'm—"

"I know," Jess said quickly. She couldn't take the soft tone, couldn't allow it to fill in those cracks inside her, to soften her barriers. They were already weak, what with the anniversary coming up, with the memories closing in. "I'm okay. It was..." A breath. "It was all a long time ago, and I just want to move on."

Brit nodded, lightly squeezing her shoulder. "I get it, babe. Trust me, I do." And considering Brit had both been sexually assaulted and blackmailed about it in a scandal that had eventually come out very publicly, Jess knew she did.

"I know," she said again.

"So, I'll go, but...I have to say this first." Another squeeze. "We get to be professionals at burying our trauma, get to be so damned good at it that we think it's shoved down so deeply that it won't ever come out. Whether we do that because it's too painful to think about, too hard to remember, or because it fills us with so much shame that it seems like it's going to drown us from the inside out, the reason doesn't change the truth." She dropped her hand, cupped Jess's cheek. "And that truth is like a fucking splinter under the surface of the skin, painfully inching its way to the surface, those buried memories *always* come out." She let go. "The only choice we have is to be in agony during that entire painful creeping, or to rip it out with tweezers." A step back. "But know, hun, I'm here with a Band-Aid no matter which way you choose."

Jess's eyes stung, her throat closed so tight that she could hardly breathe. But she managed a nod.

Brit nodded back. "I should go, Josh"—here she grinned, and Jess knew she was trying to deliberately lighten the mood— "introduced the team to hacky sack, and as you might imagine, competitiveness is rearing its ugly head."

"You love it."

That grin widened. "Fuck, yeah, I do."

Then with another nod, a whip of that blond ponytail, Brit was gone.

And Jess was alone in the video room, wondering if she was so transparent to the rest of the team.

Which might have been the scariest thing she'd ever thought.

Six

·

Josh

"Hey."

He turned, saw that Ben—one of the rookies who had been working his ass off during training camp and had a bright future in the league (and hopefully with the Gold, if management decided to keep him on the roster) was standing in the hallway.

Pale.

And appearing ready to shit himself.

Josh stopped, turned from where he'd been heading to join in on the pregame team warmup—mostly for the new guys, but he and a few of the others with solid contracts tended to join in.

It gave him a sense of where the team was, kept his instincts fresh.

And, hell, he just really liked playing hacky sack and since that was the majority of the warmup...

Josh made sure to attend.

But Ben didn't appear ready for any sort of warmup or game or mess around session with a bean-filled ball, on the ice or off it.

"What's up?" he asked, moving toward him, gripping the

kid's shoulder when he wavered slightly. "Are you okay? You don't look good, man."

"I'm fine." Ben tried to shake him off. "I just was wondering where the pregame stuff was."

Right.

Ben looked *totally* fine. If fine was equivalent to appearing ready to puke in the trash can about five feet down the hall.

But Josh had the feeling that if he pushed, he'd get about as far as he had with Jess.

Which was, suffice to say, not far at all.

"I'm heading that way. Want to walk over together?"

"I—" Ben cleared his throat. "You sure?"

"Why not?" He grinned. "I like you, kid. I especially like that toe drag you did around Blue last practice."

Ben chuckled nervously. "That was just a lucky play. I—it— wouldn't work in a game."

"Why not?"

"I probably wouldn't have enough time and—" He stopped, gaze on his hands.

"What?"

"I might fuck it up."

Ah.

This Josh was familiar with. *This* was a common stream of consciousness often flowing through his mind.

This was also something he didn't want this fresh-faced and talented player to be dealing with his entire career because, fucking hell, imposter syndrome sucked ass. And Ben might not be eighteen and first making his way into the league. He was older, having played college and then worked his way up through the minors. He already *got* the stakes were high, that it was a grind to make it to the show, to stay there.

He needed release, not more pressure.

So he shrugged, nudged Ben with his shoulder, and said, "So?"

Ben's expression was comical. "So what?"

"So, you fuck it up." Josh nudged him again. "You try a move and lose the puck. *Then* what happens?"

Ben frowned.

"You get the fucking puck back or haul ass into our own to protect Brit or check the motherfucker who took it or...hell, you do anything except stand there like an idiot, staring as someone takes off with your puck." Josh shoved him forward lightly, saw that Bernard, their head coach, was standing at the intersection of halls, and dropped his voice, not wanting to overstep. "You do what you know best. You work hard. You play. You know that you're going to fuck up, but you accept that and keep going, yeah?"

"Yeah," Ben muttered.

"And then," he said, snagging the hacky sack as it was launched his way, catching it on his foot and launching it back to Coop, before slanting another look at Bernard, and finishing, "you put your head down and do it all over again. You think you can do that?"

Ben's hand shot up, catching the bean-filled bag before it could tag Josh in the head, and finally the younger player was smiling. "Yeah," he said. "I think I can do that."

Then he joined the circle.

Josh waited another second, glancing behind him, wanting to see if Coach was still watching.

Bernard *was* still there.

Face blank. Eyes filled with some frightening look that Josh couldn't discern.

Making him think that he'd overstepped. That *he'd* been the one to fuck up by giving Ben advice.

Irony, noted.

He could barely keep his own head together.

What right did he have to give advice to anyone else?

"Fuck!" Blue called. "I hate you, Josh, for introducing us to this game."

"That's because you suck," Logan told him. "Let me start."

"Pft," Brit said. "You both suck."

"That's because I'm the best," Ethan chimed in, snagging the ball.

There was some grumbling, plenty of shit talk, and then, Josh decided he'd better take some of his own advice, if only to save himself in front of the big man. "I'm the expert," he said, jogging forward and taking the ball. "So I'll start."

He did.

And, just like on the ice at this point in the preseason, they managed to cobble together some passes, to foster just a bit of chemistry.

It wasn't what anyone would call pretty.

But it got the job done.

So Josh would take it.

———

Later that day, after he'd watched a training camp session with most of the rostered guys up in the team box, Josh was walking out of the arena as he got another call.

This time it was actually from his family and not a request for early morning skating lessons.

"Hey, Jordyn," he greeted. "How's my favorite sister?"

"You mean your only sister?" she replied tartly.

He grinned. "Only doesn't discount *favorite*."

"Hmph," she said, and he could practically hear her rolling her eyes. "I'm good. The boys are good. I just wanted to let you know what's going on with Mom."

Immediately, he was on alert. "What do you mean?" he asked quickly. "What's wrong with Mom?" He sidestepped someone in the hall, glancing up and seeing at the last minute that it was Jess. She was staring at him, her brows pulled down and together.

Shit.

Moving faster, he hustled down the hall as his sister replied, "Nothing's wrong with Mom. Or nothing major, anyway. She needs to have another surgery for her collarbone. Apparently, it didn't heal quite right and is giving her a lot of pain. I didn't notice anything because I'm half the country away and she's been avoiding Jeremy"—their middle sibling and Josh's younger brother—"but the boys and I went out for Labor Day and she nearly ended up on the ground trying to lift a casserole dish. Dad went through the roof. I guess he's been arguing with her to go see the doc again, but…"

"Mom is Mom," he muttered.

"Exactly. And she didn't want to miss Parent's Day for you or Samuel's school play." Jordyn sighed. "She says it's inconvenient to be hurting right now, and if she goes with the corrective surgery —which she's needed for a *year* apparently—then she's going to miss out on too much."

"I'll talk to her," he said. "Make her get the surgery."

"Yeah?" Jordyn asked. "Are you sure you have time for that?"

"Of course, I have the time to talk to Mom about her health," he said, and if it sounded a bit touchy, it was because…he felt a bit touchy.

"Okay," Jordyn said softly, making him feel like even more of an asshole.

Snapping at his sister.

His family questioning if he had the time to make a simple phone call.

Fuck.

He leaned back against the wall and rubbed his forehead. "Sorry," he said, and sucked in, released a breath. "I'll always have time for you guys, and you know that Mom listens to me. I'll get her to have the surgery."

"I know," Jordyn said. "I didn't mean…"

"I know," he said quickly, not wanting to hear the guilt in her voice. "So," he went on, deliberately cheerful. "When are you and the boys coming down for a game?"

She perked up, and they chatted until the boys heard they were talking and interrupted their conversation with talk of Legos and books and the latest video game they were mastering. By the time he said goodbye to them, the sharp slice of guilt had faded.

But then he opened his eyes, saw that Jess was standing there.

"Are you okay?" she whispered.

He should be thrilled that she was asking, that she didn't appear to want to stab him in the hand with a pencil. Instead, she looked concerned.

And...he hated that.

Fucking hated it.

She'd heard...too much. He should have gone outside.

He—

"Josh?" she asked.

"I'm fine," he muttered, turning away, and this time he did what he'd done earlier.

He pushed out into the night air, shoved his insecurities aside.

And tried to get on with his night.

SEVEN

JESS

She should have let him go.

Instead, she found herself pushing out into the night air, shivering in her T-shirt, knowing she was being a dumbass.

And not able to stop herself.

Of course, I have time to talk to Mom about her health.

Not sharp words, necessarily, but definitely barbed around the edges. *Hurt.*

She argued with Josh all the time, snapped at him, bickered and picked fights and...he'd never sounded hurt.

Never.

Which was probably why her dumbass was striding through the door, shivering across the parking lot, snagging his arm before he lowered himself into the driver's seat of his car. "Hey," she murmured.

He whipped back, eyes hitting hers, and the yellow-tinted lights of the parking lot didn't hide the bleakness in his expression.

Though he tried to bury it.

Though the smile he tried to bury it with was such a facsimile of his normal one that it was almost comical. *Almost* because it was definitely gorgeous, wide enough to show off for a toothpaste ad—one that could rival Brit's recent campaign. But mostly... sad.

She blamed Brit.

And her gentle advice, her not-so-subtle push, her soft uses of *hun* and squeezes of her shoulder.

She'd *learned* from Brit.

When she'd first come to the team, when she'd been pieced and papered together, the barrier between past and present so fucking flimsy that a stiff breeze could have blown through it, Jess had watched Brit, had been envious of the open way she loved her husband, Stefan, her team, her job.

Jess knew she couldn't go there with a man again.

Not when she'd—

A sharp mental shake of her head.

But she could have the rest with the team, could have her own family, her own tight circle of friends who would never treat her like her bio relatives had.

So, she was telling herself that it was Brit, or at least Brit's legacy, that had propelled her out here.

A member of her family was hurting.

She was there. She could do something about it.

"Hey," he said, and then his gaze darted away, his body started to *turn* away. "It's late. I should go."

"Do you"—she couldn't believe this was coming out of her mouth—"want me to stay with you while you call?"

Everything changed.

It was like a ripple went through him, shuddering from toes to head like one of the quakes the city was so famous for.

He turned back toward her, head tilting to the side. Misery. Guilt. Sadness.

Then gone, half his mouth turning up. "A pity case, then?"

There was a note of sharp directed at her, sharp that had her bristling, sharp that had her...relaxing.

"Definitely," she said lightly, letting the bait of an argument just sit there, not picking it up for once. Not because she didn't want to argue. She couldn't lie—fighting with Josh gave her a little thrill.

Allowed her a safe form of contact with this man.

Wow.

That was something to ponder.

Probably, also something to avoid.

But...not at this moment.

Because a small, small part of her—okay fine, it might be a bigger one that seemed like it was growing with every second she spent with this man.

Jumping into giving her a skating lesson and being far too fun and charming during it.

Offering to pop in and coach a college kid's team.

Working hard on the ice, being gentle with Dani, caring about his teammates.

Concerned about his mom and guilty and a bit hurt that his sister thought he wouldn't have time for his mom.

All of those revelations chipped away at her good sense.

Which was why she was standing in the night, stopping them both from going home, wanting to...do something that she didn't quite know *how* to do.

"Go home, sweetcheeks," he said. "It's late."

The sharp was gone.

In its place was...hurt.

And she stopped thinking and worrying and *thinking*.

"I will," she whispered, but then she did a thing. A thing that was definitely not brought about by thinking and worrying too much. She stepped forward, wrapped her arms around him and squeezed tightly.

Just for a second.

"Your family is lucky to have you," she whispered under the cool night air, the words so soft that they were nearly swept away on the wind. Then she dropped her arms, stepped back, and put some distance between them, between herself and those dangerous words.

"Goodnight, Josh."

A whisper.

Followed by her fleeing.

Eight

JOSH

"That's it," he called, as Christina carried the puck up the ice. "Go. Go! Take it. Take it!"

They were terrible.

They were a fucking *blast*.

But though the hockey was barely hockey—some of the women had fewer skating skills than Jess had begun with the other day—Josh was fucking energized. They laughed and teased and gave each other—and him—shit. They might not be able to skate well or to shoot or to connect passes, but they had their razzing *down*.

They also hadn't won a single game in the three seasons they'd been together.

But that didn't stop them from playing, from having a good time, from all that shit-giving.

And...already, he was way too invested.

Well, that was probably obvious based on the way he was yelling his head off as Christina carried the puck up into the offensive zone, closing in on the net. Was it slow and wobbly and had it come to fruition because two of the players on the other team had collided and knocked each other to the ice?

Yes.

But was she approaching the goal, moving in, and—

"Come on," he chanted softly. "Do what I told you. Do it. Do *it*."

Her shot was...not great. Her hands were pretty good. Her game sense was better. Christina had a knack for being in the right place at the right time. Case in point, snagging a breakaway when the opportunity had presented itself.

She made it to the top of the circles.

To the hash marks.

Yes. Just a couple more feet.

She wound up.

"Come on," he whispered. "Come *on.*"

And faked the shot, doing that small move he'd advised, a simple six-inch shift of the puck, from the concave forehand of her stick to the convex backhand portion, and...tapped it.

Lightly, because she didn't have a lot of experience with shooting.

But hard enough that it slid on the ice.

The goalie was moving, shifting because of the movement, stick slightly off the ground, legs apart, leaving the space between them vulnerable to tap soft shot.

This might have been the most exciting moment of hockey he'd watched in years, time having inched to a crawl as the play developed, as Christina skated and shot...

And the puck slid into the net.

Holy fuck.

Holy. *Fuck.*

The bench erupted into cheers. They weren't going to win this game, but they had just scored their first goal.

Ever.

Josh had jumped up at the whistle, at the ref signaling the puck was in, that the goal was good, joining in with the cheers as

Christina skated back to the bench, a huge smile on her face as she climbed over the boards.

"Fuck, yeah," he told her, extending his fist for a bump.

"Watch out, NHL," she quipped, "here I come."

He laughed, fucked it all and slung an arm around her shoulders, hugging her. "Damn straight," he said. "Gotta dream big."

He had.

He'd gotten there.

And maybe he was unsure of the cost, of the price he'd paid.

But...he loved it anyway.

The next line jumped on.

The game continued.

And he stood there, both part of it and completely separate, exactly as he'd felt his whole life.

Except...with Jess.

With her, he'd always felt alive, as though he'd been strung through with a live wire.

He thought about the smile on Christina's face as she'd skated to the bench, about the way he'd pushed his mother that morning to take care of herself, to live her life for *her*, and he knew.

Jess.

It was time.

————

This was it.

He took a breath, released it incrementally, trying to calm his racing nerves. He had a plan and he was going to do it and it was going to go perfectly.

He just needed to find a quiet place to talk to her.

Maybe the parking lot?

Maybe he needed to flay himself open and look pathetic and vulnerable.

That had gotten him a hug the last time they'd been together.

He should—

Okay, so perhaps his plan was less a plan and more a cobbled-together effort after his realization the night before. He'd paid attention to the guys, watched their efforts over the last few years to win over their women.

And yeah, maybe he should be patient and build on the hug in the parking lot.

But he couldn't stifle the urgency, the *need* rippling through him to stop waiting, wishing, wanting, and to start living.

It had been that smile on Christina's face.

Bright and proud and...making him realize that he was missing a huge chunk of *something*—

"Jess!"

But fuck if she hadn't surprised him, even though he had been searching her out.

He just hadn't expected to see her right there in the hallway, walking ahead of him and—

He'd yelled rather than giving her the cool, calm greeting he'd intended.

Already imperfect.

Fuck.

She turned slowly, one brown brow lifting.

And his gut sank at the blank mask clicking into place on her face. As though she thought the other day had been a mistake and she was deliberately putting distance between them.

Or maybe she was projecting.

"Yeah?" she asked.

It was neutral.

"I need to talk to you."

Double fuck.

That was a snapped-out command, his jaw tight with nerves, his words clipped bullets that came off as an order, even though it was mostly nerves.

Her brow lifted, derision dancing in her eyes. Annoyed with him already.

Or again.

Or...*always*.

Mainly because he always managed to do this.

"Can I—" He sucked in and released a breath, letting all the air out. "Do you have time to talk?"

That brow remained lifted, but maybe there was the slightest bit of thawing. "Right now?"

"I—"

Yeah. He'd been hoping for right then.

She shifted on her feet, impatience in every line of her body.

Her second brow joined the first and they carved furrows into her forehead.

"Yes," he said quickly, before he lost her, before she lost patience and walked away. "Yes, I want to talk to you *right* now."

He froze.

Because dammit. That had come out as a command.

Jess didn't *like* his commands.

He wanted to bet that she would like them in other places—okay, namely in *one* other place, that being the bedroom—but they were so fucking far from that possibility it was almost laughable.

Hug to fucking.

Yeah, *that* was going to happen.

Plus, she'd probably laugh at any of his commands—or give him that damnable eyebrow—all just to spite him.

Or put him in his place.

God, seriously, how had he *ever* thought he was good with women?

Because even if he was, he was absolute shit with *this* woman.

She smiled with everyone else. Joked and joined in and never gave *them* the eyebrow, the furious eyes and flattened lips.

But then again, he'd fucked up with her from moment one and continued fucking up.

What was that about first impressions?

Right.

They stayed around forever.

Same with second and third and *hundredth* impressions.

It also didn't help that he kind of liked when she shot fire at him, that she was sass and life and *fire*. It made him feel something that wasn't...fear or worry or stress about fitting in or doing the right thing or not fucking up on a team that demanded excellence, or worrying what the price of getting here might have cost his family.

From the outside, Josh was living his dream.

But he'd never felt more like he was grasping at straws, trying to hang on, trying to not mess up and live up to the expectations of this team.

First the new guy.

Now a potential leader of the next generation.

Every article about him expressed that he had big shoes to fill. Fuck if he didn't know that already.

And seriously, no pressure.

Ugh.

"You gonna speak?" she asked, and it wasn't quite a snap, but it was definitely this side of tart. And, for the record, he liked the tart. Liked it so much that it made the voices in his head go away, had him focused on now, on this woman, on all he wanted to do with and *to* her. "Or just stare at me all day?"

The devil got him.

"I don't know." He grinned. "I kind of like staring at you, sweetcheeks."

A scoff, her pretty eyes rolling up toward the ceiling. "Right. I'm sure you do."

He didn't agree or disagree because he wasn't trying to dig himself a bigger hole. She wasn't running, was talking with him. He'd gotten a hug, had smoothed over the worst of the orders. So he wasn't going to admit that he liked staring at her a lot.

Did it a *fucking* lot.

She was gorgeous. Curvy and with an ass that he dreamed of gripping, holding, spanking, getting his mouth on. It had brushed against him when he'd given her the skating lesson, and all the wobbles and bending had done nothing but fuel his desire to get it naked, to kiss and lick. But it wasn't just her ass, her mouth was plump and pink and made him desperate to taste. Her breasts were so fucking amazing that he could write a fucking poem and he'd only seen them through her clothes.

But it wasn't just her body.

He also liked her mind, even though it often had her sparking fire at him, leaving him feeling like he was on the back foot. He always had to be fully focused on their conversation or she would call him on it.

Plus, she couldn't give a shit that he was an athlete with a nice house and car and plenty of money in the bank—maybe because she was surrounded by athletes on a daily basis, but mostly, he suspected, because she was a capable badass who could take care of herself.

And she wasn't interested in spreading her legs just because he'd shown interest—though that probably had less to do with the fact that he'd shown interest and more to do with the fact that he'd inadvertently insulted her.

But he liked that, too.

Not the insulting and fucking up, but that instead of Jess just laughing his idiocy off and bearing the brunt of the insult, she'd pushed back. She hadn't just taken it. She'd given him...fire.

And *fuck*, he'd liked *that*.

Now if only he didn't feel like he was digging a deeper fucking hole every single time he interacted with her. They were oil and water. Mustard and donuts—was that a thing? Hopefully not because it definitely shouldn't be.

"Okay, well, as stimulating as this conversation is, I'm going to head home."

Fuck.

Shaking himself, breaking the hold of those striking blue eyes, the need to feel the shining silk of her dark brown hair dragging over his skin, his *naked* skin, he opened his mouth to ask her to dinner.

Yes, his slipshod plan for apologies and platitudes basically included the gift in his pocket and asking her to dinner and winning her over with his "charming personality" through wine and chocolate and hopefully not another repeat of sticking his foot into his mouth.

And even *that* plan wasn't going to...plan.

Even his own mind was rebelling.

He'd just told her that he liked staring at her, for fuck's sake.

So he just needed to get the ask out.

To start from there and then systematically win her over.

"Jess—"

She'd spun away from him.

And he realized he'd been doing more staring instead of talking. So much for being present. He was so far up his own ass—

Stop.

He needed to take a page out of the guys' books.

Find out what Jess needed.

Give it to her.

Don't stop.

He had the last part of that figured out. It was what had gotten him into the league. Working hard. Never giving up. Sacrificing all for that one dream. But with Jess, he didn't want to sacrifice. He wanted it all. He needed...

To watch her walk away from him.

Shit.

He hustled forward, snagged her arm. "Jess," he said. "Wait!"

She didn't stop, just shook him off and kept moving toward the exit that would take them out to the parking lot.

Fuck.

He did the only thing he could.

He stepped in front of her and used his big, bulky hockey body to block her path. It was finally good for something—well, *something* that wasn't stopping pucks from getting into the net or crushing an opposing player into the boards.

Her brows—both this time—lifted. "Really?" she asked. "I

thought we'd finally made some progress, dumbass. Now, you're going to start manhandling me?"

"Look, sweetcheeks," he began.

"Let. Go," she gritted.

"Just wait."

"Yeah, no, I don't do that anymore."

"I just—" he began.

"Let go." Icy words, a shadow in her eyes that had him immediately releasing her.

But not stepping out of her way.

He just needed one more minute to make this right.

"I know I always manage to fuck things up," he said.

"That's the understatement of the year." She laughed, and it was bitter and sharp. "Or *three* years, considering you've spent all three of your seasons with the team arguing with me."

Because she was fun to fight with.

Because that was all she would give him.

She rubbed her arm. "Just consider this a truce, okay? Less fighting, but less talking? Deal? Okay, good." She started to push by him, still rubbing the arm he'd grabbed.

Guilt swept through him. "I didn't mean to—"

A scoff. A toss of her head, eyes narrowing on his. "Oh wow, no surprise. A man trying to excuse his bad behavior by saying *I didn't mean to.*"

"Jesus, sweetcheeks. I'm trying here," he muttered, rubbing his forehead.

"Oh *wow*," she repeated. "A man who—"

Any soft had gone, leaving—

So. Much. Derision.

So. Much. Annoyance.

So much of him wondering why in the fuck he was fighting for this when she clearly didn't want him.

What was the point?

Why was he bothering?

He'd burned the bridge. Fucked up too big. She wasn't interested.

"—thinks that his *trying* means he can get away with being an asshole." Another roll of her eyes, her expression filled with bitter amusement. "Congrats," she snapped. "I'll just go and order you a trophy, ask for the nameplate to be inscribed with *World's Best Tryer.*" A slow, scornful clap.

And...as it often did with this woman, his temper reached its breaking point, splintering along the edges, shooting shards in all directions. He stepped closer, spinning her around and pinning her between his body and the wall, bending so that his face was in hers. "*A man,*" he growled, "who has been trying for months—fuck no, for *years*—to get a woman to realize that he likes her and feels like a total shit because he got off on the wrong foot with her. Because he's fucking *crazy* about her." He plunked his hand on the wall beside her head. "And a man who has had so many wet dreams about her that his fucking balls should be dry." A beat. "And that's just this week."

His chest heaved as the words petered out.

So. Fucking. Stupid.

But then he wasn't worried about his words, nor his lungs, his breath, his body or mind. He was focused solely on her face, watching as her eyes went wide, as her lips parted.

Watching in wonder when, for once, she didn't snap back at him.

Instead, she whispered, voice hoarse, "Wet dreams?"

Her mouthing those words shouldn't make his cock twitch, her reiterating his loss of control, the stupidity he'd had in dealing with her. But she was talking about his dick, so he found he didn't really give a shit.

He cupped her cheek, felt his heart skip a beat when she didn't yank her head away. "Yeah, sweetcheeks," he murmured. "Every fucking night, I dream about you."

Her blue eyes drifted up, locked with his. "You're crazy about *me?*"

"Yeah, Jess."

Those eyes went wide. Then they dipped down.

To the fraction of space between their bodies.

Toward his cock.

Which twitched again, pressed fiercely against pants.

And *that* was the moment he remembered his plan and the object in his pocket. She wasn't kneeing him in the dick, wasn't shoving him away, and GTFO-ing. She was there, actually talking to him. Sort of. But anyway, he needed to lock it down, to be less focused on his dick and more on giving her what she needed so that he could win her over, so he could convince her to give him a chance.

Convince her that he wasn't a misogynistic asshole.

His fingers hit his pocket, intending to give her the gift he'd bought for her, the small trinket that had reminded him of her. But the moment his fingers brushed the tissue paper it was wrapped in, she straightened and shifted to the side—

Wait. Fuck.

Now she was leaving?

But then she shocked the shit out of him by grabbing the tie that hung around his neck, yanking him to the side, and pulling him across a threshold and into...

A closet?

"Right," she whispered, shoving him back a row of shelves.

"Jess—" he began.

Another yank to his tie before...

Her mouth hit his.

NINE

JESS

He had the most incredible lips.

Soft and damp, still...and then demanding.

Like *she'd* dreamed about.

Josh said he'd been having wet dreams, but she'd be lying if she said the attraction she felt for him hadn't carried over into her nighttime activities—

Those activities being a very active relationship between her and her vibrator...and her and her dreams, and her and her pulsating handheld shower head because *that* little gem of technology had just the right amount of pressure and—

A nip to *her* bottom lip.

Fingers weaving into her hair, tilting her head back. Delicate prickles of pain dancing along her scalp, sending tendrils of heat sliding down her spine, curling around her middle, dipping in between her thighs.

"Pay attention," he ordered.

And seriously, her pussy shouldn't convulse at that, shouldn't tingle and jazz-hand itself into happy oblivion at the husky command. She didn't do orders. Not any longer.

So she should let go of his tie, shove him back, and get the hell out of his proximity.

Just like she had every other time in the last few years.

Except...the skating lesson, the hug.

And look where ignoring that instinct had gotten her.

In a closet, about to do something critically stupid.

Because he was a black hole.

He'd draw her in, suck her down, and she wouldn't be herself.

Not ever again.

She might come out the other end, might be able to pretend to the rest of the world. She might be able to hide behind the mask of Jess-ness and do it so well that no one would suspect.

But inside, she'd see the cracks were barely papered over.

She'd know they were one wrong bump away from all of her being shattered to pieces again.

She'd—

Another nip, this time to her throat, after tugging her head back to expose the expanse of skin.

"I. Said." He pressed his mouth to her throat and inhaled deeply. "Pay. Attention."

Her nostrils flared as she sucked in a breath, mouth parting, curses on the tip of her tongue and—

Then his large, warm palm slid up her side and cupped her breast.

It felt...

Oh God, *she* felt.

Sparks of pleasure shooting through her veins, fireworks exploding on her nerves. Fuck yeah, that was good, especially when he ran his thumb over her nipple, lightly tracing the hardened bud. But she had spine. She was a tough old—young?—bird and didn't let men walk all over her.

Not anymore.

"Fuck off with your orders," she snapped, knocking his hand away. Even though that was basically a punishment for *her* since it stopped the delicious way he was molding her breast in his big palm, especially because he'd gotten her more wet with one fucking hand and a couple of soft brushes of one fucking *digit* than her vibrator had in the months—yes, *months*—since she'd been with anyone.

Sex.

She missed it.

But sex...

She could only do it because *she* made the calls. *She* drove the action. *She* did what *she* was comfortable with and—

Her hair pulled as she slipped her head from his grip, as she shoved him back. His chocolate eyes were wild, his lips swollen, his tie askew and exposing the undone button at the base of his throat.

"Sorry, sweetcheeks," he began. "Is this too much—?"

It *wasn't* too much—unless she was allowing the tiny thrill that slid through her when the man gave her orders, or the shame that followed when she found that tiny part of her wanted to follow them.

Self-respect.

Where had hers gone?

"No," she hissed, shoving him back again, this time until he stumbled into a set of shelves, rattling the contents on top of them. "But we do this *my* way."

Before he could react, she dropped to her knees.

Flicked open the button on his slacks.

No belt.

Just one button and a measly zipper between her and the motherland.

Time to remind him that *she* was in charge here.

The *zip* was loud in the quiet space, almost as loud as his breathing, as his whispered curse trailed by, "What the fuck are you doing, love?"

What she was doing had nothing to do with love, unless that

love was getting his cock into her mouth as deeply as she could stand, to get this man's knees to shake, his legs to go weak, to have his will in the palm of her hand...and then to crush it.

Okay.

Not exactly *crush* it.

She just wanted to suck him off until he lost control, ripped her off his cock, and then proceeded to fuck her into oblivion.

No making love.

No relationships.

Just a hard release that propelled her out of his gravitational pull. Once. Done. Forever.

No more hugs.

No more skating lessons.

No more bickering because that release had been found and wouldn't need to be found a second time.

That wasn't too much to ask, was it?

But right then she didn't have time to ponder that. She was busy reaching inside his slacks, pushing his boxer briefs down, and—

"Hello, you beautiful, *beautiful* cock," she whispered.

Josh made a choking sound, one that turned into a groan when she took him between her lips, swallowed him as deeply as she could, and fuck, he was hard and big and smelled incredible, tasted like man and salt and—

Hands gripped her beneath her shoulders, yanked her up, her lips sliding off his cock with a *pop*.

"I—"

Her ass hit the shelf she'd pushed him back into.

His hand dove into the waistband of her sweats, plunged right beneath the fabric, hot fingers slipping under her panties, delving into the soaking folds of her pussy.

One second, she'd had the man in her mouth.

The next, he was playing her clit like he was a master violinist and she was a pathetic little string at his mercy.

Control.

Gone.

Pleasure.

Spiraling.

"Oh fuck," she gasped as he hit just the right spot, as his fingers strummed and her pants slid down her thighs, tangling around her feet.

"Yeah, love," he said, the husky words fueling the fire burning inside her. "Yeah, you're going to get fucked."

His fingers disappeared.

He lifted her up, and a moment later, her bare ass hit the shelf.

He dipped low, eyes hitting hers, pinning her in place with molten chocolate irises. "Yeah?" he asked. "You want me to fuck you?"

"Yes, please."

His lips twitched, and she realized she'd said that out loud.

But before she could muster something—a protest, a barb, an order, anything to save face in this situation—his head was descending, and his lips were on hers, and—

Oh.

That was nice.

That was *very* nice.

And nicer still when he stepped closer, moved between her thighs, his cock brushing her thigh, her pussy. One arm around her waist, tilting her hips.

Big and broad and strong and hot and—

In.

He was *in.*

"Fuck yeah," she breathed.

Stretching her wide, pressing deep without the least bit of hesitation. They *should* have hesitated. Or at least, *she* should have. This had gone from her being in control to her being *controlled*, to her holding on for dear life, to her struggling to catch her breath, her head spinning, that coiling pleasure inside her winding so tightly she felt as though she were going to explode—

No.

Explode wasn't a big enough word.

She was going to be obliterated.

By a big man who was fucking her hard and fast, the shelf behind her biting into her ass as he pounded into her, as the hand on her hip held her in a grip that was unforgiving. And yet, his other hand protected the back of her head, preventing her from hitting it on the shelf above her.

Brutal and gentle.

Fast and long enough to rocket her up the cliffside, to send her flying into outer space, to bring that obliteration.

"I'm going to come," she said, realizing as she said the words that it was already there, that her orgasm was convulsing through her, squeezing his dick.

"Don't come yet," he ordered, though he didn't stop fucking her.

Fuck.

She liked *that*.

"I'm going to come," she announced again, her orgasm swirling around her, starting to expand, to spark through her nerves. She ignored the order, because she fought to learn how to resist them, because fuck the orders, fuck this man—*any* man—giving them.

"Don't," he growled.

She arched against him, grinding their pelvises together, rubbing her clit against his pelvis, sending her that final millimeter into oblivion. "Don't stop fucking me," *she* ordered, leaning up and nipping his jaw.

"Fuck!" he snapped, pounding harder, sending her soaring as he just kept fucking her with that glorious dick, her pussy squeezing it tightly, her body wracked with wave after wave of pleasure. His groan—a curse, a benediction, a sound of defeat— echoed in the small space as he followed her over the edge, his cock getting harder, bigger for a few seconds until his rhythm faltered, as his body began to shake.

Not brought to his knees.

But brought down a peg. Or three.

Then he was coming and she was *still* coming, the pleasure inside her waning in ever-decreasing waves. Tsunamis to softly lapping splashes. Whirlpool to a babbling brook.

Lost in the moment to...

Her remembering where she was.

What she was doing.

Who she was doing.

H. E. Double hockey sticks.

She'd come first.

Later, she would figure that was the only reason she was able to do what she did next. Quite simply, her brain recovered from the mind-melting orgasm faster.

A shove had him staggering back, his cock (still hard, so help her God) sliding free.

She felt his cum, slick and hot, slipping out from inside her and coating her folds, dripping down and sticking to the tops of her thighs as she bent and reached for her sweats, yanking them up and over her hips.

"Jess—" he began.

No.

Oh no.

This wasn't a conversation they were going to have. This was stupid.

So fucking stupid that she—

He reached for her, and she realized the stupid was continuing, that just by standing there, by staying in the fucking closet (literally the *fucking* closet, she thought with a slightly hysterical giggle) their chances of getting caught were increasing by the second...

And the longer she stayed in his presence, his dick still

hanging out of his pants, his eyes hot on hers, those hands coming close—

The stupider she got.

Right.

She ducked under that outstretched arm.

And...she ran.

TEN

JOSH

He wound up and ripped a shot, not caring that it went wide and hit the glass with a sharp *thwack*.

Okay, maybe he felt a *little* bad that it made the woman who was watching their practice (in a very impractical glittering dress that revealed more than it covered and heels that were just begging her to get her toes sliced off courtesy of big old feet in big old—okay, *new*—hockey skates) jump and nearly topple over backward in those toe-baring stilettos.

But here was the thing—

No.

The thing was a person.

An infuriating woman who he'd declared his feelings for, only to have an ill-advised, albeit fucking amazing encounter in a closet.

And then hadn't seen or heard from her for *days*.

Ten fucking days.

A shove from behind that nearly sent him toppling to the ice. "Heads up, Rook."

"Fuck you," he muttered to Logan.

He wasn't a rookie, not by a fucking long shot.

But he *was* one of the younger guys, and had barely been out of his rookie contract when he'd come to the Gold.

Now this was his third season with the team, and they'd lost some of their staple roster guys—Blane and Max had joined the ranks of Mike Stewart and Stefan Barie, the captain who had led the team to their first Cup. Stefan was married to their goalie, Brit Plantain, so he was at the rink often and in the stands for most of their home games, their adopted daughter, Roxie, bouncing in his lap.

But word had it that Brit was going to retire at the end of the season.

Blue might join her. And word was that Logan and Coop weren't far behind them.

The old guard was transitioning out.

Rosters shifted all the time. Players were traded, young guys picked up. But the Gold had a solid core, and that core was being whittled away.

If Brit left?

If Coop, Logan, and Blue followed?

That would be...

Strange.

He'd watched the Gold play in the years leading up to getting drafted. He'd worked his ass off to get here, to get to a team that was in yearly contention for the Cup. And...he liked the guys, respected them and management and the coaches and the support staff. This was literally living the dream, and if the core of the team was gone, if they couldn't produce—if he couldn't pull his weight and help the team win, couldn't fill the spots they would vacate...

Well, that dream would be gone.

So the last thing his mind should be drifting toward was an encounter with a woman who despised him, and then had ghosted him like she'd earned a gold medal in the sport.

But it was.

It had been. *Constantly.*

And he'd been trying for *his* gold medal in hanging by the video suite, attempting to catch just a glimpse of her...and failing utterly.

Now he was letting it affect his game—

By scaring innocent puck bunnies (now *that* was an uneven statement if he'd ever met one).

Another nudge, this one to the back of his leg that had his skate shooting out, him going down onto one knee. *Hard.*

Fuck.

He was going to feel that later.

The guys—including that core of Coop, Logan, Blue, and yes, Brit was included as one of the guys—busted up laughing.

"Can't wait till you fuckers retire," he muttered.

Which made them laugh harder.

Logan clapped him on the arm before yanking him up to his skates. "Hell yeah," Logan boomed. "I can't *wait* to retire. I'm gonna buy a big ass recliner, prop my feet up, and watch Char lead you guys to another Cup."

Char being Charlotte Harris, a slightly scary but mostly kickass woman, who was the GM of the team and the reason that Josh was on the team.

She was also Logan's wife.

"Yeah, well," he grumbled. "With Char on our side, we definitely don't need you fuckers."

"Just saying"—Brit swatted him with her stick—"gotta hit the net first."

The guys laughed again, skating off and going back to what they were doing before they'd decided to come over and torture him.

"Maybe you need some pointers?" she needled, her trademarked smile on full display. "It's been years since I skated out, but I'm sure I can help you fix your shot."

She probably could, considering she made it her business to study the shots of most of the players in the league. Knowing when someone was likely to shoot or make a move was incredibly helpful when she was trying to keep the puck out of the net. For posterity, though, he flipped her off. Gotta keep his image (ha) up.

And anyway, it didn't help because he was grinning. Because that shot—under no pressure, with all the fucking time in the world—had been about six feet wide.

Fucking terrible.

But that didn't mean he was going to let the shit-giving slide. He could shovel it right back. "How about I give you some pointers on that glove hand in return?"

She clutched a hand to her chest. "You wound me."

"Yeah right," he teased, and because he might be able to throw some teasing her way, throw it the guys' way, but ultimately, didn't like the idea of someone not feeling good about themselves, he added, "Nothing gets through that impenetrable Brit Ward in front of your net."

Her smile softened, and she bumped his shoulder. "You're a good guy, you know that?"

A good guy who fucked a woman in a closet?

A woman who'd then run?

Yeah, that was the definition of a good guy.

Totally.

Another bump to his shoulder. "So you gonna tell me what's up your ass? Especially since the season hasn't even started yet."

He knew what she meant. No games to get pissed about losing. No plays to get frustrated about.

Training camp had just finished.

Preseason wasn't starting until next week.

There should only be excitement, not frustration.

"It's nothing to do with the guys."

"I know."

Surprised, he jerked his head toward her.

Her smile went mischievous and she leaned close, her helmet bumping into his. Her voice dropped to a whisper. "It's a woman."

Another jerk, and the satisfaction that crept into her eyes told him that he'd given the truth away.

She straightened, did a little shimmy that should have been ridiculous in all her bulky gear—and let it be noted, it *was* ridiculous. But it was also pretty fucking adorable, especially when she shimmied all the way back to her net, sing-songing the whole way, "I'm right! I'm riiight! How do you like *that*"—she pointed her stick at Coop as he skated by—"deduction by the future captain of this team."

"Goalies can't be captains," Coop called. "Especially not ones retiring at the end of the season."

"Maybe I'll stay around, just to torment you fuckers!" she yelled back, still doing her little dance as she prepped the ice in her crease.

He laughed at her antics.

But all he could think was that he was fucked.

Because Brit knew he was interested in Jess. Which meant the entire team would know soon enough, if they didn't already. Because the gossip train at the Gold traveled at light-fucking-speed and it took *every single stop* along the way.

Which *meant* that Brit and Mandy and all the nosy...*noses* would be all up in his business.

Wanting to "help."

Wanting to be in the know.

Wanting to be the one who orchestrated his happy ending.

And Jess—oh God—she was going to *hate* that.

And *that* meant his chances with her...well, just picture a cartoon plane imploding as it crashed into the side of a mountain, complete with sound effects.

He. Was. Fucked.

———

He got off the bike, swiping at his forehead and deciding to hit the showers. That was enough for today.

There was a lot of season left—namely all of it.

Eighty-two games.

Four rounds of playoffs.

Plenty of time for more bike time.

"How's that quad?" Mandy asked as he dropped his towel in the laundry container by the door. He'd had a minor tear in the muscle toward the end of last season.

"Feeling fine," he told her.

"Not tight? Sore?"

"No more than usual getting back into the season."

Narrowed eyes. "You tell me if that changes."

Not a question. An order, and unlike a certain stubborn woman he was pretending to not think about, he didn't get his hackles up, just agreed with a wave, and strode out the door.

Then nearly ran into Rome.

He survived training camp along with Ben, Will, and Lucas and had a legit shot of becoming a permanent part of the roster.

The future of the team.

Josh hoped.

Because that mantle was getting pretty heavy to carry, especially since he was undermining his confidence by missing the net by six feet and obsessing over a woman.

"Hey," Rome said, jumping back so he didn't get mowed over. "I—"

He broke off, eyes darting over his shoulder.

Josh turned, saw that Bernard was coming their way, nodded to their coach then turned back to Rome. "What's up? Everything good?"

More eye-darting. "I was wondering if you might—" He cut himself off as Bernard passed them.

"Might what?"

"I—" Rome cleared his throat, dropped his voice to a whisper. "I'm fucking up."

The kid wasn't. He'd had a few stumbles, but had just finished camp and a single preseason. He was gelling with the system, had been kept on, and even if he got bumped down to the Rush—their minor league affiliate—Josh knew that the kid would be back.

It was a confidence issue.

Which...

Josh knew something about.

He was just better at faking it at the moment. Better at pretending that he didn't internalize the pressure and take his own fuck-ups personally, that he wasn't freaking out that this might be his last season, if his contract wasn't renewed, that being the future, carrying the mantle forward, filling the shoes was all fucking scary.

Even for a twenty-eight-year-old man.

For a nineteen-year-old one?

That could be paralyzing.

Josh had years of pushing through.

Rome was just young enough to lack that experience and just old enough to understand the stakes at hand.

"Some advice?" he offered.

Rome's Adam's apple bobbed as he nodded.

"We're all going to fuck up. The season is too long to expect differently. But we all work together here and..."

And *now* that this was his second time in as many weeks giving this talk—first to Ben, now to Rome—he had to wonder how effective it was. Would it take ten more times for some of it to stick in his own brain? Help him work through some of the shit plunking around in it?

Though, Ben had relaxed and settled in, so maybe it *was* effective.

Josh, he began to himself. *Everyone is going to fuck up. The mantle going forward will be heavy, but you wouldn't be here if the team didn't want you.*

No.

The mental peptalk was weird.

Especially since it had begun as his own inner monologue and was ending in his agent's voice.

He didn't like it.

Probably because he was a stubborn son of a bitch and it was easier to agonize over his position on the team—and the stability of it—than to focus on the good stuff.

Except...he was watching that same agony tear these guys up, watching it mess with their minds, their game.

Maybe he should take some of his own advice.

Inwardly, he snorted.

Nah. It was easier to beat himself up, to feel guilty, to wonder if it was all worth it.

If he wasn't here, would his parents have retired somewhere warm? Gone on more vacations? Would he be closer with his siblings? Would he have missed all their big events?

Would it all be altered, but ultimately the same?

Would he still—

Or maybe he was just having a mid-life crisis at twenty-eight.

Either way, he knew that he needed to give the agonizing a break, to focus on the problem in front of him. Maybe if he helped Rome and Ben, any of the others who came to him, maybe if he mended things with Jess...

He *had* to mend things with Jess. He would do that tonight, and he wouldn't stop until he had.

And maybe if he did that and if he helped the guys on the team who needed it, who came to him, who were struggling... maybe if he did all of those things then the pieces in his own mind would slide into place.

Maybe he would find that it had all been worth it.

Maybe he would find *he* was worth it.

ELEVEN

JESS

"And then can you grab the clips on the list that Calle sent over?" Dani asked, gathering her papers and laptop and tossing her backpack over her shoulders.

Her friend looked tired.

A little pale.

Jess understood her pain.

Getting back into their routine at the beginning was always tough.

But Jess was grasping at every opportunity to pretend that what had happened between her and Josh hadn't actually happened. Which meant that she'd been working her ass off the last few days, and studiously avoiding the practice facility where the guys were.

Someone had to make sure all their equipment was set, right?

Stifling a snort, she just told Dani, "Of course." Then turned back to her computer, to the video of the preseason game they had been pulling clips from. Dani had finished her chunk of the list that they typically worked from, and Jess was almost done with hers. They were usually good about ticking items off most of it as the actual game progressed—from confirming goals were goals and checking offsides for coaches' challenges, to tagging times of plays and goals and penalties that the players and coaches would review later. They had to work with speed a lot of the time, and post-game was mostly clean up and addressing any special requests—like the list from Calle, who wanted some extra tape of the rookies that were on the bubble for making the roster. Aside from those requests, they spent a good chunk of time cataloging the video into their online system so it could be easily reviewed later on the team's tablets or accessed by the players from the comfort of their own homes.

Avoidance strategy or not, she was almost done with her post-game stuff, so Calle's list wouldn't take her long.

"Go," she ordered. "Get your man to tuck you into bed, yeah?"

A yawn. "Yeah. I think I'll do that."

"Good." Jess hit her mouse, and the game moved on her screen—

And...there was Josh.

Tall and dark with kissable lips and a giant fucking cock and—

She hit her mouse again, spun away.

Out of your brain, Jess. Keep that shit out of your brain.

That was how she survived.

It had been a stupid impulse, and look, it had very pleasurable consequences, but it had also been incredibly stupid.

First, she didn't do relationships.

Second, she didn't do sex she couldn't control.

Her terms. Always.

Except...she'd kind of liked it when he'd taken over.

So not the point.

Because one look at Josh when he'd joined the team had told her that he'd never be a man she could control. Too pretty. Too strong. Too determined and too good at issuing commands and...

too good at fucking her until she'd practically been reduced into goo and—

Dani smiled, grabbed her phone, and shoved it into her pocket. Then her smile faded, her gaze seeming to catch on Jess's face.

And Jess didn't know what the hell was showing in her expression, but it couldn't be good.

Not when she was thinking about He Who Must Not Be Named.

Certainly not when her friend tilted her head to the side, eyes narrowing, concern writing itself into the lines of her face. "Oh shit, that's too much, isn't it?" She started to shrug out of her backpack. "I'll tell Ethan to go on without me—"

"Absolutely not." Jess jumped out of her chair, caught Dani's backpack before it fell off her friend's shoulders. "I'm fine, Dani. I promise."

Dani—quiet, lovely Dani who'd taken months to win over because she was so shy—got fierce. She dropped her backpack anyway, took Jess's hands in her own. "Tell me," she demanded.

Another order.

Which, she'd made it clear, she hated.

But an order from Dani, whose confidence had grown leaps and bounds in the last few years?

That made Jess smile.

And maybe her issue was less about orders and more about the people in her past who'd given them.

Maybe with the right person.

Maybe with Josh...

She blinked when Dani squeezed her hands again, knowing she couldn't tell her friend the truth of what was flying through her mind. The conflict and concern and confusion.

And hell.

She certainly, couldn't say, *Oh, I'm fine. I just fucked Josh in the supply closet and didn't use a condom, but don't worry, once I got my head together, I hauled ass over to the pharmacy the next morning and got Plan B. So, I'm covered there.*

Oh, and bonus, my STD test came back clear.

Go me!

"I'm fine," she said instead of *any* of that.

A sigh, narrowed eyes. "*Jess*," Dani warned.

And fucking hell, Dani wasn't going to let this go. Not now that her concern had been piqued because Jess had been dumb enough to let the Jess Mask slip.

She scrambled for a moment, and then...she lied.

"Aunt Flo is being a total bitch." She laughed and massaged the lower part of her stomach, though, come to think of it, Aunt Flo *hadn't* been a total bitch.

Aunt Flo should be coming to visit any time now.

Joy.

She'd be horny, thinking about *all* the stupid things she'd done (especially—*cough*—with Josh), *and* on her period.

Yay.

At the lie, Dani's expression cleared, and her expression went sympathetic. "Aw, damn. That sucks," she said. "Do you need anything? Ibuprofen? Chocolate? Period spoon?"

The last shouldn't make sense.

Except, it did.

At least in Jess and Dani's world.

In the J and D world, they'd bonded over both using menstrual cups, but occasionally the vacuum they created made them a bit challenging to remove. They'd been traveling to join the team on a road trip—one of the rare occasions that Jess had been able to tag along (hello, Boston and the Freedom Trail and yummy cream pie, and New York and Madison Square Garden and *Broadway*). Well, mid-trip, Jess had a cup emergency. Dani had answered her urgent call...by bringing a spoon.

Miraculously, it had helped dislodge the cup.

And thus, the period spoon had been born!

"Don't worry." Jess grinned. "I'm maxed out on ibuprofen,

I've got my chocolate stocked up, and my true crime documentaries cued up and ready to go as soon as I get home." She picked up the backpack, held it out for Dani. "A hot bath. Empty calories. A dash of murder. All will be well."

"I'm sure you've got it handled." Dani shrugged into her bag then bumped her shoulder against Jess's. "But promise me you'll call if you need emergency spoon backup?"

"I promise," she said solemnly before nodding at the door. "Now go and enjoy your—"

A knock.

Jess grinned and went on, "*Man*. Who I'm guessing is right outside the door with a pack of Hot Tamales or some new mouse you wanted."

The man spoiled Dani in the best possible way.

Dani, whose cheeks went bright red. "I told him to stop buying me things."

"That won't happen," she teased as Dani moved to answer the door. "Ethan's love language is gift-giving, you know that."

Small. Large. In between.

So fucking thoughtful that it made Jess's buried, damaged heart squeeze.

"I do." Dani tossed a mischievous look over her shoulder. "And I'd be lying if I said I didn't love it."

Then she opened the door, revealing Ethan standing there...

And—fucking hell—Ethan wasn't alone.

Standing behind him was Josh. And Josh? Well, his big brown eyes hit hers a millisecond after the door swung open. She sucked in a breath, forced her gaze away, and had a heartbeat to process that Ethan did have a gift in his hand.

But then her gaze was drawn behind her friend's man.

To Josh.

To those big brown eyes and sharp jawline and kissable lips and broad shoulders and...

His giant, delicious cock.

A muscle in his jaw flexed.

And she could feel the hard line of his face rubbing against hers, the bristles of his beard dragging over her skin. She could feel his strong hands on her curves, her breasts, her pussy, could feel his body against hers, his cock stroking deep. She could hear his rough, husky voice in her ear, drawing out goose bumps on her nape, down her back.

All of that.

In an instant.

"Fuck," she whispered under her breath, whirling back to her computer, unplugging the dongle. She'd pack it up. Finish the rest of the pulls at home and upload or email them to the necessary channels and people.

Run.

She was going to run.

Again.

But the last time she'd been around this man, she'd ended up fucking him in a closet.

Running might be cowardly, but it was also prudent.

Laptop into her backpack. Straps over her shoulders. Purse slung crossbody. Phone in her pocket. She could escape while Ethan and Dani were playing kissy face and—

Warm, strong fingers wrapping around her arm.

A spicy, masculine scent in her nose.

He sidled close, chest brushing along her back.

"Running again?"

Considering she'd just been thinking that exact same thing, that she'd been planning on doing it, a bolt of annoyance shot through her.

The man just needed. To. Get. Out. Of. Her. Head.

She whipped around, glared up at him. "I am *not,*" she said, and the amount of outrage in her tone impressed even herself considering it was a big, fat lie. "I'm going to finish my work at home because I've been here since three and...I'm tired—"

His lips turned up into a smirk.

A snarky smirk that said he didn't believe her in the least.

Was she lying? Yes.

Would she admit that over her cold, dead body? Fuck, no.

Which was why she lifted her chin and dead-eyed him. *"And I'm on my period, okay?"* she snapped, loud enough that she saw Ethan and Dani break apart from their lovey-dovey embrace and turn to look at her and Josh. "So, if it's not too much to ask for your demanding hockey player ass, I'd like for you to back up so I can go home and bleed in peace."

Josh swallowed hard, eyes darting away. "I—um—"

"Now," she snapped, jabbing a finger into his chest, "is that reason enough for you to leave me alone?"

Ethan cleared his throat.

Josh studied his toes.

And seriously, it was just freaking unused uterine lining. The guys didn't need to act like she was discussing the Plague.

A cough. "We'll leave you to...um...your—" Ethan broke off, and Dani's lips twitched, her stare hitting Jess's and seeming to mirror the same thought Jess had—*Silly, silly men.* "—your..."

"Bleeding?" Dani asked dryly, no shy in sight. "Since half the world does it?"

Ethan cleared his throat. "Yes," he croaked. "Yes, exactly that. Let's go and leave Jess to her bleeding."

Dani exchanged a look with Jess, and they both bit back a laugh. "I'm on call with spoons and chocolate."

"Thanks," she told her friend. "And I'll get that list sorted out before my bath and murder time."

Josh choked.

Ethan, at least, seemed to understand what she meant (probably because she'd waxed poetic about her documentaries way too many times when they'd hung out). He just nodded and slipped the backpack off Dani's shoulders as he herded her toward the door. "Have fun with the murder. And make the bath extra hot. It helps Dani."

Jess grinned.

Then Dani glanced over Jess's shoulder, her eyes going strange.

But she didn't say anything further.

Just clutched the present from Ethan—a book whose title Jess remembered her mentioning a time or two—finger waved, and then let her man lead her out the door.

And that leading...

Left Jess alone with Josh.

Shit.

TWELVE

JOSH

S he smelled like the summer sky.

Warm skin and hot sun.

A balmy breeze skating through the trees, rattling the leaves on the branches.

But her eyes were pure fire.

They sparked up at him, flames in the blue depths, threatening to turn him to ash. Her chin was lifted, her shoulders sat proud and straight. Fury and determination had quickly taken the place of the desperation to flee his presence (and fuck, he hated to admit it, but that anger had also taken the place of a blip of fear that had written itself into the lines of her face when she'd first spotted him standing behind Ethan).

Afraid of him.

Fuck, he needed to make this right.

Was him trailing Ethan to the video suite, all under the watchful gaze of Brit, fuel for the gossip train?

Absolutely.

Because he doubted that they believed the excuse he'd given, that he was asking for tape of a preseason game that didn't even count (because preseason games were mostly for the rookies, those trying to earn a roster spot, and for the guys who felt like they needed to get their sea legs back under them).

He'd made up some excuse about wanting to check out a prospect.

But between Brit's smirk and the look Ethan had given him—and the second one that he'd slid his way when Josh had deliberately taken a step back from the door of the video suite when he'd knocked—had told Josh that he wasn't being very sly.

Blocking a certain woman's escape route and then getting into an argument with her all of thirty seconds later didn't exactly fit that bill now, did it?

But crashing the Ethan-Dani parade was also the only action he could take that would increase his likelihood of tracking down his little ghost.

And it had worked.

She was trapped and feisty and glaring at him and looking so damned sexy that he wanted to fuck her right on that desk of hers.

He'd fantasized about it more times in the last years than he cared to admit.

Ever since this little obsession began.

Ever since he'd said the wrong thing and pissed her off and... had appreciated the way she'd called him on his bullshit.

Maybe that made him a glutton for punishment.

Absolutely, that did. There was no *maybe* about it.

But he liked it, liked her. Fucking gorgeous and spicy and drove him absolutely crazy in the best fucking way and—

On her period.

No desk fucking.

Right.

He filed that fantasy away for future use.

In this moment, he let his hands drop to her shoulders and massaged lightly. She'd gone stiff at the initial contact, but the gentle stroking had her head falling back, her lips parting and tempting him to taste.

But...victory.

Because she was allowing the contact, not moving away, and... a soft moan escaped her lips.

That moan went right to his dick.

"So," he began and immediately wished he hadn't spoken because the moment he did, her eyes flashed open and she went stiff, jerked out of his hold.

He played it cool, just leaned back against the wall near the door and watched her continue getting ready to leave. She moved back to her desk, took off her backpack, and instead of the frantic laptop shoving he'd witnessed earlier, she began systematically packing her things. Pens in a certain pocket. Wallet in another. Cell phone in a third. Headphones in the large compartment.

Like she'd done it hundreds of times before.

And she probably had.

She'd been with the team longer than him, had been an assistant video coach well before he'd come to the Gold.

Hundreds might be creeping toward a thousand.

And he liked watching her do something that was so routine, loved seeing a piece of her that was normal, everyday.

It made him feel like...

He was connected to her.

"I have something for you," he said, ignoring the way she went somehow stiffer, her movements jerky as she spun around and started to shrug into her backpack a second time.

He moved, catching the top handle before she could put it fully on, and shoved the package he'd had in his pocket for the last two weeks into her hands.

She looked at it like he'd just handed her a lit stick of dynamite.

"What the fuck is this?" she asked, fingers completely flat, the small box rocking slightly on her palms.

Josh tossed her backpack over his shoulder. "A peace offering."

Her eyes narrowed.

He clamped his lips together, swallowed the extra words that wanted to come out, the explanation, the rambling that was desperate to emerge.

Fewer words.

Less rambling.

Better chance at success with this woman.

Fix this. Fix his mind. Fix the yawning hole inside him, fill it with something other than the swirling doubts and anxieties—

Jess shifted slightly and he watched her as she held her hands up, the package still resting there like some cheerfully-wrapped offering to the hockey gods.

Like it was that lit dynamite.

Or contained a venomous snake that was ready to strike. Or was—

Her fingers closed around the box and thank fuck for that because the words were bubbling up at the back of his throat, threatening to burst forth...and that would likely lead to her being even more pissed at him.

"What is it?" A much softer question, curiosity creeping into the edges of her bright blue eyes.

"Open it." That soft faded, hardness sliding in and destroying that curiosity. So he hurried to add, "If you want," he said. "It's just—" What? He'd seen it in the window, and it had reminded him of her, and he'd had to buy it, and then he'd come up with a plan that definitely shouldn't have ended with unprotected sex (which he still needed to discuss with her, though, he supposed that the mention of her period meant they'd gotten away with one, but at the very least, he should tell her that he was clean so that she didn't have to worry).

Anyway, his cobbled-together plan had been to win her over, to start again, to not put his fucking foot in his mouth for once.

And instead, he'd talked about wet dreams and had stuck something *else* in.

Hell.

"I just—" He broke off, shook his head, and...just told the

truth. Those bubbled-up words could fly free, heaven help him. "You intimidate me," he admitted. "You're really smart and funny and gorgeous, and I know I always say the wrong thing. So, that" —a nod toward the box—"it's—*that's* a peace offering."

Her brows drew together.

But she didn't launch it back at him (which he considered a victory).

Her shoulders rose and fell on a breath.

But she *still* didn't launch it back at him. In fact, she actually tore open one end of the paper.

He clenched his teeth together.

She tore open the other side, slid the box free of the paper.

His lungs seized. He tensed every muscle in his body so that he didn't leap forward and snatch it back before she actually opened it.

What if she hated it and—

Then the lid was open.

Oh fuck.

Oh fuck.

He took a step forward, but then she whipped toward him, blue eyes wide. "What is this?" she breathed. "*What* is this?"

"I—"

She took a step toward him, jabbed a finger into his chest. "What *the fuck* is this?"

It was hardly anything, just a tiny rhinestone-covered Golden Gate Bridge. Kitschy, something that was found in airport gift stores or those crammed shops down by Fisherman's Wharf. But he'd heard her mention that her favorite thing to do on her off days was bike across the huge, red landmark and into Marin.

"A paperweight," he said. "It's just a paperweight. I know you like to bike it and—"

"How?"

His brows dragged together. "What?"

"How do you know I like to ride?"

This wasn't a hug. He'd kind of, sort of, expected a thanks or a hug or maybe something more, and yeah, he was an asshole. But he supposed, he'd expected...what? Not the bewilderment and a dash of anger. "You mentioned to Dani before that you like to ride your bike across it and—" He clamped his lips together, cutting himself off when that bewilderment and anger grew, clouding her expression.

Her finger trailed across one of the studded supports. "Why?"

A whispered question.

He inhaled, let it out slowly. "Because I thought you might like it."

Silence.

Her fingers clenched on the box. Tightly. And he watched as her breaths sped up, as her gaze stayed glued on her hands. Then she moved.

Part of him expected it to be toward the door, to take off for the hall, and to run like hell.

But she moved closer.

Closer.

Until the toes of their shoes touched, but before he could reach for her, she was moving past him, walking toward her desk—

No.

Toward her trash can.

Let the box—and the peace offering inside it—fall into the gray bin without hesitation.

Thunk.

She turned back to him, put her hand out. "Give me my backpack."

He passed it over without a word.

She shrugged into it, grabbed her purse.

And then...

She walked out the door.

Thirteen

JESS

She'd parked around the corner, hidden her bike in the shadows, let that darkness carry her down into a dark place in her mind.

She'd stayed there until Josh's sleek black Mercedes had turned around the corner.

She would have preferred to hear his tires squeal as he took it too fast, fury in his driving. Fury because she'd acted like a total bitch.

Bridge. Burned.

Check.

No more fucking—literally—mistakes.

He wouldn't be giving her any more presents—no gift-giving love language like Ethan, no more peace offerings, no acts of kindness, no skating lessons, no coming to the video suite to argue with her.

No more wet dreams or stupid—cough, *fantastic*—sex.

He'd look at her like she was a bitch.

Because...she'd acted like a bitch.

What big bitch vibes you have, Little Red Riding Hood would say.

And she'd reply, *That's because this big bitch will cut you hard and deep and—*

"Enough," she whispered.

The taillights of his car had disappeared, so she hit the button to turn on her bike, flipped down her visor, and slid back into the parking lot of the arena.

It only took a moment to slide to a stop, to cut the engine.

Her keycard on the pad by the door. The lock *bleeping* as it retracted.

Slipping inside.

Navigating the empty and darkened hallways. The space quiet and absent of players and most of the support staff. A few voices told her that the equipment guys and the cleaning crew were still finishing their tasks, somewhere in the bowels of the arena. They had the toughest jobs, worked the longest hours, especially the entire equipment team—starting well before the players showed up, staying long after everyone had gone home. Loading and unloading all the gear the team needed, prepping extras and backups and planning for every eventuality that might happen.

They made sure the guys had what they needed before they knew they needed it.

The unsung heroes of professional sports.

But luckily, the equipment crew was a small group. Same as the cleaning staff.

Which luckily for *her* meant they were easy to avoid.

She unlocked and stepped into the video suite, moved quietly across the room on silent feet.

Then, holding her breath, she reached into the trash can.

Her heart squeezed as she felt around the wrappers, the crumpled Post-Its, and papers.

Then relaxed as her fingers connected with the rhinestone-studded metal. Releasing the hold she had on her lungs, allowing them to empty and fill semi-normally, she plucked out the paper-weight. It glittered softly in the dim office lights.

Still silent, still sneaking, she shoved it in her pocket.

Then she made her way back to her bike, turned on the engine, and zipped out of the parking lot.

She drove home, the cool night air whipping around her body.

But before she got there, she decided to take a detour.

And that detour was a there-and-back across a big red bridge.

There weren't any rhinestones, but there *were* glittering lights.

———————

She took a breath, released it slowly.

Her helmet was tucked under her arm.

Her keycard was in her hand.

And Josh was walking toward her.

"Fuck," she whispered. "*Fuck.*"

The final preseason game was happening in just under two hours. Josh wouldn't be playing, but he was there to watch and support the team. Which was probably why he was walking toward her, looking like a fucking snack in a fitted navy suit and crisp white shirt. It was unbuttoned at the collar, and he was wearing loafers with no socks, his slacks bearing his ankles, along with aviator sunglasses with blue-tinted lenses.

He should have looked dumb as hell.

Instead, he was an entire package of double-stuffed Oreos.

With a big glass of milk.

Fucking delicious.

And...coming her way.

Holy hell.

She had to get the fuck out of there. She needed to lock herself in the video suite and hide like she'd done the last couple of weeks. She needed to *run.*

Lifting her keycard, she whipped around to face the door and swiped it before grabbing the handle and yanking fiercely. But the heavy metal panel didn't move, and as she glanced over her shoulder, she saw the delicious snack that was one Joshua Webb was getting closer.

"Shit," she muttered as she swiped again.

No *click* signaling that the door was unlocking.

No *beep* telling her that her card was reading.

Another swipe. Another glance over her shoulder.

Fuck, he was five feet away and—

She turned back, ready to Hulk out on the door and tear it open if need be.

"It helps if you actually swipe your keycard."

His voice skidded down her spine, set her insides to fire, her hands shaking. "What?"

Fingers reaching for her shaking hands, or rather reaching to pluck the plastic keycard out of them, holding it up in front of her face, and making her see that it *wasn't* a keycard. It was a rewards card.

For wine.

God, she needed some.

Right then.

"Oh," she whispered, taking it with numb fingers when he held it back.

He leaned forward in an abrupt movement that took her breath away. Strong. Fast. Big. Every-*fucking*-where.

But he didn't jerk her toward him, didn't pin her against the door and kiss her, as she half-expected...as she—no half about it—wanted him to. Even though getting physical again would fuck up the distance she was trying to create between them, *had* created between them if the frost in his eyes was any indication.

Instead, he just pressed his keycard against the panel.

It *beeped*.

The lock on the door *clicked* open.

And then he was tugging it wide, nearly clipping her nose in the process.

He didn't say anything, just gestured her forward.

Her temper began to boil. Oh, she completely understood that she had no fucking right to be mad. *She* was the asshole here. She'd literally thrown his peace offering in the trash. But that careless gesture, that little jerk of his head and hand...*fuck,* but that made her mad.

"Go on," he ordered.

Orders.

Got her back right up.

And the fucker knew, if the bitter amusement in his eyes was any indication.

She snapped, spinning on her heel. "I am *not* a fucking dog."

His eyes narrowed, a muscle ticking in his jaw. He inhaled deeply, let it out slowly. "No, you're not. But I'm assuming that you want to actually walk through this now-open door so you can go to work."

Spoken calmly.

Without stammering or inserting his foot or the attempts to apologize that normally would have come. Without bickering or calling her on her shit or trying to pick a fight. Whatever spell he'd been under that normally had him on his back foot had broken and...she was a little sad.

But that—she knew, sucking in a breath through her nose— didn't mean that she was going to let his orders stand.

Fuck *that.*

She shoved her way under his arm, bringing her body way too close to his in the process of snagging the door away from him. "I'm *assuming* that *you* won't mind walking through a door held open by a *woman.*"

That muscle in his jaw ticked. "I don't fucking like what you're insinuating."

Her nostrils flared as she inhaled, preparing to unleash more words, more actions that were fucking immature and that she would hate later because they were fucking petty.

"But," he said before they could emerge. "I don't really give a fuck what you're insinuating." A beat. "I'm out."

He slid through the door, disappeared down the hall.

And she was left standing there, holding the metal panel.

Alone.

Like always.

Fourteen

Josh

He didn't really need to be on the fucking stationary bike, peddling like he was an action hero trying to escape a giant boulder that was rolling after him.

Or maybe a scary-ass monster.

Or—

He kicked up the resistance because he just wanted to think about how much his legs were burning and how much his body hurt and how much he fucking hated working out in general, and especially how much he fucking hated working out on a stationary bike.

Because he didn't want to think about Jess.

He'd rather be miserable.

Because he was miserable anyway.

And, funny story, adding more misery to his already miserable misery worked.

He really hated the damned bike.

But it was a necessary evil, and anyway, the final preseason game was over. In two days the regular season would start. Rome,

Ben, Lucas, and Will had all made the cut, and he'd taken the guys out for a celebratory beer the night before.

They were young.

Well, Ben wasn't. He'd played college, made his way up through the ranks, had only been at the rookie's training camp (a clinic the team put on so that the younger guys could get a feel for playing in the league) because one of the prospects had been injured and he happened to be visiting family who lived in the Bay Area.

He'd turned that opportunity into a roster spot.

Fucking good on him.

So, they had the majority of their new guys in place. The roster *would* shift and change as the eighty-two-game-long season went on, as injuries happened and fatigue built up, but the new guys had pretty much sealed their spots.

They'd also secured some solid D, a good backup goalie, and a couple of really talented forwards.

And all the new guys had exactly one season to get their shit together, to gel, to become a winning powerhouse before they lost a chunk of their team.

No pressure.

Nope.

Josh wasn't feeling any pressure at all.

Wasn't feeling like maybe none of this was worth it because his mom had an infection in her surgery site and had been admitted to the hospital that morning. He'd wanted to fly home, but she wouldn't hear it.

But swear to God, if she got any sicker...fuck hockey. He wasn't going to miss being there for his family.

Not again.

He leaned in, kicked up the resistance further. His quads were on fucking fire, and he'd probably get yelled at by Mandy for pushing it, but he wanted to be so freaking exhausted that he had to weigh whether his legs would hold him up when he managed to peel himself off this bike.

All that internal weighing was probably why he didn't notice the slender blonde with the adorable baby in her arms.

Not until she spoke anyway. "Looking awfully angsty, Joshie."

Brit's damp hair was pulled back in a ponytail, her cheeks flushed, and she was wearing a black Gold hoodie that Roxie was yanking the collar of.

"What are you talking about?" he asked—or puffed, he supposed, since he was about to fall off this fucking bike.

Brit smoothed a hand over Roxie's blond curls, used her other hand to gesture at Josh, ticking off items on the fingers of her free hand as she spoke. "You. Broody expression. Working yourself into a pile of goo. Angry eyes sent my way when the only one you normally give that particular glare to is that asshole from the Ducks who took that cheap shot on me last season." A kiss to the top of Roxie's head. "Well, just to Benedict"—that asshole from the Ducks who *had* taken a cheap shot on Brit...and who Josh had nearly plastered to the boards for fucking with his goalie—"*and* Jess. Though lately it's been reserved for Jess." A smile at her daughter. "And mostly over the last couple of days. Actually"—she tilted her head to the side, studying him—"ever since that night you followed Ethan to the video suite, you've been glaring at Jess."

Now her fingers numbered five, and her penetrating eyes were on his.

He stiffened.

Because fucking hell.

How was she *that* observant?

"I know you and Jess seem like oil and water, but"—a grin as she tapped a finger to her bottom lip—"sometimes they say that opposites attract, and you and Jess are definitely opposites, and she seems to make a gold medal sport out of trying to push your buttons." She waggled her brows. "So?"

He frowned. "So what?"

Another gesture. "So, are you and Jess—"

Not touching *that* with a fucking ten-foot-pole. With a

hundred-foot one, for Christ's sake. Jess would probably chop off his dick and throw it in the fucking trash can.

"Don't you have a slew of rookies to spend time trying to play matchmaker?" he asked, hoping that question might divert Brit from him and refocus back onto her favorite pastime—that being finding the players of the Gold their life partners.

"I don't *play* at being a matchmaker," she said loftily. "I *am* the team matchmaker."

"Pfft." Mandy, the head trainer, poked her head in. "We work together as co-matchmakers."

Brit grinned. "I'll concede that point."

"Damned right." Mandy grinned. "Otherwise, I won't bake for you anymore."

Brit sobered, and Josh felt her pain. Mandy's baked goods weren't PR-Rebecca's special homemade brownies, but the sheer breadth of yumminess that she could—and *did*—create on a regular basis meant that no one smart would risk that haul. She made Cheat Days worth it.

"My stuff might not be the prettiest," Mandy said, "but it tastes good, *and* I think I got PR-Rebecca to give me her recipe when she officially retires."

The publicist, who'd recently relinquished many of her duties to her assistant Scarlett, had a baby at home and a hockey player in her bed. She'd worked her ass off for years and deserved whatever happiness she had in her life—retired, on the job, or otherwise.

"Well," Brit said, "considering that I doubt Rebecca will ever fully relinquish her role here, I'm guessing she gave herself a loophole out."

"I—" Mandy clamped her lips together, sighed heavily. "Aw, damn, you're freaking right. She'll probably call herself a consultant and never pass it on."

Josh grinned.

Brit cackled. "Of course, she will."

"Bitches, man." Mandy huffed. "We really are a pain in the ass, aren't we?"

"I'm not even pretending to get involved in this conversation," Blane said, striding into the room and pressing a kiss to his wife's mouth.

Mandy smoothed her hand over his cheek when they broke apart, foreheads pressed together...all while Brit taught Roxie how to make gagging noises.

"Don't want to hear it," Mandy grumbled, jabbing a finger in her direction. "You and Stefan are the worst."

They were.

The couple had been together the longest, and were almost sickeningly in love with each other.

Like his parents.

His brother and his wife.

His sister and her husband.

Connections he hadn't had time to make, more regrets and missed opportunities. It was bittersweet, the knowledge that he didn't have what so many of the guys did, but it didn't take away from how much he loved this team.

The banter. The inside stories. The random connections and good-hearted teasing. They were a family who knew each other inside out, who always welcomed newbies with open arms.

And he'd never felt like he didn't belong here—at least not from the team.

His own messed-up head was another story.

Blane pressed a kiss to Mandy's forehead then stole Roxie from Brit's arms. "I'm commandeering your daughter," he said, swooping her toward the door. "Maddy needs a partner in crime."

"Just for a few minutes," Brit said. "It's way past bedtime."

A nod in agreement, a wave toward Josh and his bike, a heated look for his wife, and then Blane was gone.

Mandy shot a look his way. "Want to tell me why in the hell you have the resistance set to"—she came near and though his hand twitched toward the knob, he didn't move fast enough to avoid her lighting-like trainer references—"*max?*" she exclaimed. "And you've been riding for what?" Her gaze flicked from the screen back to him. "A fucking hour? Are you *trying* to burn out your quad?"

Trying to burn a woman out of his mind, but he wasn't going to admit that.

"No," he said, not protesting when she hit the stop button. "I just wasn't paying attention."

"He's brooding," Brit chimed in.

"I'm not—"

Twin pairs of curious female eyes swiveled in his direction.

Well, fuck.

He sucked in a breath. "I want the season to be good, and I'm willing to work hard." He unsnapped from the bike, swung himself over, and thanked the hockey gods that his legs held him when his feet hit the floor.

Not quite a puddle of goo.

#Winning.

Mandy frowned. "You know you won't be good if you burn yourself out before the season even begins."

"Yeah," he said, and because it was the truth, "You're right."

That frown turned full smile. "My favorite words to hear."

Perfect. She was happy.

Now time to GTFO.

She slanted a sly glance his way. "So...who's the girl?"

Aw, fuck.

"There isn't—"

"Jess," Brit supplied.

Mandy's eyes went wide, glee spreading across her face. "Oh my God. That is *so* perfect. Tell me every—"

"Mommy!" An adorable little girl ran into the room, arms up, light brown ponytail bouncing with each step.

"Maddy!" Mandy called, scooping her up and squeezing her tight.

"Daddy said to tell you to hurry up."

"Does *Daddy,*" Mandy asked, "have his impatient pants on?"

A solemn nod. "And *I* have my ice cream ones on." A head tilt that sent her ponytail bouncing again. "Which means we have to go get ice cream, right?" Pleading eyes and an all-too-innocent expression.

Josh's lips twitched, and he wasn't the only adult in the room smothering a smile.

Brit nodded. "It *definitely* means that we need to go get ice cream."

"Aren't you a woman with a diet plan?" Mandy asked, plunking her hands onto her hips.

"Conveniently," Brit said, "Nutritionist Rebecca wrote in a Cheat Day for tomorrow."

"But Auntie Brit, we're supposed to get ice cream today!" Maddy exclaimed, brows furrowing.

"You know what?" Brit crouched down, voice dropping to a whisper.

"What?"

Solemn eyes. "It's tomorrow somewhere."

That had him bursting out laughing. "Is it five o'clock?" he asked, glancing down at his watch.

A snort from Brit's direction, but she just patted the top of the little girl's head and said, "I'll take you to get ice cream, Maddy girl, so long as it's okay with your mom, since it *is* late, and I don't want you to be tired in the morning."

Mandy's face went soft. "Teacher workday tomorrow, so this little one"—a light tug to Maddy's ponytail—"has ice cream *and* a late bedtime in her future."

Maddy squealed, grabbed her mom's hand, and started tugging her toward the open door.

Brit stood, started to follow her.

Excellent, he would escape this conversation. He snagged his towel from the bike, swiped at his forehead. He'd cool down, shower, put the suit back on, and go home. By that time, it should be after midnight, and he'd be able to have his Cheat Day beer.

Brit, of course, had Avoidance Radar.

"You coming with?" Brit asked, brows lifting.

"I'm not sure it's five o'clock yet," he quipped. "But, seriously, I'm tired. I want to go home and chill."

She'd started to grin at his lame joke, but then her eyes narrowed.

"Is that a glare that's worthy of the future captain?" he asked, going for straight distraction.

Her face cleared, and she studied him closely. "Actually," she said. "I've decided to take my name out of the running. I think someone who's going to be around for a while should get the C."

"Like Coop," he said, mostly because he hoped that saying it would mean one of their best forwards would stay around for several more years.

"Coop is good as an assistant captain."

He shrugged, mopping his face. "Not sure we really need more than a couple of those," he admitted. "The leadership is strong on this team."

"It is," Brit agreed, walking with him out into the hall. "It definitely is."

Her expression went calculating and he braced for more Dani Interrogation.

Instead, Brit asked, "Did I hear right that you helped the guys find an apartment?"

He shrugged. "It was nothing. Now that they're on the roster, they needed somewhere that wasn't a hotel to stay."

"I hear that," Brit said softly. "I lived the hotel life for too long."

He nodded in agreement. "Having your own place makes a big difference. I hope they know what they're getting into with four dudes in one house."

Brit's lips twitched. "I have the feeling that Ben is going to play babysitter."

"Are you kidding?" he asked. "Rome is the most serious of the bunch. He was texting me with play ideas." He shifted, allowed Calle to squeeze by them. "At six in the morning."

Calle grinned. "Those same ideas you forwarded to me at six-*fifteen* this morning?" she teased.

"Kid's got talent."

Calle nodded, her expression considering. "Seems to be a lot of that going on."

"We're getting ice cream," Brit chimed in before he could ponder exactly what Calle meant by that. "Come with."

Calle grinned. "Don't have to ask me twice." Her eyes hit Josh's. "You're coming."

Not a question.

A statement.

And yeah, he might be subjecting himself to further interrogation about Jess.

But this was his team, his family...and there'd never been any doubt that he was going.

FIFTEEN

JESS

"Ice cream!" Brit all but shouted, shoving her head into the video suite and startling both her and Dani.

Dani's headphones hit the floor.

Jess didn't react, other than slowly spinning her chair around and lifting her brows at the starting goalie. She'd had plenty of experience with outbursts. She might startle, but she'd gotten really fucking good at not showing fear.

Even if inside she was a giant ball of nerves.

Brit bounced Roxie in her arms. "This little girl wants ice cream *and* the Dairy is staying open late for the team."

Now *that* got Jess's attention.

The Dairy was the shit.

Homemade ice cream and malts, frozen slushies topped with soft serve. Sundaes and mix-ins and freshly whipped cream to top all the confections. Basically, it was a sweets lover's dream.

That they were staying open for the team? Fuck yeah.

Nothing made a woman with papered-up walls and a hole inside her that would never be filled feel better than unnecessary sugar and empty calories.

Except...it *had* been filled in a little bit with Josh's gentle encouragement on the ice, the silly gift he'd given her that showed he paid attention, the way he'd quite literally filled her so full that she thought she might—

Coughing, she hit a few keys on her keyboard and then snagged her laptop. "I'm in. I can finish these at home."

Dani bit her lip, hesitation in her eyes. "*Everyone* is going?"

Brit smiled gently. "*Everyone*," she confirmed, "though, in a non-pressuring way."

Dani bent and retrieved her headphones, her movements relaxed now that she'd recovered from Brit's bellowing. "Well, I'll take your non-pressuring explanation and accept your ice cream invite, even though *I* know it's not Cheat Day yet, and you're trying to corrupt my man and his diet plan and get him in trouble with Nutritionist Rebecca."

"Nutritionist Rebecca granted a special disposition for an extended Cheat Day beginning in the next thirty minutes." Brit nibbled at Roxie's ear, unleashing the adorable little girl's giggles then glanced up, her trademark smile on display. "I think that Rebecca was swayed by my argument that it's Cheat Day somewhere."

Jess smiled back. "I know *I* am."

"Though, more likely," Brit went on with a shrug, "I'm guessing that it's mostly because ever since Nutritionist Rebecca got knocked up, she has a weakness for the Dairy."

"Win-win for us, definitely," Jess teased, shoving her laptop into her backpack, and picking up her helmet. "We've got to take advantage."

Brit lifted a fist that Jess bumped. "Damn right."

"You don't have to come," she reminded Dani. "I can always just drop by some treats for you and Ethan."

Dani had come a long way with her social anxiety, but she still struggled sometimes in large gatherings. Yeah, the team was family. But also, yeah, sometimes that family was big and loud and overwhelming. Still, just because it was overwhelming didn't mean Dani should miss out on ice cream.

Her friend's face went soft. "Ethan and I will go," she said. "Their peanut butter malt is what I dream about at night."

Dreams.

Fuck, that made her think about *wet* dreams.

And a certain man who now, rightfully, hated her.

Maybe he'd skip the festivities?

Please, God, let the universe be that kind.

Spoiler alert.

The universe wasn't kind.

Hadn't been kind.

She might be an a-hole.

But at least she was an a-hole who had ice cream.

Of course, she was eating that ice cream while sitting next to Dani and Ethan *and* trying to keep her eyes off Josh. He was licking his vanilla cone—and yes, the man had come to the Dairy with all its copious flavors and mixers and gotten straight vanilla —looking like that damned snack again.

His tongue.

She shivered.

Unfortunately, Ethan noticed, leaning close and wrapping his free arm around her. "Might want to avert your eyes if you want to avoid the notice of Brit and Mandy."

Based on the penetrating look Brit had given her when Jess had seen Josh and then promptly turned the other way, spinning right into Brit and nearly taking down their goalie's milkshake, that ship had long sailed.

"Avert her eyes from who?"

Ethan kissed Dani on the nose. "No matchmaking," he warned.

Dani snorted, and Jess grinned when she went full-on Sass

Mode. "I will matchmake any time I want to, thank you very much."

A soft reply, one Jess only heard because she was so close to his other side.

"Anything you want. *Anything.*"

Dani set her cup down turned into Ethan's side, kissing him long and deep enough that Jess slid away, would have gotten up and walked away to give the lovebirds space.

But before she could, Ethan turned back, eyes dilated, lips a bit swollen as they turned up into a smirk. "I'd say sorry..."

"Except, you're never sorry to kiss Dani," she finished.

She'd meant it as a joke, and it came across as one. Well, it *was* the truth, but it was said in a light, teasing tone that expressed how little she cared about being subjected to PDAs. There was nothing more special than her friends finding happiness.

Despite her past, she would never begrudge anyone else that joy.

She'd had it, for a split second.

Or *thought* she'd had it anyway.

So, she knew it was precious, knew how it could make someone feel like they could fly, and she also knew the agony that came from losing it.

Of course, hers had come with a side of mental and physical abuse and sexual assault, so she wasn't in the same boat as Ethan and Dani and the rest of the couples in the organization.

"No," he agreed. "I'll never be sad to be able to kiss her." He turned slightly, studied her face. "You know you could have that, too. There are a lot of men who—"

"Oh Lord," she muttered, going back to joking. "Don't."

Dani's expression was gentle. "It's true." A glimmer of humor in her eyes. "I mean, it doesn't take a *PhD student*"—she nudged her hubby who'd decided to pursue one in his free time (and don't get Jess started on the insanity of a professional hockey player thinking that he had the free time to get *another*—yes, *another*—degree)—"to know that you're worthy of someone to love you."

Jess sucked in a breath. "I love you," she told her friend. "And you, too." She punched Ethan lightly on the shoulder. "But I'm not cut out for relationships." A forced smile, her arms lifting and hands going full-on jazzy. "I like being footloose and fancy free."

Ethan snorted.

Dani looked at her. *No.* She stared at her, eyes boring into Jess's, peeling back all the layers of paste and paper. "But do you really?"

"Yes."

No hesitation.

Because on her part, Jess knew that it was all she had in her, and she was happy. Happy with the team and her friends and her job and her little house she'd managed to purchase outright last year.

She was *living*.

Dani sighed. "Jess—"

"Look," she said, interrupting her, letting her mask fall just a little. "You know how I grew up." Dani and Ethan both did, both knew that she hadn't had a normal childhood. She'd grown up in a very strict church, one that controlled every aspect of her life, from the clothes she wore to the food she ate (and thus, her weight). She hadn't been able to watch TV or go online or talk to a person outside that very small community she'd lived in with her parents. "You know that I can't relinquish the type of control that a relationship requires. I just…" A shake of her head. She'd lived that. She'd married that. She couldn't— "I'm happy." A breath. "That's enough for now. That's all I'm ready for."

"We get it," Ethan said, stopping Dani when she might have pressed more.

Her friend took a breath, her eyes concerned. "We do," she said. "And I'll just say one more thing."

Jess braced.

Turned out, rightly so, because Dani's words hit her with the force of a punch.

"If you being alone is all you want, that is totally fine," she said gently. "We love you. You're family and ours and that will never change." A breath. "But, honey, if there's a part of you—small, big, in between—that wants something bigger, something *more,* then...just give yourself the chance to consider it."

She couldn't.

Even considering it might lead to wanting it and then wanting would leave to more and—

She'd be flayed open and vulnerable, her paper and paste barrier giving way like it was a piñata breaking apart beneath a heavy wooden stick.

"I—I—"

Ethan's arm came around her again, giving her a light hug.

Dani reached over him, squeezed Jess's hand, smiled gently. "Time for more ice cream."

Relief shoring up the walls inside her.

She picked up her cup from where she'd set it on the grass next to her. "More ice cream," she said, holding it out to cheers Dani's. "And"—a breath—"thanks...for..."

Ethan pressed a kiss to the top of her head, and she felt the barriers creak, ripple.

But it was what he said that had them tearing slightly, allowing a little of the warmth he and Dani pointed in her direction to shine through, to fill in that hole.

"Anytime."

Sixteen

Josh

His phone buzzed as he talked with Ben and Rome—just call him Rookie Coordinator.

He was kidding.

The guys were cool.

But they'd definitely stayed close, and yeah, it sounded cheesy as fuck, but they looked up to him.

Probably had something to do with him finding them a place to live.

He shifted his cone to the opposite hand, dug out his cell, saw that his mom was calling. "I have to take this," he told the guys, stepping away and answering the call. "Hey, Mom."

"Don't freak out."

Surefire words to get him *to* freak out.

"Mom."

"I'm fine," she began. "The infection is under control, and they were going to discharge me in the morning."

Okay, that didn't equate with freaking out.

"However, your father is going to be here for a few more days."

"Dad—" He frowned, starting to rub his forehead, but luckily catching himself in time before he ended up sporting a vanilla cone like a third eye. "What happened?" He sensed movement behind him and turned slightly, moving further away from the group, ear glued to the speaker.

"He's fine," she said. "I just spoke to the doctor who did his surgery—"

"Surgery?"

"He's fine," she said again. "He had some chest pain when my doctor came to check on me. She saw and made him do a workup. Turns out his arteries were ninety percent blocked."

"What?" His cone was dripping down his hand, and he glanced around for a trash can, not wanting to throw it on the ground. Well, *yes* wanting to throw it, but no, not willing to be the special kind of asshole who did.

He spun further as she talked about the angioplasty and two stents that had needed to be put in, how he was awake and not in any pain and how this all worked out for the best anyway. Apparently, they'd wheeled his dad down so his parents could share a room.

"I'm glad he's okay," he said. "I'll talk with management, fly back to see you both."

"No."

"Mom," he said. "I can grab a flight in the morning and be back before the season starts—"

"I said *no*."

It was a rebuff that was sharp enough for him to freeze. "Mom," he began, the sting of her words coating his tongue, making it feel thick and useless. A soft hand touched his, taking the cone from his fingers and he looked up, saw that Jess was standing there, her expression unreadable.

But she just pressed a napkin into his now-empty palm, turned, and walked back to the group, dropping the cone in the trash as she went.

"Joshie," his mom said, drawing his focus back to the phone

call and not the strange whiplash of Jess. "We are fully capable of living our lives without you dropping everything and swooping in to save the day."

"I know that."

"We don't *need* you, baby."

That hurt.

That burned through him, zinging along all his insecurities. Yeah, he was aware of how well his family got along without him, knew they didn't need him.

"I know that," he said quietly. "But I'm in a position now where I can take time off for this stuff, Mom. The team understands, and they wouldn't fault me for wanting to come and visit you both, especially considering you're sharing a freaking hospital room."

"I don't want you to come."

It shouldn't have felt like a slap, not when she added,

"We're adults, baby. We can manage on our own. I love that you want to come, but your dad and I are never prouder of you than when you're pursuing your dream." He sucked in the breath, tried to ignore the burn, the hurt. "You dropping everything to come out for something that truly isn't a big deal would just stress us both out."

"I don't want to stress you out," he said. "I just want to make sure you're okay."

"We are." Her voice gentled. "And we'll be watching the season opener, so we want you to be playing in it, baby."

He dropped his gaze to his feet. "Yeah, Mom. I get it."

"Plus," she said. "Jordyn is coming out tomorrow. We'll be in good hands between her and the home nurses the hospital is setting us up with."

"I'll pay for—"

"Our insurance is good, Joshie. *We're* good. I promise."

"Right," he whispered, throat tight. "You'll...um...call me if that changes?"

"It won't."

His shoulders rose and fell on a breath. "Right," he whispered again. "Talk soon."

A quick goodbye.

And then there was just dead air in his ear.

He was still for a moment longer, trying to not take the words personally. His mom was right. They were adults who could take care of themselves, and he hadn't been home. He'd gone away, played hockey, pursued his dream. They were used to relying on themselves, on his siblings.

He wouldn't be the first call.

Blowing out a breath, he dialed his sister.

"It's nothing personal," she said immediately before he could speak, the background noise telling him that she was driving. "Jax is at Disney World with Sharon and the kids, and Daniel wanted to take the boys camping for the weekend. I've got nothing going, Joshie. I promise it's not inconvenient."

"Right," he said, feeling fucking useless.

"Joshie?" she asked, concern rippling through the airway. "Are you okay?"

"Yeah." A quick reply, keeping it light to temper that concern. "I'll pay for your plane ticket, okay? I know it's got to cost a bundle leaving last minute."

Silence—well, road noise—then, "I'm not going to let you pay for my ticket, bro."

Of course not.

"Jordyn."

"Joshie."

He sighed, rubbed his forehead. "I just want to help them, to be part—"

He cut himself off before he revealed the rest of it.

Outside, looking in. Never quite feeling like he was part of his family. And it wasn't a surprise, he'd been away from them more than he'd been home. He'd missed a lot and wouldn't be the obvious choice to call in a pinch.

Kind of hard to swoop in and save the day when he was flitting around time zones for three-quarters of the year.

"I just want to help."

"We know, Joshie. We appreciate it. *They* appreciate it," she said. "Our parents are stubborn, middle-aged Gen Xers who are barely tolerating me coming to check on them because they don't want to inconvenience me. And the only reason I got that okay is because they're sharing a hospital room." A sigh, and he pictured her shaking her head with good-natured exasperation. "I have the time, Joshie. I have the money." A beat. "You'll be on in the summer, yeah?"

"Yeah," he whispered.

"I love you."

"I love you, too." Then he couldn't resist adding. "Text me. No matter what time. No matter how small."

Jordyn paused. "Okay, Joshie."

As they said goodbye, he caught movement out of the corner of his eye and jerked around.

Jess was back, a fresh cone in her hand.

Her expression said she'd heard at least some of what he'd said, even though she had stopped a few feet away, as though trying to give him some privacy in the wide-open space.

He pocketed his phone.

Used the napkin to wipe his hand.

Then shoved *that* in his pocket too before starting back for the group. He'd say goodbye and—

"Wait."

SEVENTEEN

JESS

He spun slowly around to face her...

And she had instant regret.

Mostly because the expression on his face had all of that paste and paper threatening to shred apart.

But she also had a vanilla cone that was melting in the late summer air, dripping down her hand.

She didn't know what had come over her when she'd seen his face as he'd listened to that call, having left the two lovebirds to their own company. She'd been intending a French Exit, to disappear without saying goodbye like an outlaw into the night sky, to go home and enjoy her true crime podcast, her bathtub, and sleeping in late the next morning. But then she'd seen Josh on the phone, his expression grave, his tone wounded, his big, broad shoulders hunched forward.

And she'd...just been drawn to him.

Gravity yanking a boulder down a steep hill, spinning and jerking and bringing her closer to an inevitable collision at the bottom.

Because rolling, spinning, jerking had come to a halt in front of Josh.

Just in time to hear the hurt in his voice.

She *hated* that.

Because she'd put hurt in his eyes before, because if he'd spoken to her after she'd thrown the gift in the trash, he probably would have sounded like that.

Regret.

So much fucking regret coursing through her.

But she couldn't change what she'd done, couldn't do anything about what was making him sad on the phone. Except perhaps...she could make a peace offering of her own. Ridding him of the ruined ice cream, and since it had been making a mess on his hand, giving him something to clean it with.

It was nothing.

But it still felt like she was hurling herself over a cliff.

And now she was back with another vanilla ice cream, watching it melt down the edges of the cone.

"Here," she whispered, thrusting it at him.

He took it, eyes going from her hand to the treat. "Why?"

Yeah.

Why?

"You're sad," she whispered.

He brought the cone up to his mouth, licking around the edge of it with a quick thrust of his tongue that she felt between her thighs. "And you care why?"

Acerbic. His words were ice.

And...she deserved it.

"That's fair," she said, backing away. "I—" She turned.

"Wait," he said, catching her arm. Thick, strong fingers gripping her bicep, warmth seeping in through the hoodie she was wearing. "It's"—a sigh—"my parents are sick—" He stopped.

"They're in the hospital," she said gently. "Together?"

He nodded, rubbing his temple with his free hand. "My mom had surgery to repair a break that didn't heal right. Then had to stay a couple of days in the hospital when the incision got infected."

"I'm sorry. That sucks."

"Yeah." Move temple-rubbing. "And then apparently my dad had chest pain earlier today and they examined him, and he needed surgery..."

Another squeeze of her hurt. "And now they're sharing a hospital room."

He nodded.

"And they don't want you to go help?" It was a question, but she'd heard enough of the conversation to know that was the truth.

"No." And there was a note in his tone, one that spoke of an old, buried pain.

It called to her pain, her old aches, and for the first time, she wondered if they might have something in common. Her and all her messed up childhood and adolescence might have something in common with the man whose family she'd met several times over the years, who clearly loved him and was proud of him and—

Made him hurt.

She looked at this man who'd sacrificed his body on the ice, who she'd seen help his teammates, who would step in and give a skating lesson on no notice, and she understood. This was a man who lived to care for others, and his family, his parents wouldn't let him.

She wouldn't let him help her.

She couldn't.

But maybe she could help him feel just a little better. *With what?* she thought snidely, a fresh ice cream cone and some idle, uncomfortable chitchat?

"I—" She sucked in a breath. "My parents..."

He stilled, his eyes hitting hers, but he didn't say anything, just seemed like he was holding his breath as he watched her.

"They were abusive." His face clouded, and she hurried to add, "I don't mean that what you're going through is that—" A shake of her head. "I just mean...sometimes we don't get what we want from our families, and I'm sorry yours has hurt you. That's not okay. But"—a breath—"I've seen them at the arena, I've seen them with you, and I know they love you."

Still. He was still, so freaking still.

Then his question was whisper soft. "And yours don't love you?"

"Mine"—God, this was a can of freaking worms to open— "no," she said simply. "They love their church and their rules and the man who nearly destroyed me. But...no," she said again, "no, they don't love me."

His hand clenched into a fist, the tendons pressing against the taut skin.

Then the ice cream cone hit the dirt and he stepped toward her, his body towering over hers, his clean hand coming to her cheek, the other fisting at her side.

"Jess."

Her eyes were on that fist, throat going tight when he lifted it.

"Sweetcheeks."

That fist rose higher.

Her lips parted, a breath slipping out.

Then a gasp when it shot forward and crashed into the tree trunk with a sickening *thunk*.

"Josh," she exclaimed, grabbing it, and bringing it in front of her face. Which should have clued her in, right then and there, how she felt about this man, how much she trusted him, how much he meant.

But...she was too worried about his hand.

"What's his fucking name?" he growled.

Mandy was going to kill her. *Hell*, the entire team was going to kill her if he'd broken his hand. "Shit," she whispered. "I. Honey, your *hand*." Carefully, she straightened out his fingers, saw that the creamy white dessert had dripped all over his hand again.

She didn't have any napkins left.

She didn't like vanilla ice cream.

But she still brought that hand to her mouth, kissed the knuckles that were split open, her tongue darting out unbidden, lapping up the sticky remains.

"My hand is fine." He slid the one she wasn't holding into her hair.

And she looked up.

Realized what she was doing.

How they were standing.

Where they were.

Who was nearby.

What this could ruin.

Hot breath on her lips. His body moving closer, hand flexing and tilting her head back.

"Jess," he murmured.

"I—"

His mouth touched hers, just briefly, just for a heartbeat. His warm, firm lips were a shock, every single nerve in her body lighting up.

Then his palm was on her cheek again, thumb brushing along her bottom lip.

"His name."

Mutely, she shook her head.

"You'll tell me."

"No."

It was a whisper, so quiet *she* barely heard it, even though it came out of her mouth.

But he wouldn't have heard it anyway.

Because a voice rose above the pounding in her head, the pulse thrumming in her ears.

"Where's Jess?" Brit called. "She's the best at bubbles."

Because at the sound of Brit calling for her, he dropped his hand, stepped back, and scooped up the ruined cone. Scalding brown eyes on her as he straightened, burning into her, freezing her lungs, pinning her in place without laying a finger on her body.

"Bubbles, sweetcheeks," he said softly.

Then he turned, headed back to the group, the soft *thunk* of the cone hitting the bottom of the trash can mirroring the *thunk* happening in her chest.

It beat rapidly.

Punched against the paper barriers surrounding her soul.

Rip.

―――――

Someone had gotten him a third ice cream.

Vanilla again.

And seriously, that was a crime against nature.

He was so far from plain vanilla that she didn't even know where to begin.

His mind. His personality. His—

God, his fingers alone...

She shook herself, watched him unabashedly.

He and Blane were chatting, and the sadness and pain from earlier had seemingly been erased by hanging with the guys—or perhaps she'd helped rid him of some of that by her making a fool of herself with the bubbles Brit had commandeered from somewhere. She hadn't missed him watching her while she'd goofed off with the kiddos, same as he probably didn't miss her watching him now.

And, as though the thought had shot right through the evening air and plunked directly into his brain, his head whipped toward her.

He smiled.

And her fucking uterus squeezed, about threatened to explode because he wasn't just standing there chatting and smiling. He also had one big arm folded around a now passed-out Roxie, his hand spread wide on her back. She was drooling on his navy suit as he was calmly licking that vanilla ice cream cone, listening, and talking like it wasn't a big deal that he was tongue-fucking an ice cream while holding that adorable little girl.

Giving all the single women around him ideas.

All the single women being...her.

A big, sexy man holding a tiny baby.

Not giving a fuck that his suit jacket was getting ruined.

Fuck, that was the hottest thing on the planet.

But worse than her panties threatening to combust, she was getting ideas and yearnings and *thoughts* sliding through that tear in her walls, making her think about things she'd promised herself would never *ever* be something she allowed herself to want again.

Clenching her jaw, she shoved a big ass bite of her ice cream into her mouth and turned away.

It was mostly melted at this point, but it was still delicious.

Her lips curved as she watched Brit and Mandy playing with the kids who were still awake—it turned out a teacher's workday the following day meant that they could push back bedtime and all the kids could play a little hooky. A rare and special treat with the guys' season just around the corner. Soon the schedule would be intense, with lots of travel, and nights like this—pushing off bedtime, dancing under the hanging lights on the grass in front of the Dairy, cheating the diet plan, shooting the shit—would be few and far between.

All of their lives would be living and breathing hockey, going for those wins, trying to make it to the post-season, to snag another Cup. So, any relaxing before the guys and Brit needed to buckle down and play for the next seven to eight months (depending on how far into the post-season they made it) was very welcome.

So, Jess knew that Brit and Mandy didn't care that they were making total fools of themselves. Just like she hadn't given a shit.

Not when the kids were smiling.

Not when they were all enjoying this moment.

Each other.

The calm before the storm.

Her spoon came up empty from the bottom of her container, and her lip jutted out.

Where had her ice cream gone?

It had just fucking disappeared on her. And hell, she wanted another. Maybe this time around she could get mint chocolate chip instead of cookie dough.

However...she also wanted to continue to fit into her clothes. *Sigh*.

The curse of biology.

More calories in than burned off meant her favorite skinny jeans would be toast.

Another sigh as she leaned back against a tree trunk, plunking her empty ice cream cup on the grass next to her and deliberately not letting her gaze go back to a certain tall drink of yumminess.

Ethan and Dani were still huddled together, their voices soft murmurs as they spoke to each other, Dani's head resting on Ethan's shoulder. Brit and Mandy had collapsed to the grass, the gaggle of kids still running off that sugar high and making a game out of climbing all over them. Rome, Ben, Will, and Lucas were in a rookie cluster, finally relaxed amongst the chaos as they lounged in the grass. Further away, under another tree in the distance, Coop and Calle had their arms around each other. Mike and Sara, Mia and Liam, Brandon and Fanny, Scar and Kaydon, Charlie and Kacee were in similar embraces around the open space, all the couples happy and comfortable and in love.

Jealously raged through that tear.

Stupid because she didn't even want what they had.

She *didn't*.

No.

She *hadn't*.

"Right," she whispered, knowing the train of thought, the ever-growing tear in her paper and paste barriers was her cue to pack it in for the night. She pushed to her feet, said her goodbyes, exchanging hugs and waves and deliberately avoiding Josh.

Cowardly?

Yes.

Did she also have a wide streak of self-preservation?

Yup!

Because those eyes were tracking her, accelerating her breathing, setting her hands shaking, her lungs tightening, her—

Time to go.

"Wait." Dani caught her arm. "Are you sure you're okay?"

Oh she was totally fine, just coming apart at the seams, totally undoing everything she'd worked hard to lock down. But...her belly was full, and the night's mood was jovial.

She wasn't going to crush that.

So, she slapped on her patented Jess Mask, patted her friend's hand, and slipped free. "I'm fine. For reals, ice cream is everything and bubbles are the shit."

Dani's brows pulled together. "Earlier—"

"I know," she whispered. "And I heard you, okay?"

A quiet sigh. "Okay." A gentle smile. "But before you carefully craft a response to put me off, know that I get not wanting to talk about things, and I definitely get you not thinking you deserve to be happy."

"I don't—"

Dani pressed a kiss to Jess's cheek. "Don't lie," she murmured. "I know because I lived that life, honey. But also know that there's a shelf life on punishing yourself, on bottling everything up inside, okay?"

God, she loved this woman. "Okay," she whispered.

Dani stepped back, bopped her on the nose. "Good. Listen to Auntie Dani. She'll solve all of your problems *and* get you a man."

"I think there's one who wants her already." Ethan smirked as he slid an arm around Dani's waist, tugging her back against his chest. "Do I need to kick Josh's ass?"

"It's not about Josh," she said, well aware that the response was too fast, but she added more information and did it quickly—

yay for distraction! "I'm just tired. Plus"—her chin lifted—"you know that I could kick his ass on my own. I have a very specific set of skills, and those skills are excellent at leveling hockey players." An innocent—okay, not so much—smile. "As you well know."

Ethan, who'd been subject to her teasing a time or a hundred, winced. "That is very true." He tugged a strand of her hair. "Lucky for me, I can hack it."

She reached down, snagged her helmet, and tucked it under her arm, grinning. "But *can* you?"

Another tug of her hair, this time paired with a light shove. "Considering you and Dani are tight, I've *got* to."

Dani giggled and leaned into Ethan, and *fuck*. The way Dani looked at her man...

The paste and paper tore a little further. She ignored it, knowing that the barriers were bound to have an occasional shift, just by the pure chance of being around this much happiness.

It was like being surrounded by cotton candy.

She was certain to get a sugar high.

But it would fade.

She'd paper over the tear using extra paste.

And then Josh would move on, find someone who could give him what he needed.

Now sadness slid in through that tear, sweeping up and coating her from head to toe, constricting tightly, clawing up her throat. That thought hurt. That thought *was* dangerous.

But it was the truth.

He hadn't crushed her peace offering.

But they couldn't be.

No matter how much she wanted it to be.

Another wave, and then, avoiding looking at Josh, though his gaze was on her back, she slipped out of the park and walked down the quiet street.

Meandering slowly to where her bike was parked a few blocks down.

Helmet on, leg thrown over the top, engine o—

She frowned, turned the key again.

Nothing happened.

"Fuck," she whispered, trying the key a few more times before giving up and making the walk of shame back to the Dairy.

Except, by the time she got there, the Dairy was officially closed, and the grass had cleared of hockey players, partners, and little kids alike.

"Fuck," she whispered again, spinning in a circle, arms akimbo, mind wandering through her options.

Which were limited.

Nothing to do about it.

She didn't have any tools here, probably wouldn't be able to get it started without them, without a couple of hours, decent lighting, and her kit. Though considering it was late, she was toolless, and light was at a premium, she did the only thing she could —pulled out her phone and called AAA.

Then found that it would be at least an hour for a tow truck to make it over to her.

"That's okay," she told the dispatcher. "I'll come up with another plan." Which was to deal with it in the morning. She would load it up in the back of her truck, bring it home, figure out what was wrong when she had some spare time.

Thankfully, she had another mode of transportation.

But her sigh was heavy because she knew that with the season starting her spare time was going to be limited and that it was going to be quite a while before any of that spare time materialized. She ended the call then tapped on the Lyft app and sighed again when she saw it was peak hours. Of course it was—playoff baseball, basketball, and hockey preseason games all on the same night meant that she was fucked.

Just like her riding time.

The wind through her hair, her late-night drives...she'd miss them, miss the freedom.

She'd survive without them, of course. At least for a little bit.

But that survival didn't get her home, and when she saw it was going to cost her close to a hundred dollars to go a couple of miles to her place, she knew a Lyft wasn't going to either.

So, she decided to walk.

Save some bucks.

Walk off her ice cream.

Burn those calories so that her skinny jeans that all the Gen Zers wanted to rip from her cold, dead hands would still fit for the foreseeable future.

And most importantly, she was going to pretend that this was fine, that everything was fine.

No chocolate-eyed men whose pain cut through her.

No peace offerings and orgasms that threatened to melt her bones.

Just...*pretending.*

Then again, that was her default position, so what else was new?

"Nothing," she whispered as she took off walking. "Nothing else is new."

Eighteen

Josh

He pulled out of the parking lot, wishing that he'd followed Jess.

Made sure she'd gotten safely home.

"Dumbass," he muttered, knowing that would have driven her crazy, even *if* it would have soothed that feeling of being scoured all along the inside of his skin with steel wool by leaving her to drive that stupid bike down a dark street in the middle of the night.

But...

She'd come to him.

She'd shared.

She'd brought him a fucking ice cream.

So, they'd made progress.

Progress, he wasn't going to ruin by pushing her away.

Which was why he'd stifled his protective urge to follow her, instead making his own exit. He signaled, made the turn, and headed in the direction of his house.

He would have to weave through a couple of residential areas, but he didn't live far from this part of town *and* the Dairy. Actually, if he was being truthful, he lived dangerously close to the Dairy.

At least for his diet plan.

Which was why he only let himself have vanilla cones.

Josh knew if he broke his rule and started in on the mix-ins or the shakes or the specialty flavors, it would all be over.

He lived too close.

Ice cream was his downfall.

The diet plan would be ruined.

Then Nutritionist Rebecca would give him that disappointed look, the same one his mom used to direct at him when he was in elementary school and had broken a half-dozen windows in the course of a summer. That look would be *his* downfall because the Always Do the Right Thing guilt would be raging through him.

And then he'd need to sell his house and move, all to avoid that shame.

Needless to say, he avoided the entire vicious cycle and just stuck to boring vanilla cones.

"Easy-peasy," he murmured to himself. "Easy-peas—"

He cut himself off when he saw...

Her.

With that helmet tucked beneath her arm, an overstuffed backpack on her shoulders. When he'd heard her talking about riding her bike over the bridge all those weeks before, he'd assumed that it was a bicycle, not a motorcycle.

He should have known she was too much of a badass to be riding a simple bike.

But right then she wasn't riding a bike, motorized or otherwise.

She was walking.

At nearly midnight.

In dark clothes, with no streetlights overhead, and—

He'd pulled over before he even processed that he'd jerked the wheel to the side, sliding to a halt beside her, popping the door, and getting out of the car as she jumped and spun to face him.

Her mouth dropped open. "Josh—?"

"What the fuck are you doing?" he growled.

Her brows had been sky-high as she'd registered his car, him coming close, but they snapped down at his question, and he saw the fury write itself into the lines of her face, her chin coming up, lips parting as she prepared to no doubt slice him down.

So much for not fucking up that progress.

But even that thought didn't penetrate the fury.

She'd put herself at risk.

She could have—

"I know you drove to the Dairy," he snapped, "so where the fuck is your bike?"

A roll of her eyes. A huffed out breath.

But she didn't reply otherwise, just started walking again.

He grabbed her arm, halted her.

"Let go of me," she gritted, tugging at his hold.

Yeah, that wasn't happening. "Where is your bike?"

She reached up and grabbed his thumb, bent it back in a way that had his fingers spasming, opening, dropping off her arm. Pain rippling through him, especially after he'd tried to make that tree his punching bag earlier.

"Goodbye, Josh."

Then she spun on her heel, started back down the sidewalk again.

"Jess," he began.

"God!" Her head dropped back, gaze on the sky. "Why the fuck won't you *go away?!*"

That stung. He couldn't lie.

It was turning the knife his mother had deposited during their conversation earlier.

But she was still walking down the street, at night, with no fucking streetlights, a goddamned motorcycle helmet under her arm, and no fucking *motorcycle*.

So he followed her, caught her arm again, catching her other hand when she would have gone for his thumb again. "I'll go the fuck away after I drive you home," he gritted out.

She opened her eyes, her words sharp slivers of ice, "You're not driving me home."

Her tone told him that he wasn't going to get her into his car unless he tossed her over his shoulder and carried her there himself. Tempting, but also probably not the scene he wanted in a residential neighborhood at midnight. Sucking in a breath and striving for calm, he went back to his car, hit the button to turn off the ignition, and then got back out.

Closed the door.

Hit the button for the locks.

Then started following Jess again.

She'd made it to the end of the block, probably thinking that her prickly exterior meant that she'd managed to get rid of him again.

And why the hell not?

It had worked before.

But...he couldn't leave her to find her way home by herself after midnight. He *couldn't.*

Clearly, she was having a problem.

One she didn't want his help with.

Which was fine.

He didn't have to help her in order to make sure she made it home.

Maybe that logic wouldn't have made sense to the casual observer, but that was what he was going with.

Plus, the stubborn, prickly woman couldn't fault a man for just taking a nice evening stroll.

After midnight.

In the dark.

In clothes that were definitely not made for strolling.

Shoving his keys into his pocket, he used his long legs to his advantage, catching up to her before she reached the other side of the street. Her head jerked when he sidled up beside her, but the stubborn woman didn't say anything.

Which was fine.

He didn't say anything either.

Just walked right next to her, up onto that sidewalk, making a mental note to circle back downtown when they were done here and see if he could figure out what was going on with her motorcycle.

But...if she wanted silent, he could do silent.

And there were worse things than being outside on a cool fall evening, walking beside a beautiful woman.

Stars and the moon, fog in creeping tendrils across the sky, making the space around them seem quiet and hushed. He liked this neighborhood with the wide sidewalks and old-growth trees. The large front yards and the median filled with flowers. In fact, he had almost bought a house on the next street over before deciding on something a little bit bigger up the hill, wanting to have room for his nieces and nephews.

In both neighborhoods, hiking trails connected at regular intervals and green spaces backed up behind the houses. There was also a fair amount of wildlife, and he'd seen deer and possums and the occasional raccoon on his drives home.

All in all, a pretty cool space not far from the city. South of the metropolis, with better schools and less traffic. The perfect place to raise the nonexistent family he had.

But was hoping for.

He sighed.

Felt her gaze come to his profile. "For the record," she said. "I told you to go home, so the sighing accompanying the 'chivalrous'"—she made air quotes—"behavior is in poor taste."

"What happened to the sweet woman in the park?"

She slid to a stop.

And there he went, shoving his foot in his mouth again.

For the record, he deserved the glare she tossed up at him, the barbed words. "I didn't ask you to walk with me. My bike wouldn't start, but my legs work, okay? I don't need you to solve my problems." A jab to his chest. "Which brings me to what I've said once, and I'll probably say to you a hundred more times"—she tossed out an arm, indicating the quiet street—"you can just fuck right off down the road."

Why did that make him want to smile?

Because...he loved the fire inside her, the no-holds-barred way she was always herself. He liked that she had spine and never gave him an inch.

He liked *her*.

Which was probably why he started blabbering. "Do you ever want something so badly that you can almost taste it, but it always stays just right out of reach?" He risked a touch to her cheek. "So that the smell of it is in your nose, the feel of it brushes your fingertips, the outline of it, the shadows of it are at the corners of your vision, teasing, tempting, but—" He shook his head, cut off the idiocy.

It was late and he was tired, and both of his parents were in the hospital and this woman—

A breath.

Breeze through the tree leaves.

Moonlight through fog.

Keep on walking.

"But what?"

The quiet question shot through him like an arrow. Soft and gentle, so like that moment in the park.

He cleared his throat, both trying not to hope that the question meant something, and unable to deny her anything. "But," he whispered, "you know that even though it's almost there, almost in your grasp...you know, *know*, it's still going to slip away."

She slid to a stop.

He halted, too, turned to face her.

She was a marble statue gilded in the moonlight. Sharp cheekbones, delicate lips, a proud nose, and...haunted eyes.

"How?" she whispered.

"How what?" he whispered back.

"How do you know that?"

He opened his mouth to reply.

Then saw a flash out of the corner of his eye, and those words dried up in his throat.

Nineteen

Jess

She faintly heard a rustle in the bushes behind her, but Josh's words were rattling through her head, making her feel even more unhinged than normal.

"How do you know that?" she repeated.

Another rustle in the bushes.

Probably a raccoon getting ready to be an asshole, and she should start moving away.

But...

What he'd said...it rocked her to the core.

He'd encapsulated every *single* thing she'd been feeling for years. No, for her entire life and—

His brows were drawn down, gaze drifting behind her, but suddenly those curved swathes of dark hair flashed up, eyes going wide, and he shot forward, fingers gripping her arm tightly, dragging her toward him, and—

Instincts flared.

He'd moved too fast.

Was being too rough.

She jerked against him, fought that hold, kicked out and used her nails and—

"*Ow!* Fuck, Jess," he growled. "Just stop for a second. There's a—"

"Let go of me!" she hissed, fighting harder.

Don't stop. Can't stop. Never give in. Fighting and then stopping only makes it worse in the end, makes the punishment worse, makes—

All of a sudden she was off her feet, held tight to his chest as he spun them around.

"Let. Go!"

Then it hit.

Not him.

Something wet, splattering against the side of her face.

And a second later the *smell* slamming into her nostrils.

Every bit of fight left her as the stench crowded in. It was rotten eggs and sulfur, and it burned her nose and—*oh hell,* she accidentally gasped, sucking in a deep gust of air, and gagged.

"Shit," she hissed, trying desperately to wipe her face, trying to get the moisture off, but all she managed was to get the stinky spray on her hand and spread the smell around more.

"F-fuck," Josh sputtered, grabbing her again, this time hefting her up and over his shoulder as he took off running. The bouncing of her stomach against his body did shit all for the nausea suddenly gripping her, and it was a double *fuck you* when Josh's running made the air run around them, the stench wafting up and hitting her nose over and over again.

She gagged.

Again.

"Hang on," he gasped out, and her body shifted as he bent slightly.

She heard the *bleep* of locks, felt another jerk of movement, and then he was dumping her into a seat, reaching around her and buckling her belt. The door closed.

And immediately, the smell was a hundred times worse.

The driver's side door opened, cool air pouring in, giving her a momentary reprieve.

But then his door was closed, and the odor flooded her all over again. She lifted her hand, wanting to plug her nose, but her hands were worse than her face.

"Fuck, that's foul," he muttered. "Hang on."

The engine rumbled on.

All the windows rolled down, and then the AC was on and blasting.

It helped...marginally.

Especially when Josh pulled away from the curb and began driving down the road, fresh air blasting through the windows and vents, and thankfully, tearing the scent out of her nose.

"You can shower at my place," he called over the rushing air. "I think I have tomato sauce or beer or whatever you're supposed to use for skunk spray—"

"Fart squirrel spray."

Not a correction, per se. Just a random thought.

Anything to take her mind off the smell.

He turned his head. "*Fart squirrel?*"

"I—" Well, truth be told, she had a bit of an obsession with finding new animal memes online—Danger Floofs (Grizzly Bears), Trash Pandas (Raccoons), Duck Puppies (platypus—platypi?), Danger Noodles (snakes), Sea Flap Flaps (stingrays), and yes...Fart Squirrels.

Why did her brain work this way?

No clue.

But it had coalesced to this moment, with her blurting out *fart squirrel spray.*

Cool.

She was *so* cool.

"Never mind," she muttered, probably quieter than he could hear, especially with all the air blasting through the interior of the car.

"Not *never mind*," he said, slowing slightly, which meant the air slowed, too, and *that* meant the smell picked up.

"Don't stop driving," she snapped. "Dear God! *Don't* stop."

His foot hovered over the gas pedal, mischief creeping into his expression. "Or what?" he taunted.

"It smells like—" She broke off, coughed. "How can you stand it?"

A grin. "I grew up in the locker rooms, sweetcheeks," he said. "I can stand a lot of bad-smelling things."

"Well, I can't," she snapped. "So, unless you want your car to smell of skunk *and* vomit, I'd suggest you speed up again."

That grin didn't fade, but he pressed his foot down, his car accelerated, and her urge to puke dissipated. *Slightly.*

"And you're not taking me to your place," she told him.

"Well, I'm not leaving you on the side of the fucking road, smelling like ass, to walk home."

Okay...so the smelling like ass part didn't feel great. Yeah, it was the truth, but also, yeah, it still stung a bit. Who liked hearing they smelled? Even if that *smelling* was making her gag.

Also, yes, this just in, she was going in ridiculous mental circles.

They'd begun upon the first moment of attraction to him.

She'd spun faster when she'd begun to respect him.

Then even faster when he'd told her how he'd felt, when they'd...well, done their business in the supply closet.

Became dizzying with the peace offering and the skating lesson and—

Started moving at tornado speed with the sex in the supply closet, and tonight...

Now she felt like she was moving so fast that she was almost standing still.

Or maybe she was frozen in the eye of that tornado, the world rotating around her while she was imprisoned by winds whipping around so rapidly that they might kill her if she tried to push through them.

And she still had to come up with an answer about where they were going.

"My place," she blurted.

"What?"

There was a glimmer of mischief in his deep brown eyes, but just a glimmer, so she couldn't tell if it was still due to Fart Squirrels, or if it was because he'd actually heard her and was enjoying her squirming.

"You can drive me to my place," she said, loud enough to be heard over the gusting.

They were almost there anyway.

"If you're sure," he said, less mischief this time and more serious.

Actual concern.

Fuck.

She didn't want to see that.

It pushed at the edges of the paper, extended the rip.

"I'm sure," she muttered.

A nod was the only response she got in return, and since her place was right around the corner, she had to start giving directions.

Otherwise, she would probably end up at his place.

Which would be...

Disastrous? Dangerous? Fucking stupid because she might learn something else about him, something else that would make her like him more and might convince her that paper and paste were as cracked up as they had always seemed to be.

Which was...a perfect trifecta of stupidity.

More than the singular entity of allowing him to drive her back to *her* place?

The jury was still out on that one.

A quad-fecta?

A—

Focus, White.

"Turn right here," she said as they approached her street. "It's the last house on the left. The one with the white shutters."

Another nod, the same response he'd given as she'd rattled off the directions.

And then he was pulling into her driveway. The engine turning off. His door opening and closing before he rounded the hood. The smell increased again, and she fought with her seat belt.

Desperate for escape.

Then her door was open, and he was walking with her up to her house.

She smelled like shit.

But, for some reason, her heart was racing.

Because this—the car door, the walking her up to her porch... it was all...too...

Intimate. It was too *fucking* intimate.

Which was probably why the next thing she did was something incredibly stupid.

She unlocked her door, started to step inside, and paused.

Josh had waited on her porch...because, *of course*, he had waited on her porch.

Too nice.

Too fucking nice for *her*.

"You got a ride to the rink for the morning?" he asked once she'd flicked on the light.

"Yeah," she whispered, and even though she didn't owe him an explanation, even though she never would have normally given it to someone who pressed, especially not to a *man* who would press her for information—and she knew Josh would press her for information, make sure she wasn't bullshitting and actually *did* have a way to the rink in the morning, she added, "I'll take my truck."

Brown eyes on hers, holding for a second.

Then another nod.

And a step back, a gesture to her door. "Lock up."

Her heart, the traitorous fuck, squeezed...and here was where stupid came in.

Her lips parted, words bubbled up, "You should come in and shower here. I-I—have deodorizer for your car. We can let it work while you clean up, and then you won't have to ride home in..."

She trailed off because his face did something weird.

Okay, not *weird*.

It was soft, and it slid through the paste and paper, wrapped around her heart, and squeezed.

And...she was tired.

Really fucking tired of pretending and being alone and frantically wallpapering her soul, hiding behind the layers. And burying, always *burying*. Being fucking Sisyphus with a shovel. Digging and digging and *digging* but never making any fucking progress.

Because she never really changed.

"...something that smells bad," she finished.

Then waited as he studied her.

Resisting the urge to go back to her frantic papering over and expecting him to push her on her sudden change of heart.

He didn't.

He just...gave her another nod and stepped over the threshold.

TWENTY

JOSH

Stepping inside her house felt like he was leaping out of an airplane.

Dropping thirty thousand feet and crashing toward the ground.

Jess whirled the moment he'd crossed the threshold, so he took a minute to lock his car—though with the windows open, he suspected that the smell of the Fart Squirrel's special sauce was going to be a bigger deterrent than any locked door or window or alarm system he could buy. After the *bleep*, he moved further inside, closed the wooden panel, flicked the dead bolt.

Her place...

Gave him a strange feeling.

Jess was bright and fun and a strong-willed woman, and this space was clean and organized and...very, very beige.

Oh, there was *some* color in the throw pillows on the couch, a purple ombré blanket folded over the back of the armchair, books on her shelves. But there weren't any photographs on the walls, just neutral art that seemed way too safe for the woman who called the guys on their shit regularly.

He expected rich reds and electric blues. He expected sparkles and flames and freaking rainbows.

He expected the space to be *Jess.*

Not this tastefully decorated and neatly appointed with the proper *Interior Designer Digest*'s accessories, beige-filled space.

Hiding.

Even here she was hiding.

She moved down the hall and reached into the room at the end, flicking on the light. "My shower is in here," she said, stepping out of the way so that he could see the stall shower behind her. "If you, um, toss your clothes out here, I can bag them up so that you don't have to smell them."

He shrugged out of his jacket, almost laughed when her eyes went wide. "This is as far as I'll go," he said. "I don't think you'll want to bag up *all* of my clothes."

A lift of her chin, the barest hint of pink on her cheeks. "I have a pair of sweats that'll fit you," she said tartly.

Fuck, he loved that bit of fire. "What? They pink and tight?"

"Purple, actually," she countered, flipping her hair. "Because, clearly, that's the better color."

"Okay."

Her head cocked to the side. "Okay what?"

"Okay, you pick out the clothes," he said, knowing he was all but signing his own death warrant, especially if any of the other guys got a whiff—no pun intended—of this, "and I'll wear them."

And, yeah, her expression went wicked. This was definitely going to be blackmail material. A shrug. "Your funeral, Webb."

Fuck, he *loved* when she called him by his last name. "I'll pick out the casket."

She grinned, gestured toward the bathroom. "Guess you'd better start stripping."

Well now, *that* he could do.

He dropped his jacket to the floor of the hall, reached for the buttons on his shirt, began flicking them open. One by one by *one*.

Her eyes went wide, lips parting as she released a shuddering breath, one that was trailed by an equally shaking inhalation when he let his dress shirt hit the floor as well, baring himself from the waist up. Fuck, he wanted to kiss her. Even with the skunk smell surrounding them, sinking into his skin. That must be a fucking miracle, that his dick still worked under the current circumstances. But maybe not, considering that this was Jess and she'd always had this power over him.

When he reached the button of his slacks, she spun on her heel, rushed toward another door, opened it, and disappeared inside.

He got one glimpse of a bed before the door slammed shut.

Right.

He moved into the bathroom, closed the door. Phone and wallet on the counter. A flick to open the button, a tug to drag down the zipper, and then his slacks hit the floor. One shove and his underwear landed next to them. A moment later, he tugged the handle inside the shower, turned the water on, and as it warmed up, he searched through the cabinets until he found a towel and hung it over the glass.

Then he spent a couple of minutes on his phone, researching skunk spray and the best way to be rid of its aftereffects.

By the time his cell's screen fogged up, he had learned more about anal glands and the chemical components of thiols than he'd ever wanted to.

But he'd also learned something else.

Hydrogen peroxide. Baking soda. Dishwashing detergent.

That was the ticket to have them smelling fresh again.

At least, that's what YouTube told him.

And, as luck would have it, he'd seen some...

"Yes," he said, opening a cupboard he'd snooped through and pulling out the brown plastic bottle. Plunk, onto the counter.

He snagged the towel he'd hung on the glass, wrapped it

around his waist, yanked open the door, and nearly mowed Jess down.

She was standing on the other side of the wooden panel in a ridiculously fluffy robe. Tucked under one arm was a stack of clothes (and yeah, he caught a glimpse of bright purple). Beneath the other was a black trash bag.

She teetered back on her heels.

"Right," he said, steadying her before snagging the clothes and setting them next to his phone and the peroxide. Another quick series of movements had his stinky suit in the bag, the plastic drawstrings pulled tight. "Now that's taken care of, we need baking soda and dish soap."

She stared blankly up at him, so he decided to take matters into his own hands.

He'd passed a perfectly-appointed beige kitchen on the way to the bathroom. The last two Fart Squirrel dissuader ingredients had to be there. A few steps took him into the space, a few more to the cabinet below the sink. Score. Dish soap. Next, he tried the fridge for baking soda. And *there*, on the top shelf, shoved way behind some plastic takeout containers, was a flash of orange.

Baking soda. Double check.

Opening and closing a few cabinets brought him a bowl and spoon, and then he was standing in front of her again.

"What are you doing?" she whispered.

The steam and skunk mixing in the hall weren't doing either of them any favors.

But he'd been around stinky fuckers his entire life; he could hack it.

"Fart Squirrel Detox," he said by way of explanation, wrapping his fingers around her wrist and tugging her into the bathroom.

He wasn't much of a cook, but he could mix a simple part-to-part-to-part recipe.

So he did.

Then set the bowl in the shower and reached for the tie of her robe.

Her face paled and she gripped the material tightly. "No—"

He stilled, left his hand where it was, extended but not touching and let his eyes move back to hers. "Trust me," he asked softly. "Just trust me to help you for fifteen minutes, okay, sweetcheeks?"

A shake of her head, her feet sliding back an inch.

"Please, baby," he whispered, gut sinking, twisting tight. Even here, even now, the people in his life wouldn't let him help. "Let me help you."

Teeth pressing into her bottom lip. Another shuddering breath. "I can't."

Damn.

That shouldn't hurt.

She'd set the boundary. He would respect it.

But...it stung like hell, twisted the implanted knife again.

"Okay," he whispered. "Use the soap. Be careful. I'll wait in the hall."

He turned away, reached for the knob.

"Wait."

A whisper. Barely audible over the shower streaming down in the background. Slowly, he spun back to face her, not daring to say a word, not moving toward her. Just spinning around and waiting, all but holding his breath.

"I—" Her eyes darted away, back, and then they were soft again. Seeing too much. Knowing too much. "Maybe you can help me with my face and arms?"

He'd help her with anything, but he didn't say that, just nodded and reached for the bowl, scooping up a small amount and smoothing it over her hands, rubbing it into her skin. Then drawing her to the shower.

Towel on.

Robe on.

Both of them getting splattered and soaked through, but she

was trusting him with this, and he wasn't going to push her further than she was comfortable with.

Her hands into the water, rinsing the solution off.

Then repeating the actions—bubbling mixture on, washed away in the hot water—until her hands and arms smelled clean.

Next, her face.

Spreading the mixture onto her skin, smoothing it in lightly, scooping water into his palms and lightly dribbling it over her cheek. Rinse. Repeat.

Until she smelled like *Jess* again.

And maybe with a dash of the clean, fresh scent of Dawn.

Quiet.

She was so fucking quiet, so still, so unlike herself, so—

She lifted up on tiptoe, her lips brushing his.

And aside from half of him still smelling like shit—the half of his body he'd used to block Jess from the worst of the blast—this wasn't the time for that.

This was...

Him taking care of Jess.

Watching out for her.

She was giving him that gift.

He wouldn't abuse it.

So, he carefully pressed her back, nudging her back down onto her feet. "No, sweetcheeks," he said when her lips had slid free.

Twenty-One

Her heart was pounding.

Her robe was damp at the bottom hem, at her forearms where he'd pushed up the material to clean her palms, along the neckline, the fluffy fabric sodden from his ministrations in washing off her cheek.

But when she kissed him, he didn't try to take her robe off, didn't seek out any of the explosive chemistry they'd explored in the closet, and his towel remained firmly tucked around his hips.

"No, sweetcheeks," he said, when she reached for him again.

"Why?" she asked, genuinely dumbfounded.

As he'd touched her, the pulse between her thighs had intensified, her skin had prickled, need was washing over her.

The desire, that want for him was familiar. Safe.

She knew how to scratch the itch, how to satisfy the urge, how to enjoy an orgasm.

She'd spent a long time after...everything had happened, getting to that point.

Of course she was going to go there, to seek out the release, the oblivion.

Because she didn't know how to deal with him taking care of her.

Strings, strings all around, snapping into place, *snicking* themselves into her palms, her elbows, her shoulders and hips and knees and feet, turning her into a puppet, a toy to be used and manipulated and...abused.

Winding around her neck, tighter and tighter and—

"Stay with me, sweetcheeks," he whispered, brushing a strand of hair back, tucking it behind her ear. "Stay with me."

Her knees went weak and crouched down in the stall, water pinging off the metal, ricocheting up to coat her face, to soak into her robe. Her throat worked hard as she swallowed as she tried to just be and breathe.

"I don't know if I can do this," she told the bottom of the tub.

A movement had him crouching in front of her, more water splattering onto her as it splashed off his back and shoulders. "Do what?"

She closed her eyes, breathed, a curl of misery crawling up through the tear in that paper and paste, wrapping tight. "*This,*" she whispered.

"This?"

A breath. "Yes, *this*. Be with a man, be in a normal relationship." Her throat convulsed, halting any chance of further words.

"Because he hurt you?" he asked.

"No." A breath. "Not physically anyway."

"Being hurt emotionally is still a hurt."

"I know," she said softly, knew that *he* knew that, too, that his family loved him, but that they'd hurt him, too.

He didn't speak, just crouched next to her and waited.

And that gave her the strength to continue. "Because he—no because *they,* my ex-husband, my family, my church, they all worked together to control every single thing I did. Because it took me a long time to break free, longer to figure out who I was without it, without them I—" A breath, that misery growing. "The therapist I found helped me a lot, but I don't think I'll ever be able to be open and vulnerable and..."

Words got hard again.

Josh waited.

But when she didn't go on, he asked, gentle as could be, "Isn't that what you're doing right now?"

Her head jerked up, eyes locking with his. "I—"

No. She wasn't being open and vulnerable, she was trying to put him off...by being open...and yeah, vulnerable.

A palm cupping her jaw. "Yeah," he murmured. "You know, I knew you were beautiful the first moment I laid eyes on you."

She frowned both at the conversational shift and the words themselves. Not that she thought herself particularly good-looking, but because they didn't make sense. He'd seen her from the moment he'd first laid eyes on her, so he'd known what she looked like, for good or bad.

"On the outside, yes," he said. "But also here"—a tap to her temple then another to the spot on her chest, just above where her heart was currently pounding against her rib cage. "And here. But more than that," he added, "about thirty seconds later, I knew you weren't just beauty, but fire and strength, and not just because you put me rightfully in my place." The ghost of a smile. "But because it radiates out of you, fills the space around you."

"I don't feel strong," she whispered. "I feel like I'm wearing a mask and running scared *all* the time."

"Aw, sweetcheeks," he said, kneeling down and tugging her close, wrapping his arms around her shoulders. "You telling me what you told me, you being open and vulnerable"—a pointed look—"shows me that even though you may be scared, that you never lose that steel at your core. Scared doesn't mean weak."

Scared doesn't mean weak.

Those words rattled around in her head.

As they did, he straightened, scooping one big, broad hand

into the bowl, slathering it up his sides, his stomach, his chest. This should be the least sexual thing ever.

She was a fucking mess, he'd turned down her advance, she'd shared...what she'd shared. Hell, the smell of skunk was still clinging to the air.

But this man was beautiful.

And he was different.

And...he made *her* feel different.

Which sent her pulse skittering again, the urge to jump out of the shower and run for her fucking life, for her fucking sanity, for the safety of her mind and heart ramping and—

He was struggling.

She blinked, dropping back into the moment, seeing him trying to reach behind his back, to spread the mixture on the skin there.

Skin that smelled like ass because he'd spun her away, taken the brunt of the spray.

The fear faded, and she moved without thinking, scooping up some of the bubbling solution, and closing the distance between them as she spread it over his back. The first touch of her hand had him stilling, his gaze shooting to hers.

But she simply pressed lightly, had him turn completely away.

Then she washed his back.

Over and over again. Until the odor was gone. Until he was clean, and his skin smelled fresh...at least the skin on his back.

Because his legs still had the perfume of Fart Squirrels.

She moved from his back, shifted to his front, and reached for the towel.

His hands closed over hers, stilling her. "No, baby," he said. "Not tonight. I—"

She slipped them free. "I know," she said then had to promptly clear her throat. It had been too long since she'd spoken, too long staying silent. But she could speak then. "I know," she repeated. "I just..." Her gaze hit his. "Trust me?"

No hesitation.

Just, "Yes."

Her pulse sped as she removed the towel, tossed it up and over the glass. Then she washed his legs, his hips, his butt.

His cock was hard, glistening from moisture and precum.

She wanted to wrap her hands around it, to stroke it, to take it deep and taste his spicy male scent on her tongue, but...he was trusting her.

So, she worked around it, not really ignoring it, because how the fuck could she ignore that glorious thing?

It was impossible.

Instead...she looked but didn't touch.

Ugh.

Life was hard sometimes.

And suddenly, she had the insane urge to laugh, to giggle. Life was *hard?* Yeah, right at that fucking moment it was hard as hell.

Fingers on her chin. "What?" Not demanding.

Gentle. Genuinely curious.

He wouldn't be mad if she didn't answer, wouldn't lock up the food in the fridge, throw away her favorite dress, forbid her from seeing her friends. He wouldn't yell and scream and crack through her papered-over walls, shattering her as quickly as she tried to put herself together. He'd just ask, and if the answer turned out to be no, then he would let it go.

So instead of throwing up another layer of paste and attempting to fill in the cracks, she just...

Trusted.

In this moment.

This man.

And she stepped outside of the protective barriers.

Showed a glimpse of the real her—not the big, brash Jess for show, not the quiet, broken one that lived inside. Just her...on her couch reading a book, cooking in her kitchen, sitting in her back yard, enjoying the stars twinkling overhead.

The *her* she'd been trying to find for years.

She could joke and laugh, she could be serious, she could be in between without having to worry about how this man was viewing her, what he would think of her, how he might punish her later.

He'd seen her at her worst.

And somehow, he didn't hate her.

His brows lifted, and she popped out of her own mind, back into the conversation, and deadpanned, her eyes flicking down and then back up, "I was just thinking that life was hard sometimes."

A flash of bright, white teeth. "Around you?" Another flash, his grin growing. "Fuck yeah, it is. *Always.*"

Her breath caught.

He was so fucking gorgeous.

She wanted to kiss him again, but more than a peck, a brush of their mouths, like in the park. She wanted to drag him into her room and fuck him properly on a bed. But then again, she'd take him *in* the shower, on the floor, on the counter or against the wall or—

Anywhere.

Which he seemed to recognize.

Because his eyes darkened, his throat worked, his cock bobbed. But all he did was smooth his fingers over her cheek before turning and cranking off the water, slipping through the shower door and grabbing two towels. Then he was back in front of her, fingers on the tie of her robe.

"Sweetcheeks?" he asked, waiting for her to give him the go-ahead.

She swallowed the urge to drop to her knees and...well, *swallow*, nodded.

He tugged the tie loose, slid the robe down her arms, dropped it to the floor. Before the cold even touched her, the towel was wrapped tight, his palm sliding up and down her back, warming her, drying her, keeping his body close to hers for long moments.

Then he stepped back, tucked the other towel around his waist, almost in an afterthought, before he drew them both out of the shower.

"Get dressed, sweetcheeks," he ordered softly.

And for once, that order didn't make her bristle.

She just...reached for another towel, used it to catch the drops of moisture sliding down his chest and torso that he hadn't bothered to dry off. "There," she whispered, leaning up and pressing her lips to a scrape just above his heart, the light brown skin rubbed pink. From hockey, no doubt. Probably something that he dealt with all the time, something that was no big deal.

Jess didn't even understand why she did it.

Not really.

Or maybe she just didn't *want* to.

Either way, she didn't focus on her confusing, out-of-character actions. Instead, she gave him an order of her own.

"Get dressed, sugarplum," she said lightly.

Brows lifting. "*Sugarplum?* Really?"

She smirked, raised and dropped one shoulder in a casual shrug, even though her pulse was thrumming in her veins, heart thundering against her rib cage, and she felt about as far from casual as could be. "Now you know the rule—you don't get to pick your nickname—"

"—you just have to live with it," he said, finishing the Gold mantra.

The same one that had ended up with him earning the moniker, Spidey.

Because Webb and speed meant Spiderman, but that was too long to say.

So...Spidey.

"Exactly," she said, tossing her hair and spinning toward the door. She grabbed the handle, let herself out, and closed it behind her before she did something stupid like throwing herself at Josh again.

He was too tempting in that white towel, all those muscles on display.

He was too tempting with all that *caring* on display.

And that was so cheesy, so sappy, so *true* that she almost gagged.

Luckily, she had better things to do.

Like getting dressed.

TWENTY-TWO

JOSH

He was sitting on that beige couch, the bag of skunk clothes in his trunk, his car still in the driveway—though it was currently airing out from the large amount of deodorizing spray they'd doused the inside with.

So that he could breathe when he drove the rest of the way home.

Which, as it turned out, was less than fifteen minutes away.

He could probably make it if he really wanted to.

But...he didn't want to leave.

He was afraid that the next time he saw Jess she'd be like before. That this spell would be broken. That...

He'd be fending off barbs and spikes and trying to break through walls again.

Jess was sitting in the armchair, a blanket wrapped around her, eyes looking heavier by the second.

He should brave the fumes, leave her to get some much-needed sleep, see what he could find out about her bike, but... circling back to not wanting to go.

A soft snore had his gaze going to her face.

Those eyes had closed fully, softening her expression. Beautiful in sleep, gentle and quiet in a way that made this room make a little more sense. She could be soft too, self-reflective, and fuzzy like that ridiculous robe of hers, so different than that mask of hers she'd talked about. Her hair was piled on top of her head, loose brown waves escaping to frame her face. Lips slightly parted, forming that O from which the snore had escaped.

Her head lolled to the side; her fingers were relaxed where they rested on top of the blanket.

Another quiet puff of sound.

Right.

He needed to go.

But first...

He moved over to her on quiet feet and bent over her, his movements partly hindered by the tight purple T-shirt and plain gray sweats she'd given him.

Her period sweats, she'd teased when he'd emerged from the bathroom to find her holding two cans of deodorizing spray like she was a gunslinger in an old spaghetti western. There'd been a trace of uncertainty in her eyes, like the time away from him and the cocoon of the bathroom had given her time to think (and that time hadn't fared all that well for him). But he hadn't commented on it, had just snagged the trash bag from the floor, caught the can she'd tossed him, and then they'd gone to town spraying the fuck out of the interior of his car.

The leather might be ruined, but he didn't care.

Not when Jess was next to him, giggling when he'd sneezed (apparently jasmine and his sense of smell didn't mix all that well), and spraying like a fiend, then giggling some more when they'd both run like hell from the cloud of scent that was trying to get them again.

They'd escaped into the house.

She'd given him a beer, taken one for herself.

And for the first time *ever*, he and Jess had talked. No fighting. No jabs or prickly exterior.

Just bullshitting about TV shows and the season and her job and nothing important, but also *everything* important. The getting-to-know-each-other shit he'd bungled with her from the beginning, finally being able to tell her, "You know I respect what you do for the team, right?"

Her eyes had warmed. "I know," she'd said. Then she'd surprised the shit out of him by adding, "It was just easier to pretend you didn't."

A heartbeat later, she'd talked about the season opener that would be happening in two nights—one now, he supposed, considering it was well after midnight at this point. Hell, they were nearing the *middle* of the night.

And he still just wanted to stand there and stare at her.

But if she woke up and saw him staring at her like the fucking creeper he was?

That would set him right on back.

So, instead, he lifted her from the chair, keeping the blanket wrapped around her, and carried her down the hall. Pushing open the door, scouting the darkness for any obstacles, and seeing none, he strode across the room and set her gently on the bed.

She moved slightly, nestling into the pillows, and he tugged the comforter over her, made sure she was secure and tucked in.

And then he spent just a few more seconds being a fucking creeper.

Committing this moment to memory.

Summoning every bit of self-control he could manage, Josh started to turn away. She needed her rest, needed—

He halted at a glimmer, his feet sliding to a stop on the carpet, body halfway rotated toward the door.

A glimmer.

A sparkle.

His heart squeezed tight when he saw the replica of the Golden Gate bridge, the fake crystals shining faintly from the light of the hallway, sitting on the nightstand.

Not in the trash.

Not lost to some landfill somewhere.

But his gift sitting right between her phone charger and bedside lamp.

In a place of some importance.

And *that* was the moment he realized that every single thing he'd thought he understood about this woman up until this point was completely wrong.

He had no clue—no *fucking* clue—what was going on in that head of hers.

Only that...

She'd kept the gift.

———

He'd managed to lock the front door, flicking the bolt and exiting through the garage—hitting the button and making a mad dash over the concrete floor, contorting himself as he avoided the sensor and the metal panels sliding down. Now he got in his car, started it up.

The windows remained down even though the middle of the night air cut *right* through the clothes that Jess had loaned him.

Frankly, he didn't know which was worse. The skunk spray itself or the mix of flowers and fruit *and* skunk spray that was currently occupying the interior of his vehicle. This could take on hockey funk—and win—any day of the week.

Still, he was thankful that he'd crammed his big old feet into a pair of Jess's fuzzy purple socks, so at least his toes weren't going to freeze off.

Freeze off.

In California.

Fuck, he was getting soft.

It was maybe forty degrees. Which should be shorts and T-shirt weather. Bare feet and jumping into the local lake. Not shivering in his borrowed clothes and being relieved that his tootsies were sort of warm.

Luckily for him *and* his soft blood, he managed to survive the windows-down drive home.

He parked in the garage, hoped it wouldn't stink up the space, and then moved into the house.

Clothes that didn't make him feel like a sausage casing? Check.

Socks and shoes for his cold tootsies? Check, check.

Then he grabbed the keys for his second car—yeah, yeah, he was a fancy professional athlete with more than one car, feel *oh so bad* for him. But the second vehicle made things easier for him when his family came to town during the season.

Less coordinating schedules and making them wait on him, plus his family didn't have to waste money and rent a car when they came to visit.

Driving the spare car—a minivan—didn't do much for his street cred, though.

He backed out, his eyes feeling heavy as he navigated the short drive back to downtown. He started at the Dairy, began circling through the side streets, first in small circles and then in larger ones. Until he spotted it.

That sexy black and blue bike.

The one that had made his dick twitch when he'd watched her pull out of the arena parking lot headed for the Dairy earlier. Sitting astride it like a total badass, revving the engine, zipping right through the cars with a confidence that was pure Jess—

He stopped, wondered about that.

Wondered about the Jess he thought he knew and the glimpses of the woman he'd seen tonight, been *given* tonight. The softness of her space, her past, the fear and vulnerability she felt about the future. But then there was the glittering bridge on her nightstand, the way she'd seemed shocked that they'd shared some of the same thoughts, same experiences, how she'd held his hand and cleaned his body and—

The woman was a puzzle.

An intriguing mix of carefree and prickly, of open and closed, a set of interlocking metal pieces he needed to move around until he managed to get them all free.

But that puzzle needed to be solved on a rested mind.

For now, he just pulled out his phone, called AAA, and spent the next hour waiting for a tow truck.

Then he fired off a text to his friend, Marco, calling in his favor.

He'd gotten Marco tickets to a Gold playoff game in exchange for future auto work. Something Josh had never expected to recoup on. He'd met Marco on the street, they'd gotten to talking about life and kids and hockey, and Marco had mentioned that he was saving up for a ticket for his son for next season, since Jericho was a big fan.

It was what he hadn't said that Josh had picked up on.

Not asking for a favor, not saying playoff tickets were too expensive.

Not commenting on the fact that he was saving up for one seat for his teenage son when he'd just told Josh his was a family of five—him, his wife, and their three kids.

It had been nothing to get Marco's number for "future auto needs."

Barely anything to get the whole family tickets and have them sent via text to Marco's phone.

But he'd never asked for anything in return, never even planned on it.

Not until that morning.

For Jess, he'd call in any favor.

He just hoped that Marco could deliver.

Twenty-Three

Jess

She woke up sweating, light pouring in through the window, arms and legs pinned in place.

She was—she managed to pull back the blankets enough to sit up—tucked into her bed?

Josh.

She rolled the fringe of the blanket that had been on her couch the night before between thumb and forefinger, the soft fabric tickling her skin. The last she remembered was sitting on the chair, fatigue pulsing through her, trying to argue with Josh about the merits of her trash TV shows, and...

Now she had been tucked into bed and the sun was shining in through the window.

Groaning, she rubbed her eyes, thankfully only catching the faint whiff of Fart Squirrel Stink No. 5. Josh's YouTube video had come through, and it was easier to think about that than the street and their conversation before the skunk attack. Certainly, it was easier to think about the odor instead of the shower, the vulnerability, the way paper around her heart was tearing, how she'd wanted to take Josh's pain from him in the park.

Her phone was on her charger, where she'd left it the night before, so she grabbed it and headed to the kitchen.

Coffee first.

Bike second.

Worrying about Josh and all her carefully constructed rules a distant, distant third.

Which was why she took her coffee on the back porch, putzed around her garden, pulling the odd weed that was poking up through the pavers on the small patio. Why she took a long shower—ignoring the fact that the bowl they'd left inside the night before had disappeared only to turn up in her dishwasher after she'd opened it to stow her coffee mug, and how the components of that special potion had all been returned to their proper spots.

"Who is this man?" she asked, seeing the orange box of baking soda tucked neatly back onto the top shelf of the fridge.

A demon? Sometimes it definitely seemed that way, especially when he managed to push all of her buttons.

An angel? She didn't believe in those.

Her own personal hell?

Maybe.

That certainly existed, at least in her universe.

Deciding that she needed to put it—and him—out of her mind, she decided to take advantage of her last day off for a while and shoved her feet into her shoes. She'd bring her truck downtown, get some breakfast, and then see if she could get her bike into the back of her truck. The ramp wouldn't exactly make it easy—it was heavy and could still tip from side to side if she wasn't careful. But she wasn't the Hulk, couldn't yeet the motorcycle into the bed, so it would be impossible to get the bike in without the ramp. And anyway, she'd managed it before and could do it again.

She could do anything!

Cue her spinning in an empty field, a la *The Sound of Music*.

Snorting, she snagged her keys, headed for the garage, hit the opener...and stopped.

Because her bike was in her driveway.

"What the fuck?" she whispered, moving toward it, spotting an envelope taped to the seat.

Inside was a business card for a local mechanic, and a scrawled note saying they'd replaced some fuses and cleaned the carburetor and though the battery looked good, since they didn't have the key, they couldn't be certain it would start up now, but to just call if it didn't.

The motorcycle fairy had struck.

"What the fuck?" she whispered again, half-expecting Josh to pop up Whack-a-Mole style.

When he didn't, she dug her key out of her purse and tried it on the bike.

It purred to life.

"Of course," she said. "Of *freaking* course. Interfering, stubborn man."

Caring man, whose love language was acts of service.

Frightened woman, who nearly ran for the safety of her house and drank herself into oblivion just for thinking about Josh and her and *love* languages.

But she shoved it down, walked calmly for the house, and instead of the wine, she picked up her riding jacket, packed a lunch, shoved a blanket in her backpack.

And she was smiling when she made her way across the Golden Gate.

———

She was sitting on the blanket, ocean breeze whipping her hair around when her cell rang.

She should have been on guard.

Should have *known* that the moment things seemed to be getting good, her past would lurch up and slap her down.

She was *always* on guard, always checked the caller ID, always screened her calls.

But in that moment, she was content. Happy, even.

Watching the froth of the waves below, the boats in the distance. It was one of those warm fall days where the wind whipping around her felt good, cooling her down just when she was getting too hot. However, the sun was peaking, starting its downward descent, and soon the wind would be chilly instead of refreshing.

Thinking about the weather, relaxed from the sun and wind, enjoying the quiet and the simplicity of a peanut-butter-and-jelly sandwich, a bag of chips, and a semi-warm can of soda meant that she picked up the phone when it rang, didn't look as she swiped and put it to her ear.

"Bitch."

Frost through her veins.

But she managed to react quickly, to hang up her phone. It rang almost immediately again, and she hated that her hands shook as she blocked the number, hated that she looked around and half-expected him to come up behind her.

Hated that her peace had been shattered.

That she'd fought so fucking hard for it, and it was gone in one fucking second.

She curled her knees into her chest, squeezed tightly until she felt like she wasn't going to fall apart, and dropped her head down.

A protective ball.

She hated that it brought comfort.

But...it did, and she needed it right then, needed to hold herself together.

Until the wind began to chill her skin. Until she managed to unfold her stiff arms, to push up to her feet, ignoring her shaking legs. Blanket folded and stashed along with the remnants of her lunch into her backpack.

Helmet on her head.

Body on her bike.

Driving home.

Only this time as she drove across the bridge, she wasn't smiling.

And that night, when she slept beneath her cozy comforter, the nightmares returned.

Twenty-Four

JOSH

He hesitated at the door of the video suite, fist lifting to knock on the frame.

But he froze, standing in the opening, when he saw that Jess was inside, her head in her hands, the brown locks trailing over her fingers.

Her entire demeanor was...defeated.

And he knew, *knew* that she wouldn't want anyone to see her like that.

Not big, brash Jess. Not the quieter vulnerable one he'd met a day before. They might be polar opposites, but they were both strong as hell.

Right.

It went against his every instinct to turn away, to head back to the locker room, but he had to do it anyway.

Because he had to use his brain with this woman.

Not always his gut.

Of course, even using his brain didn't work, because the moment he had begun to turn away, Mandy popped her head out of the training suite. "Josh, come in here before you suit up! I want to check out that quad."

Jess's head shot up, eyes connecting with his.

And what he saw inside them had his feet all but gluing themselves into place.

They were empty.

Dead.

He glanced at Mandy. "I'll be right there."

And then...

He ignored his brain and went with his gut, slipping into the video room and closing the door behind him, leaning back against it as he looked at her.

Hoping that she'd let him in.

The emptiness was gone.

The dead had become *alive,* bright and sparkling, and a little dizzying.

She popped out of her chair, smiled at him as she perched on the edge of her desk. "You're trying to rack up favors, aren't you, Spidey?" she asked teasingly.

His brows drew together.

"The ride home, your odor remover, my bike?" A giggle that was so not *Jess* that it prickled down his spine as she tossed her head, ponytail shaking. "You're really doing your best to dig yourself out of the hole you made, aren't you?" The tone was one he'd heard her use with others. But not one she used with him. This was all friendly and none of her tart. This was...not *his* Jess.

But he decided to play along. "Which hole? The one from when we first met? Or another in the line of the many I've dug since?"

Her smile didn't dip. "I think you've filled in a few with your actions from yesterday."

A shrug. "It was nothing."

Her eyes went warm, and for a second, he caught a glimpse of the vulnerable woman from the shower, the one who washed him so gently. "Not nothing to me." Then that flash disappeared.

"And anyway, I've decided that I have to hate you just on principle, at this point. You're too nice and pretty and good at hockey."

A glittering bridge.

A bright persona.

Hiding...what?

One half of his mouth kicked up, but he decided not to push on that front, at least not yet. Instead, all he did was say lightly, "I think you'll change your mind when you see what I've got for you."

A flicker of uncertainty, of regret and guilt. "I think we both know that the gift-giving didn't go so well last time."

"No," he agreed. "But that was before."

She went still. "Before what?"

Before he'd seen the crystal bridge on her nightstand. Before the park and shower and the glimpse of the person inside, before this half-stranger stood in front of him, the woman with so many different faces that he didn't quite understand how they all fit together.

"Before I discovered that these are your favorite."

He reached into his pocket, tossed her a package...of Twix.

She seemed to catch it instinctively before her gaze dropped to her hands, held for one long moment. Then she glanced back up, lips curving at the edges. "Yeah," she whispered. "They are."

A knock on the door behind his head.

The knob turning, the wooden panel shifting as someone tried to push in.

He started to push up. "Jess?"

Her gaze had gone back to her hands. Now, it lifted again, eyes full of emotions. "Yeah?"

"You don't throw that away and I'll consider the hole *you* dug to be filled."

Then he stepped aside, allowed the door to open, and—

Came face-to-face with Dani.

———

Dani's cheeks had gone pink, her eyes considering as they'd flicked between him and Jess, but she'd been no nonsense, thankfully, as she'd stepped into the video suite.

Not that there was much to see.

Two fully-clothed adults.

One copper-plastic-wrapped treat.

But loads of tension and interest and plenty of fuel for the gossip train.

Well, fuck it.

What did he care?

Maybe that extra fuel would help him find the correct path through the maze that was Jess.

"Quad!" Mandy hollered, standing in the open door of the training rooms, curiosity written into the lines of her face.

"Really?" he asked.

"It's an old, potentially nagging injury," she said, innocently. "I should make sure it's healthy to start the season."

"You didn't do that the last few weeks?" he asked, following her into the room.

"Of course, I did." A grin. "But if I let you wander off down the hall without interrogating you, then Brit will have one up on me and I'll never be able to hold my head high next girl's night."

"Why's that?" he asked, playing dumb.

"Because there's obviously something going on with you and Jess."

"I don't know what you're talking about," he said, sitting on the table when she pointed and letting her guide his legs through a series of movements.

"Of course, you have to say that," she said, having him take off his pants. "It's a time-honored tradition that the current couple in progress pretends that nothing is happening. Hell, I was the master at it." She blew on her knuckles, buffed them on her shoulder. "But the sparks from you and Jess have threatened to melt the ice for three full seasons now."

"All we do is bicker."

And fuck in supply closets.

And bond over buried pain.

She smoothed a strip of kinesiology tape down his leg. "I believe the saying is from bickering to bed."

He frowned. "*Whose* saying?"

"Well, *mine* obviously," she said and smiled, tossing him his pants. "That's why it's brilliant. Now"—she hopped up onto the padded table next to him—"tell Auntie Mandy all about it. How are you going to win over the woman who wants to snap your neck like a teeny tiny twig?"

"That's..."

"Brilliant?" she asked, cocking her head to the side.

"Disturbing," he finished.

"You say po-tay-toe, I say po-tah-toe."

He hopped off the table. "I'm going to go play hockey now."

A beatific smile. "Probably a good idea." A finger wave. "Ta-ta now."

Laughing, he shook his head and moved to the door.

"Oh, Joshie boy?" she called.

Heaven help him.

He stopped, glanced back. "Yeah, Mandy?"

"Just for the record, you're *totally* into Jess, right?" She hopped down herself, feigned casualness as she straightened supplies. "Like have been into her since the beginning?"

He dropped his head back, searching those heavens—okay, the ceiling—for inspiration...or well, really, for patience.

"Yup," she said, victory in her tone as the P popped. "It's been since the beginning."

Since she already had his answer, he just stifled a sigh, left the training suite, and got ready for the season opener.

Time to play some fucking hockey.

TWENTY-FIVE

JESS

The boys had brought it, she thought as she grabbed the last goal—a one, two, three from Blue to Josh back to Logan.

The slap shot from the point had happened so fast that she'd nearly missed it.

And she had it on replay *and* in slow motion.

She was playing catch up during the commercial break, grabbing another angle of the wind-up before the game started again, and...she found herself pausing the clip on Josh's celebration. The way his entire face had lit up, even though he hadn't gotten the goal (that had gone to Blue, who'd had a nice freaking tip right in front of the net), made something happen in her heart.

Okay, not something.

Feelings. *Fucking feelings*.

That was what she had.

Ugh. This might be the stupidest thing she'd ever done to herself.

Forcing herself to focus, she let the tape roll at normal speed, logged the rest of the normal data necessary (they had a tagging system for each clip), and the offensive, defensive, and goalie coaches all had preferences to be grabbed, tagged, and be available for review.

Certain players—like Brit—always asked for tape, so Jess made sure to catalog both the shots and Brit's saves, even if the opposing team's attempts went wide.

Brit had a method to her madness, and that meant studying lots of tape.

Jess respected the process, busted her hump through the rest of the plays, and managed to catch up just as the puck dropped after the commercial break.

Because of the speed of the game, she and Dani didn't talk much other than to advise with tagging, or the occasional, "Got it," if they needed to rush a clip down. Rarely, they'd toss in a "Missed it." But those were few and far between because they'd worked together for so long at this point. They had a system, and that system had been refined over the years.

It wasn't all smooth sailing.

For example, they struggled late in the second to get another angle from the truck (not exactly a truck any longer, but where the network processed all the feeds and where they pulled their video from). This led to cursing on both their parts, several new gray hairs emerging from Jess's scalp, but thankfully managing, in the end, to get the clip down to the tablet on the bench in enough time for the D coaches to review.

Ultimately, opting to challenge a goal that had squeaked in on Brit.

And because they'd gotten the angle that had captured the interference (contact from the opposing player, knocking Brit out of position), the goal had been reversed.

That was the shit that Jess loved.

When she'd gone back to college and studied broadcasting, she'd never imagined ending up on the technical side.

But she loved it.

The speed. How every night was different.

How this organization made her feel important and part of the team and not just an employee coming in to punch the clock.

Of course, that meant the losses stung and the heartbreak of losing a Cup hurt like hell.

But, it also made her belong.

And after her childhood, after spending years being picked apart and shoved down and reduced to broken pieces, after the *hell* she'd been through, Jess needed to belong somewhere.

And yet...

She felt like it was always going to be torn away. Like if she fucked up or pissed someone off or let them glimpse the mess inside her head that...

They wouldn't like her.

She would lose the family that had taken her in when her own had kicked her out.

Like having her friends in her life was precariously balanced on the tips of her fingers. A stiff breeze, a jerky movement, if she even *breathed* wrong, it would all come toppling down.

Josh had described the turmoil perfectly.

And he'd gotten a glimpse of her, of the *real* her...and he hadn't run—

"Offsides," Dani called.

Shit.

Jess blinked, pulled herself out of her head, quickly grabbed the couple of seconds of video, scrambled for the angles, and put them in the proper folder.

Which meant that she was then scrambling for several long minutes.

Because, just that quickly, she was already behind.

And now instead of the truck and its slow ass feed giving her the gray hairs, she'd done it to herself.

Her fingers flew on the keyboard. She practically gave herself carpal tunnel on her mouse. But she eventually caught up, and by the end of the game, she and Dani were on track, flying through their list.

No erroneous thoughts of sexy men and their smiles, of their hands moving on her skin, of how good it had felt to take him inside her.

Just clips and tags and running through their list.

And they would do it for another eighty-one games, and hopefully sixteen more playoff wins to take home the Cup.

It had been a few years since they'd won, and they'd ended up in second place just two years before after a—no pun intended—heartbreaking seven-game series against the Breakers. Heartbreaking because they'd been so close they could taste the win, and then had watched as that future, the joy, just slid off the tips of their fingers. But also, *not,* in a way. Because most of the Gold's players had already won a Cup, and the Breakers' win had been for their former captain, Oliver James, who'd suffered a devastating, career-ending injury in the previous season's match.

There had been tears.

From both teams.

And joy...from both teams.

Oliver had gotten the moment he'd deserved.

But that meant last season the Gold had been hungry for the ultimate win, and then had fallen short. So, this season, *this* freaking season, they were running on all cylinders, wanting the win and willing to bust their asses for it.

Jess wasn't going to let them down.

She'd pull her weight, do her job, and if they did manage another Cup, she would be cheering as loudly as her voice would carry.

"Finally," Dani said about ten minutes later as they both finished with their lists and were signing out of their computers. Her friend slid in her keyboard tray, rolled her shoulders, leaned her head from side to side.

Jess hit the button to upload the clips to the cloud, did some stretching of her own. "Whew," she said, "I think we need to have some preseason training of our own. My hands are cramping."

"You need a new mouse?"

Dani was nothing if not practical.

"I might try that one you have," Jess said, lips twitching. "But it's not urgent."

"I was hoping you would say that." Dani tugged open a drawer, reached in and tossed her a package. "I blame what happened earlier on why I forgot to give this to you until now."

Jess caught the box, frowned. "What happened earlier?"

"Open it first."

She tore open the paper, grinned. "A mouse that's just like yours!" She clasped it to her chest and fluttered her eyes ridiculously. "What a surprise based on the context of our conversation."

Grinning, Dani balled up a piece of paper and launched it at her.

Jess ducked.

"But seriously," she said quickly, carefully stowing the mouse in her backpack, "thank you, that's very thoughtful."

"You're welcome."

"Okay"—a clap of her hands—"tell me what happened earlier?"

A dash of nerves in Dani's eyes, and shit, Jess had been too wrapped up in herself and had missed something about her friend.

God, she was an ass.

Then Dani's cheeks went pink. "It's no big deal. Really," she said quickly, probably because Dani saying it was *no big deal* meant that it *was* a big deal, which meant that Jess's stomach began twisting.

"Dani," she warned. "Don't make me withhold your Hot Tamales stash."

"Meanie," Dani said, and the light tone had Jess relaxing.

Or maybe it was the twinkle in Dani's eyes, crowding out the nerves, that brought it.

Because whatever had happened wasn't bad news.

"I'm pregnant."

Jess was still sitting in that relief of it not being bad news, so it took her a minute for those words to process. "Wait," she said, straightening in her chair. "*Wait.*" She jumped to her feet. "What?" she gasped. "You're—?"

A nod.

"Holy shit," Jess breathed. "Holy *shit!*" she rushed across the room, caught her friend up in a hug. "Dani, oh my God!" There was no description for the sound that crossed her lips. Part squeal, part gulp. Part gleeful giggle.

Her friend was pregnant.

Yes, she was jumping up and down like a toddler excited for an ice cream—a woman approaching thirty who was desperate for her shake with mix-ins from the Dairy. But anyway, she was laughing and gasping and squealing. She was—

"I am *so* happy for you!" She threw her arms around Dani, squeezed her tight. "Oh wait, I"—she pulled back—"shit! Am I hurting you? The baby?"

"No, Jess." Dani's arms wrapped snuggly around her in turn. "My baby is the size of a strawberry. I'm fine."

"Baby," Jess whispered. "Oh my God, my best friend is pregnant."

"I know," Dani whispered back. "I'm fucking terrified."

Jess pulled away from the hug, gripped Dani's shoulders. "You're going to be the best mom ever."

"I don't know about that." A breath. "But I'm going to try my best."

Which was why Dani was going to *be* the best. Or one of them, anyway. She cared. She loved. She was soft and sweet and had room in her heart.

And Ethan...

She smiled.

Ethan was going to be great, too.

A knock.

The door flying open.

People on the threshold, smiles on their faces, Brit doing an impression of an excited toddler wanting that ice cream cone herself.

They started to rush in, and when Dani jumped, staggered back, Jess moved to put herself between them, between her friend and the group of love and noise and players and women, all of whom had clearly heard the news, no doubt from Ethan.

All of whom together might be too much for her shy friend.

But...Dani had come so freaking far.

A hand on Jess's shoulder. A light squeeze. "It's fine," she whispered.

Which was just as well, because the women were streaming around her, gathering in front of Dani, exchanging hugs and squeezing arms and hands and—

Excitement.

Love.

Joy.

Ethan cupping Dani's cheek and pressing a light kiss to her forehead. Dani staring back up at him, wide open, love shining out of her every pore.

There.

Right *there*.

Jess couldn't do that.

She *couldn't*.

And her future, the one that was balanced on her fingertips, teetering to and fro...it slipped away, dropping off, sailing toward the floor.

Going, going, *gone*.

She slipped out into the hall.

Then *she* was gone.

TWENTY-SIX

JOSH

He'd seen Jess's face when she emerged from the crowded space.

Stark again.

Dead eyes again.

It wasn't even a second thought to follow her. This was brain and gut working together, moving after her.

"Jess," he said, catching up with her before she pushed through the door. "Wait."

She stopped, turned those eyes on him.

Watched as the dead in them shattered, fell away to reveal a deep, old pain. One so big and intense that it took his breath away.

"Please," she whispered.

"What?" he breathed.

Her lids slid closed, a single tear gathering on the corner of one. "Please." Her voice was barely audible. "Please, just make it go away."

He inhaled sharply.

Then he took her hand. "Okay."

He'd gotten her in the car, but she still hadn't spoken.

Just buckled in, stared straight ahead.

A muscle in her jaw ticking.

He didn't comment, didn't do anything other than click his own seat belt into place, turn on his car, and start driving.

Questions bubbled in his mind.

He bit them back.

And drove to the only place he could think of.

Through the remnants of the arena traffic, down the highway, getting off on an exit close to the one they would take to get to their houses.

Then he was winding up through the residential streets, zipping through a darkened country road, and...turning into a parking lot.

He'd stumbled onto this place last season, while going for a drive after a frustrating loss, winding through the roads, trying not to think about all the crap that had gone wrong. Attempting to think instead about moving forward, being disciplined, focusing on the small details, following the team's plan.

Of course, all he'd been able to focus on had been what *he'd* done wrong.

Maybe he shouldn't have pushed earlier. Maybe the candy and the bike and the shower and tucking her into bed was too much, too fast.

Maybe that was why his parents didn't let him step in to help.

He jumped with both feet, overwhelmed...

He'd gotten himself into full beat-up mode when he'd spotted the lights in the distance.

Lights where they shouldn't be, considering this was the middle of the boonies and there should be nothing but sleeping cows and rolling fields dotted with the occasional oak tree.

But months ago, he'd turned the corner, seen the glittering lights and...

He'd stopped.

"Come on," he said now, unbuckling and opening his door, and when she still hadn't moved by the time he'd rounded the hood, he opened *her* door, unbuckled *her* belt. "Sweetcheeks."

She blinked.

Then turned to him and got out. "Where are we?"

"Trust me?"

A sigh. A spark of inner fire. A sliver of vulnerability. Plenty of tart. "I got in the car with you, didn't I?"

He grinned. "Yeah, you did. Though"—he shrugged—"I assumed that was mostly because you wanted to see if your deodorizing had done the trick."

Now her mouth curved, and he felt the jagged piece inside him that had been stabbing him over and over again from the moment he'd seen her leave the video suite, her face a lesson in stark agony, retract, allowing him to breathe easier, to think, to tuck his issues away and to focus on her.

"It's pretty amazing what four cans of Febreze can do, isn't it?" she said.

He chuckled. "Mix the scent of skunk and flowers?"

A tap to her nose. "Got it in one." Then she turned toward the hill, the glimmer of the lights faintly visible in the distance. "What is this place?"

He lifted his brows. "This is you trusting me?"

"You only going to answer my questions with questions?"

"Would it matter if I did?"

A grin. "Ridiculous man."

"Am I?"

Jess sighed then surprised the shit out of him by weaving their fingers together and drawing him toward the entrance. "Show me why you brought me here."

So...

He did.

———

He'd rented two blankets, bought her an annual pass.

Not that he was hoping that she would come here with him again.

Just...giving her options in case she found peace here.

And maybe an excuse for their paths to cross.

Then he'd led her through the entrance and had waited for it to hit her.

It hadn't taken long, and he hadn't been disappointed. The moment they'd crested the small rise by the ticket booth, and she'd gotten a glimpse of the light display illuminating the surrounding hillsides, he'd known she got it.

Felt it.

"It's like every single hill is covered in fireflies," she said.

"Or sparkles," he murmured. "Like those sneakers you like to wear."

"Well, we do work for a team called the Gold."

That sent laughter bubbling up in his chest. "True, sweetcheeks. Very, very true." He jerked his chin toward the path. "Should we?"

"We should."

Fingers laced together, they started walking.

"I still don't get what this place is," she said as they began weaving their way through the trails.

He hadn't at first either. Not until he'd gone home and looked it up. The old art installation made permanent, lights planted in the fields like flowers, glimmering and powered by tiny solar panels didn't make sense for the area, but he wasn't going to question it, not when it brought him—and hopefully Jess—peace.

The different colors and sizes came together to create patterns ranging from simple to intricate, and yet each of them stole his breath.

"It's..."

He told her about the artist and the installation. About the small solar panels and how the special bulbs were supposed to reduce light pollution so that the native wildlife wouldn't be affected. He told her how the first part of the exhibit had been erected illegally on this property and that people had added to it over time, how it had become so loved that the entire acreage had been donated to the artist in the previous owner's will. And he told her how the profit from ticket sales now went to after-school programs teaching the arts and science to local school kids.

Then he shut up.

Let her enjoy the effect.

They walked around the entire space, up and down every path, crisscrossing every field, until they'd ended up in his favorite spot.

And that was where the blankets came into play.

One on the ground, the other around her shoulders.

"So, this is what you do after games?" she asked softly.

"Most nights," he admitted.

"No clubbing or picking up chicks for you, you big hockey stud?"

A chuckle bubbled up in his chest. "Does this mean we're back to more questions, sweetcheeks?"

She sank onto the blanket. "Or one could say, more avoidance?"

"Who? Me?" he teased.

A flash of white teeth.

He lounged back next to her. "How about tit for tat?"

Now she started laughing, flipping over to face him. "Is this going to be your new way to annoy me?"

"No." He smoothed a thumb over her cheek. "But it *is* my new way to get you to smile."

She fell quiet at that, her gaze returning to the rolling hills in front of them, the lights that would shine until the sun came up. A shriek of laughter caused both of them to jump, but her smile made a reappearance at the sight of the little toddler in pajamas taking off down the path, his parents in hot pursuit.

They'd passed each other several times already that evening, and though it was late, and they were clearly failing in their attempt to get their kiddo to fall asleep in the stroller, they'd now left abandoned as they'd taken up that chase.

But they were happy.

And they'd have this memory.

And...

"My family used to do stuff like this," he whispered. "I never really got how precious it was until I was a teenager and had moved away for hockey and started missing out on it. Now as an adult"—he nodded at the toddler, forced his voice to be light—"running through a field in my pajamas doesn't garner exactly the same reaction."

Waggling brows. "Because you sleep in the nude?"

That made him laugh again. "Well *that*." He paused.

"What?" she asked.

He stared out at the lights, mind a million miles away. "Hmm?"

"What else?"

His brows lifted as he turned toward her. "What do you mean?"

"I mean, what are you missing out on now?"

That hit a little too close to home. "Besides the pajama running at midnight?"

"Josh," she warned, though her lips were twitching.

He tugged a strand of her hair. "You already heard that my parents didn't want me to come home." An awkward one-shoulder shrug since he was reclined on the blanket. "It didn't use to be like that. They...I don't know...after I left to play it was like they moved on without me, like the family was the four of them and I was..."

She turned back to him, eyes locked onto his, waited.

"An outsider, I guess," he said. "Stupid, huh? They came to my games and sent me care packages and *still* come out to watch me play. I just...it's like they don't expect me to return the favor.

Like they think I'm too busy for them, too busy to take care of my family, and I just..."

"What?"

"I miss them. I miss what we had and—"

Her hand covered his.

"I don't know how to go back, to *get* it back. I know they're not trying to hurt me, but every time they tell me to live my life and not worry about them..."

"It hurts."

"Yeah." He blew out a breath, picked up her hand, and squeezed lightly. "Ignore me. I'm just a big baby."

One minute she was next to him, the next she was pushing him back, her hand resting on his chest, her expression fierce. "You're not a baby," she said. "You care about them, and you want them to know."

"It's selfish."

"No. It's you." A press of her fingers. "You like taking care of people"—a small smile—"even if they're too stubborn to accept it, and it doesn't feel good to be on the outside looking in, to not quite fit in."

"Yeah," he whispered.

"And you care about them, about *both* your families. Your bio one *and* your Gold one. That's a good thing, so maybe just cut yourself some slack."

"Yeah," he said again, but even he heard the uncertainty in the word.

"And, you know, you can always talk to them about how you're feeling"—a shrug, a small smile—"as painful as that is."

Fingers through her hair, skating down her spine. "So, the girl I'm into is smart as well as beautiful."

A roll of her eyes. "Don't try to be charming."

"I don't have to *try*."

Jess snorted. "Ridiculous man." Another flex of her fingers. "Also, don't think it's gone unnoticed what you've done for the rookies, how you've helped them settle in. Your family might not be receptive to your help at this point in time, but the guys are, and the team is the better for it."

He tucked her a little closer. "I don't know about that."

"I do," she murmured, resting her head on his chest. "And I wouldn't be surprised if they voted you in as captain for it."

Josh went still, his fingers clenching in her hair. "No, that's crazy. They'd definitely pick one of the core guys," he said. "Not me. I'm new and still figuring things out."

She lifted her head then lifted a brow. "After three years?"

"I—"

"After making it to the top line?"

"Jess."

"After the new guys coming to you?"

"It's only because they're new and not used to the others. They'll look to Logan or Coop soon..."

"Right." Except, she didn't sound convinced, but before he could say anything else, she sighed, dropped her head against his chest again. "Thank you," she whispered. "For tonight."

"It's nothing."

Her arms wrapped around his middle, squeezed lightly. "It's not nothing to me."

"I know."

"You don't," she whispered. "I...tonight...just, seeing Dani so happy, knowing that she was moving onto the next step of her life and seeing how far she's come in the last few years..."

He held his breath.

"I got sad. Really, really sad." Her voice dropped. "Because I don't think I'll ever get there. And I just hate that...I won't, that I can't get there and—"

She broke off, fell quiet.

And he wanted to tell her that she *would* get there.

He wanted to believe it.

Because, fuck, look where they were, what they were saying to each other.

But...

Life.

It wasn't that easy.

TWENTY-SEVEN

JESS

He'd turned into a yummy statue of a hockey player.

Still and hard and quiet.

"Sweetcheeks," he murmured, sliding his hand down her spine. But he didn't immediately disagree with her outright, and she respected him for that. It wasn't like she could just flush her past down the drain and pretend it didn't affect her now, wouldn't affect her in the future.

She knew exactly what he'd taken from her.

That would be...everything.

Until she didn't know who she was, or who she should be, or—

A breath.

A part of her wanted to blurt out her baggage, all of those dark things held in with paste and paper.

But...then he wouldn't look at her like he was now.

His expression gentled. "You're not ready," he said. "That's okay."

"I should—"

"I'm going to stop you right there—"

"I hope you don't think that you're going to give me orders, Webb." She narrowed her eyes at him. "As I've mentioned, I've already been there, done that, and I'm not going there again."

His lips twitched. "I'm just going to give you one teeny tiny order, and it's totally up to you if you follow it or not."

"Not," she muttered.

He tugged the end of her ponytail, grinned. "You're perfect the way you are. I like you the way you are. There's no *I should be* another person *for* someone else. If you want to be someone different, because in your own mind and heart you want to make that change, then more power to you. But if you think that *I* want someone different than the prickly, strong, funny, never-gives-an-inch woman I'm just starting to know, or the woman I've fought with for three years because I couldn't keep my foot out of my mouth, then you're wrong."

"Josh," she said, rolling her eyes, but her heart was pounding.

His words...they slid right through the tear, curled around her heart, cocooning it in bubble wrap.

"We've known each other for *three* years, sweetcheeks," he said, smirking, "and I've been trying to make peace with you for two years and three hundred and sixty-four days of it."

"Sixty-*five*," she corrected.

He shook his head.

"Just saying," she told him, "one of those years was a leap year."

Grinning, he just shook his head.

"You did say you like the never-giving-an-inch part of me," she pointed out.

"That is very true." His hand slid down her back, dipped into the hem of her sweats. "You know what else I like?"

Gripping the edges of the blanket as his fingers stroked over the curves of her ass, she said, "No."

"The parts of you that I haven't met yet."

His words kept sneaking up on her. In this beautiful place

that he'd shared with her, with this beautiful sentiment and his beautiful body and fingers and—

She jumped to her feet, moved out of the circle of lights.

"Jess, baby. What are you—?" He started scrambling after her, catching her hand when she would have disappeared into the trees behind where they'd been sitting.

She didn't wait, just spun around and kissed him, throwing her arms around his shoulders, jumping up and encircling his waist with her thighs.

He groaned into her mouth, spinning and pinning her against the tree trunk.

And seriously, she was finding a newfound appreciation for native oaks, especially with Josh keeping her there, one hand behind her head, the other behind her back. Protecting her and holding her close.

His tongue speared into her mouth, tangling with hers, kissing her with an intensity that instantly stole every bit of breath in her lungs.

"Fuck," he muttered, tearing his mouth from hers, dragging his lips along her throat, his voice rasping on her skin. "You are the sexiest fucking woman I have ever seen."

Heat.

Need.

Her thighs trembling and her pussy clenching.

She slipped her hands beneath his shirt, raking her nails over hard abs and squeezable pecs. Then down to the waistband of his slacks as his mouth worked her throat.

"No," he growled, dropping her feet to the ground. Then he was on his knees in front of her, hands pushing up her shirt. His teeth gripped the edge of her bra, tugging it to the side, lips closing over her nipple and—

"Oh fuck," she whispered.

That was...

Too much to process because then his hand was unbuttoning her pants, gliding his fingers into her folds.

Then he froze.

"Shit," he whispered.

She could barely see she wanted this man so much. "What?"

"Are you still on your period, sweetcheeks?"

She winced. Fuck, she'd forgotten about that, about the lie, about the fact that she *hadn't* had her period yet.

He started to pull his hand away. "Do you want to hold off?"

"No," she said, snagging his wrist before he could fully withdraw. "I'm...um...not on my period." Another wince because she was a total asshole.

A tug back. "It's okay—"

Her fingers tightened. "I didn't have it the other day, either. I...I was just scared and acting like a bitch because I didn't know what to feel, and—" She bit her bottom lip. "I really *am* sorry I was such a bitch. You know I love it, right?"

"The bridge?"

She nodded.

His eyes hit hers and he smirked. "Yeah, sweetcheeks, I kind of got that considering that you have it displayed on your nightstand. And it's nothing, baby. Truly. Over and done with—"

"Over and do—*ah!*"

He'd speared one thick digit inside.

"Oh fuck," she whispered again, head falling back against the tree trunk. "I need you, baby. I need your cock inside me."

The push. The burn. The stretch.

His body pounding into hers.

His hands gripping her tight.

"Oh fuck," she whispered for a third time, legs starting to shake.

He groaned against her skin, and her head jerked as she took in his scorching eyes, the promise rippling through his expression. He pushed another finger inside her, and his mouth latched on her nipple, sucking it deeper, harder, and—

Lights behind him, sparkling across the darkened sky.

The cool air on her skin.

Thick fingers inside her, curling as he fucked her with them fast and furious. A mouth on her breasts, sliding down her stomach, delving into her pussy.

Voices echoed in the distance.

It would be so easy for them to be caught.

It would be so easy for her to *cum*.

Already, she was dancing along the edge of her orgasm, her thighs clenching, her back arching, wanting more, wanting him deeper, wanting—

His fingers disappeared, and she cried out in disappointment.

But even as the sound crossed her lips, he was spinning her around, bending her at the waist, coaxing her to hold onto the trunk.

The sound of a zipper.

A crinkle of a condom wrapper.

Movement behind her hips.

And then he was kicking her feet apart, thighs straining against the fabric of her sweats, biting into the skin.

And *then* his cock was pressing into her.

That stretch and burn, the hard brand.

"Oh fuck," she whispered again.

A nip to her ear, her jaw, her throat. "Fucking best pussy I've ever felt," he gritted out, thrusting deep, pulling back slowly. "Tight. Wet. Hot." Each word marked a stroke that drove her closer to the edge, that had her tossing her head back, her hips meeting his movements, his breath staccato, body hard and unforgiving.

But it was when he started to lose control, when his rhythm began to falter, that her tap-dancing on the threshold of an orgasm turned into a swan dive.

Right up and over the edge.

Flying up, crashing to earth, falling to pieces.

"Oh fuck."

The only two words she could speak, apparently.

The only two words that encapsulated everything that she was feeling as she unraveled, pleasure shooting through her, tingling along every inch of skin, scorching her from head to toe, as he groaned and shattered, his big arms wrapping tightly around her, his breath rapid and erratic as he came.

A moment of quiet.

Of stillness.

Then her legs gave way—

And even then, he maneuvered them so he was on the bottom, so she landed in his lap, so he was protecting her.

Keeping her safe.

Her.

The paper and paste in her chest tore wide open, leaving her totally and completely open.

He pushed the hair back from her face, rested his forehead on her shoulder.

"Fuck," she whispered. "This is *so* my favorite place ever."

Another hockey player statue.

Then that statue came to life and laughter filled the air...

And filled her heart.

To bursting.

TWENTY-EIGHT

JOSH

The phone rang through the speakers of his car, two, three, four—

"Hey, honey," his mom said, voice a little breathless as she answered. "We're fine. I'm fine. Don't worry."

It was the morning after the lights, after he and Jess had talked —and other things—fucking hell, he needed to get this woman in an actual bed. He'd left her in her bed again, though instead of having to do his garage Ninja Warrior skills course, she'd told him the code for the keypad tucked into one of the sides.

Put in the numbers. Hit the Enter button and *presto!*

Access to Jess's place.

And also the ability to leave without those acrobatics.

"How's Dad?"

"He's fine, too. I said, don't worry. Jordyn has us both covered, so just go back to your—"

The words triggered something inside him.

Maybe it was the conversation the night before.

Maybe it was just that Jess, who had so much reason to keep him out, had let him in finally.

Maybe he just knew that he couldn't do this anymore—sit in his own guilt and memories wishing things were different, that he could go back and handle them differently.

"Mom. Stop."

Miraculously, she did.

"I love you, but you have to stop." A breath. "I know you're fully capable of taking care of yourself and Dad and our family. I know Jordyn is there to chip in and that, normally, Dad is good, too." His fingers gripped the steering wheel. "But I've spent a lot of the last years away from you guys. I want to make sure you're taken care of and when you push me away, it hurts."

"Baby," she began, voice trembling in a way that had guilt shredding his insides.

But he had to do this. To tell her.

"I love you guys. I know I've missed a lot, but I'm in a place where I can help you, and I *want* to. If that's time off, the team will understand."

"But—"

"They put family first, Mom," he said. "I know that the places that I played in before weren't like that, and I wasn't in a position to demand time off unless it was for the most dire of circumstances. But the Gold are different. *I'm* different. I've—"

And as the next words made their way from his mouth, he understood that they were true.

"I've earned my spot on the team. I belong here, and they respect that."

He sat in that for a beat.

Let that truth wash over him as he said the next words. "They understand that life happens, and I can step away because you guys are more important than hockey." He gentled his tone. "I know I didn't do a good job of making it seem that way before, but I'm trying to make that right now, have been for a while now, truthfully."

His words shut off, fingers clenching on the wheel, heart pounding, throat working.

"So please let me," he whispered. "Please, let me help. I need to feel like I'm part of you guys again, not just living my life parallel to your guys' lives with a convenient cross-over for a week at the lake every summer and a few hockey games in between."

Silence was his only response.

Right.

Fuck.

This probably wasn't the best time for demanding a change in their relationship, for unloading all of this. She'd just gotten out of the fucking hospital, for Christ's sake.

"Mom—"

A sniffle that sliced right into his gut.

"Shit, Mom," he said quickly. "I shouldn't have said that. I—"

"Joshie, baby. I'm sorry."

He froze, nearly missed the Stop sign in front of him. Braking hard, he made his way through it and then pulled over. "No, Mom. Don't apologize. Just ignore me. I'm fine. Everything is fine with us and the family and—"

"Josh." In Mom Tone now.

One that had him straightening and looking sharp, even though she was fifteen hundred miles away.

"I'm sorry."

He inhaled.

"I was so worried that you would feel obligated to us, that we'd hold you back, that I...I don't know, decided to shove you out of the nest."

He exhaled.

"I never *dreamed* that you would feel disconnected from us. I just knew you were busy and working hard and had enough on your mind that I didn't want you worrying about the small details at home when you were trying to do something incredibly difficult."

"I know," he said. "But I couldn't have ever done it without you guys driving me to practice and paying my league fees and buying me new skates when my feet grew three sizes in one season."

She laughed and he hated that it sounded a little watery.

But the fact that this was the most honest conversation he'd had with his mom in...well, in maybe forever, had him sticking with this.

So he did.

"I...baby," she whispered. "You know I had you young."

"Yeah."

"My biggest fear was always that my age, not being established in our careers or having a house or nice car or having to scramble for those two pairs of skates in one season, would hold you back. *I* didn't want to be the reason you couldn't achieve your dreams." Her voice broke. "I pushed you, yeah. Away and hard, and I thought it was the right thing."

"Mom, it was—"

"No, Joshie. It wasn't. You didn't get to where you were because you felt isolated." A breath that rattled through the speakers. "In fact, it probably made it harder."

They both fell silent.

"I can't change."

His heart ached and his insides felt shredded.

"I can't go back and do it differently."

He stared out the windshield.

"But we can do it differently now."

His gaze flicked back to the dash, as though he could see her voice, even though all he saw was the clock and knobs and buttons.

"Can we do that, Joshie Baby?" she asked gently. "Can we try to do something different moving forward?"

Those slices of his insides began knitting themselves back together. "I'd like that very much."

"Me too."

A beat.

A breath.

Then, "Want to come around Saturday and mow the lawn?"

———

He pulled into the parking lot of the team's practice facility feeling about ten tons lighter.

Part of him couldn't believe he'd just had that conversation with his mom.

But he had.

And...it might be okay.

Progress anyway, he thought as he parked and began walking inside. The smaller rink had all the necessary equipment and staff for any days that the team wasn't at the arena, and while a lot of the support staff had offices in both places, Dani and Jess's setup was solely at the Gold Mine—the local's name for the twenty-two-thousand-seat arena that was the Gold's home ice.

There was no reason for them to drive together to work that morning, no reason to *not* leave her in her bed hours before, letting her catch up on her sleep.

No reason except that he'd hated to leave her.

But right now he needed to focus, to get through practice, do what he needed to do on and off the ice, finish his post-practice workouts, his game prep and video review, and then he wanted to get back to Jess.

He had plans.

And this time, he thought he could manage them without ending up with a foot in his mouth.

"Spidey!"

He reacted without thought, catching the hacky sack that had been launched his way.

Good reflexes.

But also his fault.

He'd brought the sack. *Heh.*

He'd gotten the guys hooked on a pregame and pre-practice hacky sack session. They all worked together—which was a relative term depending on how much time they had and how much shit they wanted to give each other—to connect twenty passes.

Today, the quantity of shit being dished out—and he could gauge this purely on the sheer number of smirks surrounding him —was going to be a lot.

Dropping the bead-filled bag, he caught it on his left foot, balancing it for a few seconds before lofting it across the lobby and toward the cluster of his teammates. Brit caught it on her foot, threw it up, and Ethan snagged it beneath his chin, holding it for a moment before he let it fall to his foot and passed it to Coop who tossed it high in the air and...

Three.

Two.

One.

Impact.

It beaned Blue right in the side of the head, just as he'd strode up to join the group, his gaze on his phone in his hands and as thus, completely unprepared for the sack attack.

Double *heh.*

Josh smothered his laugh, enjoying Blue's reaction if for no other reason than because Blue had laughed his ass off when Josh had gotten tagged in a similar move a few weeks back.

Of course, the guys weren't as circumspect. They busted up, and Blue glared at all of them, even though his lips kept turning up at the edges into a smile—a smile that turned evil when he sneak-launched the hacky sack at Logan (the one who was laughing the loudest at Blue getting beaned upside the head). Logan, bent nearly at the waist, his guffaws echoing through the glass atrium of the lobby of the practice facility, took the shot off the side of his head like the tough-ass defensemen he was, barely blinking as it ricocheted off his temple and dropped to the floor.

Josh could make a comment here, about defensemen having useless brains because they voluntarily dove in front of pucks, trying to block them without goalie pads, but he was letting it go.

Mainly because he'd blocked a shot—or hundred—in his career himself.

Plus, if he were comparing brains, Logan had one of the smarter ones on the team, so it wouldn't be very fun to try to take on the older player, academically or otherwise.

But all that *letting it go* didn't mean that he stayed out of it.

He slid forward before the game could dissolve into chaos, used the tip of his shoe to draw the ball to him, scooping it up onto the top of his foot, then he tossed it to Liam. "One," he called.

Liam stepped up the challenge, catching it, and flicking it to Kayden. "Two."

Kayden to Coop. "Three."

Coop to Brit. "Don't fuck this up." And then he lofted it. "Four!"

Rolling her eyes, she caught it effortlessly, held it for a moment, bounced it to Ethan. "Five."

And around they went, running, passing, giving shit for a missed ball. Starting the count from one again, building up, working until Brit caught the twentieth and did a little happy dance.

Sweat had begun to prickle on his skin, and he knew his teammates had fared the same—a combination of the sun coming in via the glass surrounding them and innate competitiveness. To get to twenty. To not be the one to fuck up and drop the ball, even though it was a stupid game that meant absolutely nothing.

"Catch," Brit called, tossing it his way.

He snagged it, shoved it into his pocket.

She rolled her shoulders, shook out her arms, and took off. "Let's go, bitches!"

Groans followed her...but then so did most of the guys, trailing her lightning-fast ass as she began running bleachers.

Another ritual that they all participated in as often as possible —barring Mandy's orders or old injuries that would be aggravated by running the flights of stairs. This one had begun long ago as a post-game, post-practice activity, but over the years had morphed into their warm-up of sorts.

Warm-up meaning hell.

Good times.

Because if playing a round of hacky sack had them all just beginning to sweat, they would be absolutely drenched by the time Brit finished with them and they peeled off to get ready to hit the ice.

Brit was *fast*, even a year away from retiring.

She set the pace and it was brutal.

But just being with the guys, shooting the shit, talking an equal amount of smack, goofing off and turning up the effort at regular intervals...all of it was a hell of a lot better than sitting on the stationary bike for an hour. Even if it meant trying—and failing—to catch up with Brit for the better part of it.

Usually, she threw them a bone right before they all cooled down and stretched and let them get within five feet of her.

Go them.

Grinning, he made sure the hacky sack was secure in his pocket, checked that his shoes were securely tied, and took off after his teammates.

But as he pushed through the door into the rink, he happened to see Bernard, the team's head coach, standing against the wall by the entrance, arms crossed, face serious, head tilted to the side, considering expression on his face as he...

Stared at Josh.

Nodded *approvingly* at him.

What the fuck?

Jess's words came back to him—

I wouldn't be surprised if they voted you in as captain.

Yeah. No. That didn't make sense. That didn't—

Brit laughed, and he blinked, shook himself, and decided that he'd think about that later.

Right now, he had a certain svelte, blond, pain-in-the-ass goalie to catch.

TWENTY-NINE

JESS

Her bike hummed between her thighs.

She'd gotten a ride in, that wind whipping around her, and had made it back to her house with no drama, no work, no certain male hockey player who made her blood sing waiting on her porch like she'd half expected.

Half hoped.

Sighing, she pulled her bike into her garage, hit the button, waited for the heavy metal panels to close, then went inside.

Helmet on the rack in the mudroom, jacket on its proper hook.

Hands washed.

Fridge opened.

House...empty.

Normally, that was a good thing. She liked her little bubble, not having to pretend to put on a happy, light front at all times. But...Josh didn't seem to mind her lows, her tears and panic and—

He didn't seem to mind the woman she was inside.

Or at least the glimpses she'd given him beneath the plaster and paste.

"And that means what?" she muttered, pulling out a pack of chicken breasts from the fridge. "That *he's* different?"

Yes.

That was exactly what she was thinking.

Which was...stupid, because in her experience, men were men and they took what they wanted, when they wanted, *how* they wanted.

Her father.

Her brothers.

Her...ex-husband.

A hard-fought battle to escape and her subsequent victory. Years and years of trying to extricate herself, and years of stumbling through until she'd gotten her job with the Gold, until she'd learned what family could be.

Until she'd seen that men weren't like the ones she'd grown up with. Like the one she'd married.

And she'd seen that over and over again.

Which was why wanting Josh to be different *wasn't* stupid.

He was one of the good ones.

She knew that.

What she was struggling with now was why it was so hard for her to believe that a man like that might want *her.*

That was what she was pondering with a beer in her hand, a couple of chicken breasts roasting in the oven, the weight of her past sitting heavy, uncertainty creeping in when her doorbell rang.

She couldn't lie.

Her pulse sped up, heart squeezing in her chest.

Josh.

He'd come and—

She put her beer down, pushed out of her chair, and hurried to the front door.

But it wasn't Josh.

Dani and Mandy, Brit and Calle, Sara and PR Rebecca stood on her porch. They had bags and curious expressions and—

Barged right into your house.

"Board Game Night!" Brit declared.

"Don't you have a baby at home to fawn over?" Jess began.

Began because they pushed right past her, marched down the hall and into her family room, dropping the bags on the table before Mandy and Brit went to the kitchen and tracked down her blender and margarita glasses.

"Um..."

Dani patted her arm. "You know as well as I do that it's better to just go along with it. Plus"—she smiled—"you love Jenga."

Because she was good at balancing things.

Good at shifting blocks, moving them around, giving people what they wanted, so the tower surrounding her never collapsed and—

Dani frowned. "What's the matter?"

"Nothing," she said. "I just"—the expression on Dani's face went full-on concerned—"my period is freaking awful this month. I'd planned on beer, bath, and bed," she added quickly, blurting out the lie, even though...now that she thought about it, her period still hadn't started.

"Didn't you just have it?"

Jess blinked, shook her head. "False alarm." A forced smile. "Remember what I said when it was the period from hell? She's an evil B."

And no freaking wonder it was late.

What with the stress of her rethinking the entire way she viewed her mind and heart. Well, *that* along with her realization that she didn't actually hate *all* men. Because she didn't hate Ethan or Blue or any of the guys on the team and—

She really didn't hate Josh.

She actually...kind of liked him.

Eek.

Anyway, she thought, shaking herself, it wasn't exactly a shock that her period was late.

Her cycles went wonky when she was emotional and stressed.

"Well, since tomorrow is a game day," Dani pointed out, pulling her out of her brain. "I'll make sure we leave early enough for you to get that bed and bath, though I'm not sure what will happen with the third B. Brit brought enough tequila for an army, even despite not being able to drink it."

Not a Cheat Day then.

And with the season officially underway, Brit didn't play.

Which meant that Jess wasn't surprised to watch the goalie sip water through the entire round of *Cards Against Humanity* and then *Phase Ten*. Nor was she shocked when Brit avoided the bowls of junk food the girls had poured into bowls (and yes, they'd been over enough to know exactly where they were kept), instead snacking on some roasted nuts and pomegranate seeds as they played a half-dozen rounds of *Jenga*.

The woman was here for *all* the things that made her an excellent hockey player.

Code for Brit being a total badass.

Or maybe less code and more truth because—

Her phone buzzed, and she pulled it out of her pocket, swiping and squeezing it between her ear and shoulder as she prepped for her turn.

That block six levels up was loose. She could get it out, she was sure of it, and it would leave just one piece there, which would basically fuck over Brit who was on her right and played board games like she played her hockey.

Fiercely and with absolutely no holds barred.

Jess was concentrating on the game.

Which meant she *wasn't* concentrating on the call, and certainly not on Caller ID.

"You *fucking* bitch."

She gasped.

The cell fell from her ear, bounced off the edge of the table.

There was a crash as the tower collapsed, the pieces and her phone falling to the carpet, littering the space around her.

Silence descended.

Brit recovered first, rounding the table and crouching down next to her. "What is it?"

"I—" A shake of Jess's head, trembling fingers reaching out, making sure that the call had disconnected. "Sorry about that," she said, and cleared her throat since it sounded like she'd swallowed sandpaper and forced a smile. "Just this really persistent telemarketer who keeps calling."

She smiled until her cheeks hurt.

Then she opened her mouth to do what she always did when things got a little bit awkward and she was responsible for the tension in the room. Opened her mouth and prepared to tell a self-effacing joke.

Only this time, Brit said, "Cut the shit."

Jess blinked. "What? I-I'm not shitting you—"

"Oh, you are," Mandy said, eyes flashing. "You're lying, and it's not about what we thought."

Now Jess was frowning. "I don't know what you're talking about—"

"Yes, you are." This time it was Dani who cut her off. Dani who did it while looking fierce as fuck, a proverbial Wonder Woman prepared to slay monsters with her bare hands.

For *her*.

Her eyes stung.

"You're lying," Dani said, voice gentling as she reached for Jess's hand. "And you know *exactly* what we're talking about."

Fuck.

"I thought it was the baby," Dani said, and though her voice was gentle, it was still plenty fierce, pinning her in place, any response to try and get the focus off herself stuck like fly paper on Jess's tongue. "I know it's going to be a big change and Ethan and I didn't tell anyone we were trying, even though you and I usually share everything…"

That unstuck Jess—at least a little.

But before she could reply, Dani went on. "That's why I agreed to come to the board game interrogation in the first place. After you slipped out last night...the look on your face...those dark circles under your eyes." She slipped the phone from Jess's hand and set it on the table. "But it's not about the baby at all, is it?"

Jess shook her head.

"And it's not Josh," Mandy murmured. "Though we know there's something going on between you two, and we're not going to forget to interrogate you about that later."

"No," Jess agreed. "It's not."

PR Rebecca clicked her bright red nails on the tabletop. "Obviously, it's whoever was on the phone," she said. "Which bears the question: who the fuck are we killing?"

THIRTY

JOSH

He'd called but had been bumped right to voicemail.

Then he'd decided to drop by her place, but when he'd rung the doorbell, the voices inside had drowned it out.

Female voices.

Brit's car in the driveway.

Apparently, they were having a Girl's Night.

He'd started to turn away, to leave Jess to her fun, but then he'd seen the door.

It wasn't closed all the way, the wooden panel sitting slightly ajar, and he was moving before his brain fully processed the action, pushing it open, walking down the hall. He'd just make sure that everything was good before leaving the women to their night.

"Which bears the question: who the fuck are we killing?"

Maybe he should have turned away.

Instead, he moved faster, protectiveness pulsing through every inch of him and—

Jess's eyes hit his the moment he stepped into the opening,

and he expected...anger, distance, fury? But the only emotion on her face was...resignation. An emotion he lost when she turned back to Brit as their friend began talking.

"We've let the masked Jess exist for years," Brit said. "We haven't pushed"—a breath—"because you're fucking awesome and fun and the glimpses of the women we get beneath all the secrets is awesome. Because *you're* awesome, and"—she swung an arm out—"we *all* have secrets, all know that those secrets deserve to remain that way until you're ready to share them."

Having been the victim of her own secrets being exploited in a very public way, Brit was well-versed in this topic.

"We were willing to wait until you were ready to share everything. Wait forever if that was your choice—and it *is*," she added quickly before her voice gentled. "But this is more than just secrets, isn't it? This is something dangerous."

The tension in the room ramped up.

The tension in *him* ramped up.

He took a step forward.

Jess's gaze came to his again. "It is dangerous," she said. "*Caleb* is dangerous."

That protectiveness in him surged anew as he took a step forward and then another, *another*. Until he was knocking game pieces out of his way, dropping onto his knees in front of her, and taking her into his arms.

He expected her to push back.

To give him the fire and barbs and prickly exterior. To tell him she could handle her own life on her own.

But she only leaned into him and whispered, "I'm tired."

So, he did the only thing *he* could—wrapped his arms around her and held her tight. "Then take some of my strength."

A shudder.

A hitch of her breath.

And then her words came.

"You know I was married," she said into his chest. "Married young and to a man who wasn't good. His family was powerful in the church, and my parents liked the status that came from me dating Caleb. But we were kids and horny and stupid. We got caught having sex, and a month later, I was married."

He braced.

Because as fucked as that was, it wasn't what brought the bleakness to her eyes.

"It didn't take long for the comments—not a good cook, not a good wife... Hell, I didn't even know how to organize a dishwasher properly, and"—her head came up, lips attempting a smile—"I probably still don't, in case that's a worry."

"It's not." He lightly traced her jaw with his thumb. "Plus, I'm good at taking care of things, dishwasher loading included."

"I know." It was barely audible, lids sliding closed. "You have been with me"—a breath, a forced smile—"look where we are now!" Laughter. Fake.

"Don't," he said softly.

Her brows dragged down, another laugh that he knew wasn't the real Jess.

"Don't," he repeated. "Don't hide from me, sweetcheeks."

That had her going still. "What?"

"Jess. Baby." Her pretty blue eyes on his. "You don't have to hide from me. From *us*."

"I'm not. You know—*they*"—she swept a hand around the room—"know my family was abusive. That I was messed up from it." A toss of her head, her hands pushing against his chest. "It's not like I'm hiding my past—"

Brit snorted.

Because there was about as much certainty in Jess's statement as a male Karen telling Brit he could do a better job in net than her.

"Maybe you told us the bare facts," Sara said. "But you've glossed it over, honey, you know that. It's all in the past and totally fine because it doesn't affect you now. But you know it does. That kind of trauma doesn't go away."

Insight from Sara.

A gold medalist. A talented skating coach. A woman with secrets and pain and the authority to speak on dark pasts with toxic people.

"I..." For a second, Jess was off her game, those brows dragging further together, uncertainty in her words. But then the mask slapped back in place—a coping mechanism, the ultimate armor. A wide smile twisted her mouth, and her tone became just a bit too...polished. "Of course, I know that. I mean, I still see my therapist once a month. And I know you all would have my back. You guys have been nothing but supportive to me from the moment that I walked through the door. But...it's exhausting focusing on that all the time. Don't you all just want to move forward and stop drowning in the past?"

"Yes," Sara murmured. "Of course, we do. But if your past is shadowing your present, you need to stop and consider what actions you're taking."

"Like with the mask," Brit said.

"And the minimizing." Dani.

"And helping everyone else, but not accepting help in return." Calle.

All of those statements were true.

But they weren't the crux of the problem, he'd finally realized.

"They do that with everyone."

The focus of the room jerked toward him.

"What?" Jess asked.

"They welcome everyone," he told her. "And they're so freaking nice and supportive that it's almost like you've entered an alternate universe." His lips twitched. He knew because he'd experienced it too.

Because he'd wondered how he could possibly deserve it, live up to the expectation.

Except, this woman had helped him recognize that he *did* deserve it.

Now he needed to return the favor.

Her chest expanded, froze...then contracted, a hissing breath released.

"You wonder what *you* could possibly have done to deserve it," he said quietly, smoothing back her hair, holding her close to him. "You wonder why they're giving *you* that chance when you don't think you should have it. You wonder if it'll go away."

Silence.

"No."

His stomach tensed, and he wondered if this would be the moment she shut him down, tossed him to the side, made it so that she could stay in that protective coating.

"No," she said again. "You *know* you'll lose it the moment they realize the you they know isn't the full you, the *real* you, but instead just a curated image you show to the world because you feel so freaking broken inside that you know you can't give that to people. So, you are determined to be fun and positive and the one who drives the conversation if it's waning, and is never down or sad because there's too much of that in the world, and always tries to spread cheer because life is hard a-and—" Her chest hitched. "Because you *know* that if you aren't that person, then it *will* go away."

Dani slid forward, pressed her side to Jess's.

Josh expected her to pull her away from him, to tug her friend into a hug.

He *didn't* expect her to say, "Bullshit."

He blinked. *Jess* blinked. Hell, he thought he saw the entirety of the room blink in surprise.

"What?"

"That's bullshit, and you know it." A breath. "You're scared."

Jess shook her head.

"You *know* that we don't throw people away because they have trauma and secrets and pain in their past and present. You *know* that." A stern glare that had Jess straightening away from Josh, her eyes going wide. "But you don't trust it, and you're scared because the people in your life who were supposed to watch and care for you and *protect* you, abused you instead." Dani leaned in. "And you're scared to let us try to love you because if you lose that love, you'll never recover."

"Which we get," Sara said gently. "It's not easy to let people in through the shields, to be vulnerable, to risk losing everything."

"No, it's not easy," Brit agreed. "So, we wouldn't push you to share..."

"But if you're in a situation where you're not safe, then we *need* to know," Rebecca said, putting her cell down on the coffee table and speaking for the first time since Josh had heard her voice echoing down the hall.

"Exactly." Calle reached across the table, squeezed Jess's arm. "You need to be safe." Her voice gentled. "And you deserve it."

"That's..." A long pause. Jess straightened and wrinkled her nose. "Just...*God*, it feels like such a cop-out because I'm going to say it's hard. Hard to change. Hard to be open in that way—" Her eyes hit Josh's, and he knew she was thinking the same as him— that it had been hard, but that she'd been doing it.

With him.

"It is hard," Calle agreed. "But you owning that truth doesn't mean that you're wrong."

Jess sighed. "Well, it's hard and it's stupid and *I* feel stupid."

"Because you don't believe that?" Dani asked.

"Because...I spent so long hearing that I was bad and terrible and unworthy that I started to believe it." Jess's eyes went glassy. "Because it took me years to bury that deep and realize I *wasn't* trash. And because two fucking phone calls brought me right back there."

"Where?" Dani asked.

"To the marriage and Caleb. To my childhood and never being good enough. To the day-in and day-out grind of feeling like I was losing myself more and more with each breath I took, wondering what would happen when I looked in the mirror and didn't recognize the reflection in the mirror. But his voice—" Her voice shook. "It took me back to the night I left." A pause. A sigh.

"So, if you all want to know the rest of it, you'd better hold on. Because it's here and it's intense and—"

Her eyes closed.

"If I'm being honest, it still haunts me sometimes."

Fire in his veins.

Steel in his limbs.

Coming together to form a molten mass that threatened to explode.

"He wanted sex. I didn't." Her throat worked. "We fought and he hit me...and tried to rape me. He wrapped his arms around my throat and told me that he would squeeze the life out of me unless I had sex with him." Jess shook her head. "I don't know why then, why I fought back then when I'd been so compliant before. Maybe I'd just reached the end of my rope and had finally had enough. Maybe it was that he was so angry and I thought he was going to kill me. All I know is that I screamed and screamed until he got so fed up that he stopped, that he left, and when I stumbled to the bathroom, looked at myself in the mirror, sae the handprints around my throat, the tear tracks on my cheeks...and I was a stranger." A breath. "I called my mom, and she..." Jess shook her head. "I don't know why I expected her to protect me *then*. She hadn't protected me my entire life. She put my dad on the phone, and his reaction...the utter dismissal of what Caleb had tried to do...and I knew he didn't care about anything except for consolidating his power in the church, that he thought my body belonged to Caleb...I just snapped." Her eyes came to Josh's. "I got dressed, packed a bag, and went to the bank, withdrew the maximum amount of cash. And then I went to the police station. They weren't—" A shudder. "The entire process is...not designed to be kind to the victim. But the bruises were there and—"

She broke off, gaze dropping.

His stomach twisted.

Because he knew the rest of it was going to get worse.

THIRTY-ONE

JESS

Her heart thudded against her rib cage.

Her eyes and throat burned.

She hated to admit this, but it kind of felt good to get it all out.

Josh would hear. The girls, too.

The last of what she'd buried would be done and over with.

Dropping her gaze to her hands, she realized she was twisting her fingers together, clenching at the skin, turning it red and white, red and white. God, she hadn't done that in years. Not since she'd sat at the police station, telling the officers what had happened, hearing that there wasn't much they could do to protect her, not unless the DA was willing to press charges.

They hadn't been.

Caleb had copped a plea and gone back to his life and she'd... well, if she was finally being honest, she was still trying to get over it.

She jumped when Josh reached forward, carefully untangled her fingers, lifting them from her skin and each other, placing them on the outside of his, offering up his skin, his body for her.

"I'm tough," he said, brushing his fingers along hers. "I can take it."

And *that* more than anything that had happened that evening made her want to cry.

Caleb. The police station. The charges being dropped because her fucking *parents* had vouched for his character.

The DA hadn't wanted to ruin his life.

And what about hers?

Hers had been in pieces, and she was expected to put them back into place and just move on. To struggle to find a place to live, food to eat, to get a job and go to school and to move on.

Alone.

But here, in this room, with the people she loved around her, she wanted to purge that from where it had been buried beneath paste and paper. So...she told Josh and Dani and the others about that struggle. Told them about losing her family, her church, her house, her *dog* in the divorce.

She just purged *all* of it.

All of the harassment and pain, the phone calls at all hours and showing up on her doorstep, threatening her.

And she told them how now, how when she'd finally begun to think that there was a chance that her future could be different, that her past was coming back, trying to drag her down.

When she'd finished, she expected them to look at her different, with pity or disappointment or...hell, she didn't know, just *different*.

She hadn't expected them to look ready to take up pitchforks and storm the castle.

"I'm sorry this happened," Brit said, leaning close and touching her cheek lightly.

"It's not your fault," Dani said.

Jess knew that, of course. Had heard it from a caring nurse at the hospital, from the female officer who brought her home and had given her a place to stay until she'd gotten her feet under her, from the counselor at the college when she'd been accepted on a full scholarship.

But she wasn't truly sure that she believed it.

Not until then.

Until her *family* said it.

She swallowed hard, looked around the room. "There's not anything I could do to make you guys *not* love me, is there?"

Dani—still pressed to her side—squeezed Jess's waist. "Now you're getting it."

Brit smiled her sponsor-securing grin. "Well, that's not true."

Mandy gasped and threw a chip at her.

Brit caught it, popped it in her mouth.

"Damned glove hand," Mandy muttered.

A smirk on Brit's face. "I'm just calmly pointing out that if Jess starts rooting for the Ducks, we're going to have a real problem keeping up the love."

"Or the Breakers," Calle muttered, referencing the team who'd most recently beat them out for the Cup.

"Or maybe hockey isn't the most important thing here," Josh pointed out.

That got *him* a chip lobbed at his head (for the record, he didn't manage to catch it).

"Hockey is *everything*," Rebecca stated confidently.

"No," he said firmly. "That's family."

Rebecca leaned back, something almost calculating crossed her expression, but before Jess could process that, Brit was coming close again. "Sap master to the extreme or not, he's right." A smirk and she knew that the guys were going to hear about Josh and his penchant for sappy words (which was certainly going to result in shit-giving). "And Ducks fan, or not, we love you, Jess."

She nodded, touched and raw and her paper and paste shredded to dust.

And loved.

She was loved for *her*—broken or not, open or not, snarky or happy or sad or all of the emotions in between.

But...she was also done with all of the focus being on her.

She was ready for a topic change (and *then* some). So, she went with Brit's teasing. "Just because I went to school in L.A. doesn't mean that I'm a Ducks fan."

"L.A.?" Mandy stage whispered. "Damn, I didn't realize we had a traitor in our midst."

Jess mock-scowled at her.

Mandy just smiled, took the conversation even further from Jess's past and asked, "How're those shoulders? Need a massage?"

They were tense as fuck, as the sports therapist probably knew. Not just the normal tension from working at a computer, but also because drudging up her past didn't exactly have her burping rainbows and frolicking with unicorns. "I don't know," she quipped back. "If I say yes, will you massage a traitor?"

That got her a Mandy grin—sort of crooked, all kinds of joyful, and one that hit a spot inside Jess, one she hadn't realized was even there, filling the shadows with sunshine. "Only if *you* share your Jenga trickery."

She grinned. "Deal."

Josh started to get up. "I'll let you guys—"

She clutched his hand in hers, took a deep breath, and made a conscious step to continue moving forward, to continue putting her past behind her. "Will you stay?"

Warmth in chocolate brown eyes, and he settled down beside her again.

"Always."

———

The knock on the door came just as they were washing out the final bowls, searching for any stray game pieces (their last round of *Sorry* had been in-*tense*).

Rebecca put down the towel she was using to dry the bowl and moved into the hall. "I'll get it."

"Wait," Josh said, and Jess didn't blame him.

She'd explained the phone calls in between games, how she didn't normally answer numbers she didn't know, but how she'd been off her game and picked up two of them. Which had led to her having now blocked *two* different unknown numbers, being freaked the fuck out from her ex, and all the while, Josh had gotten very tense.

"It's fine," she'd said, striving to be nonchalant about the whole scenario. "I'll report it to the detective who helped me before, make sure the restraining order is still in place." Something she should have done that the moment after she'd hung up on him when he called the first time. "This happens every once in a while."

Of course, when it had happened before, the calls had been a precursor to Caleb showing up on her porch to yell at her, to threaten her.

But she'd handled it, had called the police, stayed in her car, or refused to answer the door. The cops had always responded quickly, coming over and hauling him off, and it had all been good.

Like most bullies, he needed to get the vitriol out, and she was an easy target.

Plus, she'd moved several years ago and no one from her past knew where she lived now.

Though, she thought with a niggle, she'd also changed her number since then and no one besides the people in her life now knew the number, so he shouldn't have been able to call.

Shaking her head at herself, knowing she'd handle it—and hey, that she would have help in handling it if she needed—Jess picked up the towel Rebecca left behind, hung it on the edge of the sink.

"Cool your alpha hockey player protective vibes," Rebecca said, turning back and softening the admonishment with a smile. "That sells the team, and we like that very much. *But* I know who is at the door." She held up her cell. "He texted me, and I always check through the peephole or window before opening, okay?"

Josh's bristling calmed.

Somewhat, Jess supposed.

Because his response was to step back to Jess's side and haul her close.

Rebecca's face was calculating again—the emotion there and gone. "Oh man, I have *got* to get Scarlett on selling *that.*"

"I have an agent," he muttered. "And I don't need to sell anything."

"No?" A beat before the bell went again.

Jess inched forward. "Should I go get—?"

"No," Rebecca and Josh said at once.

Rebecca pointed a finger at Josh. "Your agent needs to up his game."

"He's fine—"

"You need sponsorships, commentating contracts—"

He sighed. "Scarlett's already given me this spiel. And so has my agent," Josh said. "But I'm just one part of the team, and I just want to play hockey."

"Yeah, doesn't everyone?" Rebecca tossed up her hands. "But sometimes the sport doesn't love you back, so you need to plan for every eventuality and—"

"Oh look, everybody," Sara announced, having apparently gone to answer the door while Josh and Rebecca argued. "Pascal's here!"

Jess didn't know who Pascal was, but she *was* done with the hard sale from Rebecca (though she didn't disagree with the other woman's statements and thought it might be worth discussing with Josh at a later point...when the earlier point *wasn't* rehashing the trauma from her past). She turned to see a tall man who screamed danger walk into the room.

His eyes immediately came to hers, and she shivered, causing Josh to tuck her closer.

"Pascal does security. He helped me during my...troubles," Sara said softly. Turning, she lifted a brow at the former publicist. "Apparently, Rebecca thought that he might be helpful here?"

Rebecca's red lips tipped up. "Gotta watch out for my girl." She moved to the tall and dangerous man, lifted up on her stilettos, and pressed a kiss to his cheek. "Thanks for coming. I need you to set Jess up. She's got an asshole ex. Josh needs to know she's good when he's traveling with the team. *She* needs to be secure in her own home so the asshole can't take anything else away from her."

Pascal wiped the lipstick away with practiced ease then turned to Jess, and she nearly cringed at the ice in his eyes. "This is true?" he asked in a faintly accented voice.

"I—" She cleared her throat. "My ex is an ass. But I'm fine."

He turned to Rebecca, who rattled off, "Ex was abusive. Her parents too, and they decided to take on extra asshole points by taking his side. Charges filed came to nothing. A restraining order is in place. Now the ex is calling again." A beat, Rebecca's eyes hitting Jess's. "Did I miss anything?"

"I—" She swallowed, shook her head. "No, that's basically it."

Pascal had been still before, or so Jess had thought, but Rebecca's list had turned him into an absolute statue. Then he rotated toward Jess again, and his eyes weren't cold this time. They were hot, blazing, *furious*.

"Tell me about the phone calls."

THIRTY-TWO

JOSH

He was lying in bed with Jess, both of them fully clothed —though he was in sweats and a tee and she was in an adorable pajama set dotted with rainbow-wielding unicorns, and they were doing something he wouldn't have thought possible just days ago.

Relaxing together.

Talking about nothing.

"So," she said softly, "how do you feel about your first girl's night?"

His lips turned up, but he didn't stop stroking her hair.

She'd curled into him under the blankets while he remained on top of the covers. But she was soft and near, her scent surrounding him, her eyes empty of shadows.

No walls. None of the past.

Just *her*.

He curled a strand of hair around his finger. "I thought there would be less tequila."

She giggled.

She'd been pushed pretty far tonight, and he knew it would

take time for her to process all that had happened that evening, including the fact that Pascal absolutely wouldn't take no for an answer about putting in a security system and tracking down Caleb to find out where he was, what he was up to, and if he was likely to cause trouble for Jess.

Josh appreciated that, hadn't even gotten to the point to realize that he would have been freaked the fuck out to leave with the team when the guy who had assaulted *his* woman—yes, Jess was his, just like he was hers—was out there, making harassing phone calls and potentially plotting to do more.

Rebecca might be pushy as fuck, but she planned through every eventuality, so he had to give credit where credit was due.

"So," Jess whispered a few minutes later. "What is the likelihood I get to see *this*"—she ran a hand from his pecs down to the waistband of his sweats—"gleamed up and in a pair of tighty whities on a billboard sometime soon?"

Considering Rebecca's superpower was getting things done—even in her mostly retired state—he thought the possibility was very likely...to absolutely.

But he wasn't going to admit that.

"Nil," he said instead. "But I'm happy to give you a glimpse of all that gloriousness now."

She giggled.

And that was exactly what he wanted from her after the night she'd had. Happy and relaxed. Giving him shit. The only other thing missing was an orgasm.

Pleasured and limp and taking advantage of actually being in a bed for once.

"What?" she asked, and he realized he'd been staring.

"Nothing." He rolled over to kiss her. "Or rather *something*," he said and kissed her deeply, his cock hardening, need coiling in his stomach.

But...the night she'd had.

He pulled back, tucked her into the crook of his arm.

A hand on his chest, pushing herself up. Hot eyes on his.

Swollen lips. "Um...is there a reason we're cuddling instead of tearing my clothes off?"

That image...

Fuck, it made him want.

"It's late, sweetcheeks, and you've had a night. I should probably go home and let you rest."

"That's a no."

He blinked.

"Look. It took me a long time after Caleb to get comfortable with my body. But I am." Her lips curved. "As much as any woman can be comfortable with it, that is. I went through a phase where I *didn't* respect it, where I slept around to try to feel something, but ultimately, I realized this is better when I'm with someone who I feel something for."

"You're fucking amazing, you know that?"

Her thumb traced his mouth, as though she didn't know what to do with the words that had just come out of it. "Meh," she said lightly. But then her face softened. "I was thinking the same thing about you. Mostly because you didn't ask how long it took for me to figure it out."

Now confusion was sliding through him, gripping his mind, sinking into his brain, and making it move slowly.

"In the closet," she whispered while the wheels were slowly turning. "With you."

A groan. "Fuck."

A blink. "What?"

"How do you make me feel so *fucking* much?"

From the beginning, it was like she'd rigged his emotions with bright-ass LED Christmas lights. The ones that made people hate their neighbors because they were always shining through curtains and waking them up in the middle of the night.

But he loved it.

Maybe loved *her*.

Humor on the edges of blue eyes. Pride in a lush smile. "It's my job." She buffed her knuckles on her shoulder.

"Also, I should make it clear that you rock at your job. Even though I fucked up saying that the first day we met."

And he was a special brand of dumbass for reminding her of a time she'd been mad at him when he was trying to get her into bed...*er*...okay they already *were* in bed. But—

Fuck. He didn't know what he was blabbering about or thinking or—

"Josh?"

"What?"

Her hand on his jaw. "I don't care you fucked up."

He blinked. "I...*what?*"

Her hand slipped to his chest, resting above his thudding heart.

"I don't care what you said that day. You owned up. Apologized. We've moved on."

Right.

It didn't matter he'd messed up, that he'd said the wrong thing. Okay, that wasn't *one hundred percent* true. Words did matter and could hurt, could destroy. But...maybe he could be muddled and make a mistake and move on and still *do* the right thing, still care for her, still make a place for himself in her life.

Do. *Show.*

Not just tell.

That sank into his belly.

Because it wasn't just with Jess. He could show, *do* with the team, with his family.

Not just wait for the invitation or take the rebuttal.

He could show up.

He *would* show up.

"Josh?"

"Yeah?"

Her hand slid down his stomach. "You with me?"

Fuck yeah, he was.

Grinning, he caught her hand, pressed a kiss to her palm. "I'm with you." A nudge so that she was on her back. "Now relax and pretend I'm not here."

Laughter in the air. "Why would I do that?"

He tugged her shirt up, nipped the side of her torso. "Because then we won't bicker when I make you come?"

She jumped. "But"—she leaned up, arms winding around his shoulders—"I like it when we bicker."

He was grinning. "Yeah?"

So was she. "Yeah."

"Okay, now that *that's* established, it's time to orgasm me into submission." She reclined back on the bed, took his arm, and brought it to her belly, guiding it toward the waistband of her pajamas. He allowed his fingers to slip under the edge, to tease at the soft skin there and—

"Sweetcheeks?"

"Yeah?" she breathed, and he could see her pulse starting to pick up, fluttering rapidly at the base of her throat.

"How about that orgasm now?"

"Only if you promise to have one, too." A whisper, her eyes dilating.

Just like that, his cock was hard.

And it was the easiest promise he'd ever make. "Fuck yeah, baby."

He slid his fingers down.

Slid them *in*.

THIRTY-THREE

JESS

The man fucked like he played on the ice.
Hard.
Fast.
A little rough.
And a whole lot smart.

Or so she'd thought after the closet, after the tree...after he'd exploded into a frenzy of movement in her bed that meant the blankets had disappeared, her shorts had hit the floor, her tank top following suit a second later. She'd gone from wearing her cute pajamas to naked and exposed under the brightness of her recessed bedroom lights in under a second.

She hadn't been lying before.

She liked her body.

And she liked the way he stared at her body, took in every inch, worshipped it with his gaze, devastated her with the heat in his molten brown eyes. Melted chocolate dripping along her skin, heated drops that he'd lick up with hot, sleek darts of his tongue.

But she liked it better when he *touched*.

This was where he'd surprised her.

He hadn't spread her legs, feasted on her like she was a buffet (though she was going to request that again as soon as possible). Instead, moving slowly and deliberately, he'd *touched* her. His calloused fingers starting at her jaw, tracing slowly down her throat, across each collarbone, along her breasts.

One side.

The other.

"A bed," he murmured. "Fucking *finally*."

She grinned then arched up, her breath catching as he closed in on her nipples in ever-decreasing circles, coming closer but not actually touching them, despite the sensitive tips beading into tight points, practically begging for his fingers and mouth. But all he gave her was one brush on each side with his thumb before he began running his fingers over her rib cage, as though he were counting each one. Then he moved down, dancing them over her stomach, dipping into her belly button, light touches on her hip bones.

Her pelvis canted, pussy seeking that touch, light, a little rough, or otherwise.

He brushed her clit.

A quick, fleeting touch.

Then he had moved to her thighs, one big palm on top of each of them, massaging lightly, coaxing them apart. Skating down, over her knees, massaging her calves, her ankles, her *feet*.

"Josh?"

"Mmm?" he asked, seemingly inspecting each of her toes and making her glad that she'd gotten a pedicure the week before.

"Is the whole orgasm thing going to be happening any time soon?"

A ghost of a smile. "You know I *hate* to give you orders—"

She snorted.

"But..." Those fingers tickled the bottom of her feet. "I like giving them in bed. I like making my woman crazy with need. I fucking love hearing her desperate for my mouth, my tongue, my fingers, and"—one of his hands left her, cupped the tent that he had going on in his sweats—"my cock."

She shivered.

Because Josh touching himself was almost as good as him touching *her*.

"I don't mind a little desperation." She kicked out, pushed him back until he was sprawled on the mattress, and she was clambering on top of him. "Because," she said, leaning close, bringing their mouths a hairsbreadth apart. "I *know* that you're as desperate as I am."

He laughed. "Fuck, baby. I know that I'm *way* more desperate than you. Now"—he wove his hands into her hair—"fucking kiss me."

An order.

But one that she didn't mind.

Dropping her head, she slanted her mouth over his, tongue delving deep, body flush to his.

She'd made a critical error in not getting him naked first.

But then he was kissing her back and his hands were on her naked body and she wasn't thinking about that...

Instead, she was focused on how freaking amazing he felt.

And a moment later, she was flat on the mattress, he was on top of her, taking over the kiss, one elbow bracing him above her.

"Touch me," she demanded.

"Yeah?" he asked.

"Now."

A rough chuckle. "I like those kinds of orders, sweetcheeks." He lifted his hand, cupped her breast in his palm.

"*Wait.*"

"Less fond of those ones."

She grinned. "Wait," she said again. "Because I want you to be naked, too." A beat as she reached for the drawer on her nightstand, pulled out a box of condoms. "*Then* I want you to get on with fucking me."

Now his expression matched what she was feeling—hot,

ready, playful. It might have been the sexiest combination she'd ever laid eyes on, but she didn't get the chance to truly study it. Not when he was taking the condoms from her hand, not when he was suddenly on his feet, stripping down at warp speed.

Not when he was tearing the box open, pulling out a plastic square, tossing it on the bed next to her.

Not when...

He climbed back over her and asked, "Now, where were we?"

Mouth on hers, fingers between her thighs, this time not just glancing over her clit. But instead, they were arrowing in, circling and pressing and taking her breath from her in a few rough, *smart* touches.

She arched back, breaking the kiss, but he didn't take her mouth again, just trailed his down her throat, along her collarbones. Lips on her breasts, sucking deeply at her nipples. Pleasure cascaded through her in ever-thickening ropes of sparking need. He knew just how to send her spiraling in the best possible way, using the flat of his tongue, suckling in a rhythm she felt directly between her legs. Using his thumb and forefinger to increase the pleasure.

And just when she thought she was going to explode...he stopped.

A gasp through her throat.

Fingers gripping his hair as a distant thought in her mind advised her to be careful because she wouldn't like to see him bald.

But then he was moving down her body, no gentle or teasing touches to her belly.

Just a big, hot man between her thighs.

A big, hot man devouring her like licking her pussy was his last meal on this planet. Long, firm strokes of his tongue, hard sucks on her clit, a thick finger pushing inside her.

Already, the edges of an orgasm were on her.

"Josh," she gasped.

He broke contact, staring up at her, need burning across his face. "Fuck now, suck later?" he rasped.

"Please. Fucking. *God,* yes."

The words came out in a jumble, barely processing her own thoughts and need and desperation. But thankfully, he seemed to understand the words, or at least he wanted to fuck her as much as she wanted *him* to fuck her, and a moment later, he was grabbing the plastic square, rolling it on the hard length of his cock.

"Yeah?" he asked, poised between her thighs.

"Now," she ordered.

A smirk that was fucking beautiful...and then he was pushing in and—

"Oh God," she whispered, neck arching back again. Spreading her wide, gripping her thighs, riding her deep and fast and with that little bit of rough, so that each time he thrust forward, his pelvis brushed her clit, and he was hitting all the right spots, both inside and out.

Finger digging in.

Hips pistoning forward.

Eyes on her breasts bouncing as he fucked her. *Hard.*

"Fuck, sweetcheeks. Best fucking pair of tits I've ever seen." She sucked in a breath, felt his gaze on her nipples, her breasts, like it was an actual physical touch. "Tightest, wettest, sweet fucking pussy I've ever tasted, ever felt."

Her breath caught.

"Smartest, most beautiful woman I've met."

She moved against him, bracing her hands on the headboard, meeting his thrusts, clenching around him because it felt fucking incredible, because it had his eyes rolling back, his rhythm faltering, curses falling from his lips.

He clenched his jaw, the muscles there flickering, and he tensed, his biceps bulged, his triceps became sharp slashes all along the backs of his arms.

"Faster," she coaxed.

"Jess." A groan. A plea. "Jess. Baby. Jess. Fuck. *Fuck.*"

"Josh," she whispered his name like it was a prayer, and maybe it was because this man was winding her pleasure higher, ramping it up until she couldn't see straight, lighting a fuse that was...so...close...to...exploding. "Please. God. *Please.*"

And then the fuse burned down, closed in on that stored fuel inside her.

Boom!

She came apart.

Burst into glittering sparks, filling the room, her body, her mind. A ball of pleasure. A chunk of feeling. Not human. Not a woman. Not right then.

She was just sensation, and it was fucking glorious.

Then, slowly, incrementally, she was a woman again, her man over her, working deep and fast, his movements uncontrolled, the jerking thrusts sending her into the atmosphere again—more sparks, more feeling, more *pleasure.*

Hers *and* his.

Josh watching her and finding pleasure in hers. Her doing the same for him. A give and take she'd never experienced before.

It set her on fire.

It made her want to flip him over and see if they could do it all over again.

Two bodies. One moment. Together. Not alone.

Him.

It was always supposed to be him.

That feeling sank down into her bones with a certainty that had her arms tightening around him when he collapsed on top of her, that held him fast when he would have gotten off. That rewrote so many things she'd thought about herself, her life, her...future.

Future.

Because for the first time in forever, she thought she might be able to have one that didn't end with her being alone.

Thirty-Four

JOSH

He'd never thought that his schedule sucked. Not until he was getting up in the middle of the night having to leave the woman he'd kept up until a bare half an hour before.

Three games over seven days.

A week without Jess.

What if he came back and she hated him again?

The thought had him grinning—kind of. He hadn't dated much during the season. Not ever. Most women didn't like that he was there and gone for a good chunk of the year, hated that the schedule was set in stone so he couldn't always make work events or be around for birthdays, anniversaries, friends' weddings, holidays.

But he and Jess had the same schedule.

If she didn't travel with the team, she was at the arena, watching the games, gathering clips, and sending them to the database so the players, the coaches had what they needed. Otherwise, she was on the plane, at the hotel, at the rinks.

With him.

Or, well, she *would* be with him.

But Jess wasn't going on this trip, and they would be apart and...he was feeling very clingy.

A small part of it was the sex—hot as fuck, their chemistry off the freaking charts, all the fucking time (*all* the fucking time). Any chance they had, they were all over each other, and they'd made a point out of *making* time.

So that part was great.

The rest of his clinginess came from the fact that the more time they spent together, the more he liked her. There wasn't any drama, and each day, each hour, each minute he was with her, he was able to see more of the woman she was beneath the snark and sass. And look, he loved the sass, loved the snark, but seeing who she was without any barriers, without her trying to bury anything, was pretty fucking special.

The final part of what was making his stomach churn was the fact that it had been two days since Pascal had begun to track down Caleb Monoham and so far, there wasn't a whisper of the man.

That was why Jess would be staying at his place during the trip.

He'd been surprised when she'd agreed—but then again, he was finding that Jess was very reasonable, especially when he was asking and not ordering, *and* when he'd stopped putting his foot in his mouth.

Victories.

Both on the ice *and* off.

On the ice, the team was 3-0 (three wins, no losses, all on home ice, so the Gold Mine had been *loud).* Being in front of the hometown crowd was always awesome, and the guys were hopped up for a new season, so he was ready to keep on rolling.

The only weird thing so far being that they hadn't chosen a new captain now that Blane had retired.

He would have thought that either Logan or Coop, both of whom were assistant captains, would have been bumped up.

But the coaches hadn't asked anyone.

And the team hadn't voted.

Brit had stopped talking about her future captainship, none of the other guys had thrown their hats in the ring and well, it wasn't that they needed an official captain wearing that C. They had a lot of veterans on the roster (though fewer than in the past) and the captain role really was just to help keep the guys motivated and on track, a supplement to the coaching staff.

The guys were *already* on track. They didn't need someone riding their ass when they were working hard.

Plus, they had plenty of leadership to look to between Brit (and her non-captaining) along with Coop and Logan. They'd all been in the league for years, helped keep the rookies on track, even though he was still getting shit about being the Rookie Wrangler. But anyway, there were teams who never even appointed a captain at all. Just had assistants and called it good.

Rubbing the sleep from his eyes, he filled his carafe with coffee then got the next pod ready for Jess.

He'd left her sleeping, worn out and limp.

His own legs were Jell-O and he'd be lucky if they recovered in time for the game, but...wouldn't take the night back for anything.

They'd gone on a date.

An actual date to a restaurant, eating one entire meal, with no bickering.

Then he'd given her a tour of his place—including skinny dipping in the hot tub in the back yard, which had, no surprise, led to them touring his bathroom and shower and mattress and closet floor, all very, very intimately.

Best night ever.

He slipped into his jacket, headed for the garage.

"Wait."

Spinning, he saw that Jess had come downstairs and was standing in the kitchen doorway looking sleepy and adorable in one of his shirts, the hem fluttering around the tops of her thighs. Tempting. He needed to fuck her in that.

But another time.

Because he was out of condoms, and she was tired and probably sore and—

Mental note for next time.

Fucking. T-shirt only. Done.

He plunked his cup on the counter, moved toward her, pushing back her hair, and pressing a kiss to the top of her head. "You should be sleeping, sweetcheeks."

"I wanted to say goodbye," she murmured.

"We did that a half hour ago."

"Always got to argue, huh?" This time it was a mutter, but she was burrowing into his hold as she did so, bringing the scent of her into his nose and her curves flush against him, and reminding himself that he needed to pick up more condoms before he got back into town. Hell, he was going to order some to both their houses the moment his ass hit his seat on the bus. "I'm trying to be sweet here."

He wrapped his arms around her. "Like your cheeks?"

A snort. "I never did ask you why, sweetcheeks."

"Honestly?"

Jess rolled her eyes. "Have I ever given you the impression that I want anything other than that?"

No, she hadn't.

Which was why he grinned, tugged a strand of her hair, and said, "'Cause it made you mad."

A beat. A wave of her hand, gesturing him forward. "And?"

He lifted his brows. "And what?"

"And nothing." A shrug. "I liked making you mad."

She sidled closer, pricked his chest with her nails. "That's *it?*"

"That's it." But he ruined the joke with a smile that had her sighing, those nails digging just a little bit deeper. "That tickles," he said, snagging her wrist and pressing a kiss to her palm.

"Tickles your *cock,* you mean," she grumbled.

Fuck, his woman was funny.

He burst out laughing, nipped at her fingertips, and told her the rest. "Whenever you were mad, you actually looked at me."

Her breath hitched.

"And when you looked at me, eyes flashing, fury in your expression, I knew that I had to find some way to win you over."

"Well that worked, didn't it?" she asked with a grin.

His phone buzzed—the alarm telling him that he needed to be in his car, heading to the rink (where he'd get on the bus that would take the team to the airport).

"I should let you go," she murmured.

"This sucks," he murmured back.

"I'll be on the next trip."

"Thank fuck," he muttered. "I need to fuck you in a hotel room."

Laughter in the air and then she was stepping away from him, reaching for her purse and extracting a wrapped box that fit into the palm of his hand. "My peace offering," she said when he glanced up at her, brows raised. "That's not going to melt," she added, giving him a small shove in the direction of the door. "Open it on the plane. Now go. I don't want to be the reason you're late for the bus. I'll never hear the end of it from the rest of the guys."

Curiosity piqued, he pocketed the box, kissed her lightly on the lips. "Okay, sweetcheeks." He turned for the door then spun back, cupped her jaw. "You'll be safe? And careful? And call Pascal and me if there are any problems?"

A gentle smile as she rose up on tiptoe.

Then a slice of devil as she nipped his bottom lip. "I can take care of myself." She soothed the sting with a kiss. "But also, yes to all your questions."

Jess dropped back onto her feet, nudged him again. "Now go, Josh. I'll be fine, and we'll have lots of I Missed You sex when you get back."

"With you in my shirt." It was a grumble and a demand...and an order.

One she didn't seem to mind because she just smiled, nodded, and shoved him out the door.

And when he texted her:

Back to bed

Before he hit left the driveway, she responded with:

You and orders. Hope you're ready to obey some when I see you next.

Which brought to mind the image of her in a dominatrix outfit, sporting a whip—so not his thing. Except, with Jess *everything* was his thing.

So he typed out:

Anything for you.

Then he hit the road.

THIRTY-FIVE

JESS

"I have it on authority that Josh may be out for blood," Dani said into Jess's earpiece.

"Why's that?" she asked innocently, cueing up her program and beginning to work her way through her pregame checklist.

"Don't play stupid with me, Jessica White. You know *exactly* why Josh is getting *all* the shit." Dani was trying to sound stern, but the effect was ruined by the fact that she was attempting—and failing—to hold back giggles. "A ball tickler? Really?"

"I thought he might be lonely on the road," she said, still going for innocent.

Dani cackled. "And you told him to open it on the plane?" More giggling. "Where all the guys would see?"

"For inspiration," Jess said, "just in case the guys wanted to get something special for their ladies. You know it works on clits, too," she added stoically...a placid demeanor which lasted all of a second before she lost it and started busting up completely.

Dani joined her.

"You going to let him try it on *you?*"

Jess grinned and leaned back in her chair. "I'd let the man try *anything* on me."

More cackling, only this time she joined in...along with all the guys from the control truck. Whoops. She'd forgotten they listened in. Now *she'd* be hearing about ball ticklers for days.

Oh well, totally worth it.

Especially since apparently she'd be paying for her little stunt in orgasms.

As in, Josh planned to orgasm her into submission for her antics.

Oh, the humanity.

Mentally, she held the back of her hand up to her forehead, swooned a la old-timey Hollywood starlet.

Grinning, she went to load up the video feed when her stomach began to churn. "Oh," she murmured, rubbing a hand over it.

"You good?" Dani asked.

"Fine."

But she didn't feel fine. She swallowed once. Twice. Saliva pooled in the back of her mouth. Her stomach roiled...and she tore out her earpiece, turned to her trash can, and heaved up everything she'd had for dinner.

"Fuck," she whispered, knowing that she shouldn't have had that salad.

She'd been trying to be good, trying to eat something green and healthy.

But her body didn't do healthy.

And salad coming back up wasn't good.

It hadn't tasted right from the beginning. Ugh. Well, that would learn her. No more premade grocery store salads. Probably, someone hadn't washed the leaves properly or it had sat too long on the shelf...or maybe her stomach wasn't designed for salads, premade or otherwise.

Likely the last.

Tying the bag, she popped into the hall to dump it in one of the big cans then hurried back to her desk, slipped her earpiece back in, and got to work.

"You good?" Dani asked again.

"I'm good," she said. "Though, in case you were wondering, my body is *not* a temple, and it is not a fan of anything green that's not artificially dyed."

"Like mint chocolate chip ice cream?"

Mmm. Ice cream.

She was *so* stopping at the Dairy after this. Mint chocolate chip ice cream with brownie bit mix-ins and topped with chocolate syrup.

Yes, please.

"Precisely," she said, just as the guys came onto her screen, dressed and warmed-up and ready for puck drop.

"All set?" Dani asked.

"All good on my end," she confirmed. "You?"

"Yup." Dani ran through a quick check with the guys in the truck and the interns who were traveling with her to learn the ropes of how they functioned on the road.

A few minutes later, the puck dropped, the game got underway.

And Jess was working her ass off.

Grabbing plays, fingers flying, tagging, and saving and sending off clips.

It was three hours and change of *moving* without actually getting out of her chair. Maybe that didn't make the least bit of sense to anyone else but herself, but to her own brain, that was the only logical way to describe it.

By the end she was even more exhausted than normal.

Though she blamed that on the salad and Josh keeping her up late the day before. Plus, last night it had been hard to sleep in a strange house without him by her side.

Addicted already.

Yet, that didn't scare her.

Because...Josh wasn't Caleb. He wasn't her father, her brothers.

He was a good man, one she'd spent years getting to know, years fighting the attraction, and now that she'd given in, he'd shown her time and again that she could trust him.

So...one day at a time. Looking forward instead of closing down.

See how mature she was?

Well, besides the ball ticklers that was.

Grinning, she finished up, closed out, and wasn't surprised when Pascal met her at the arena exit and walked her to her car.

"Do you really think this is necessary?" she asked.

A long pause, as though he were wondering if it was even worth it to talk to her.

The man limited his words like he'd gotten the last malt at the Dairy and was savoring the satisfying treat.

She, on the other hand, had no issues guzzling it down—

Ew.

No guzzling.

Just...*enjoying*.

"In my experience," he said, drawing her out of her thoughts, "restraining orders don't work with crazy exes."

"Right."

"So, until I track the fucker down, I'm not taking any chances."

"I just..." She sighed. "I don't want you wasting your time when it turns out to be nothing."

Another long pause, his dark eyes pinning her in place. "If it turns out to be nothing, then I would be really happy."

Shadows in his eyes, etched into the deep lines of her forehead, the C's around his mouth, and she didn't like them, didn't like the heavy sadness there.

So she teased him.

"But would you smile?"

The man was so cold and frosty that the mere act of smiling might crack his face in half.

This time he didn't bother answering, just shined a flashlight in the back of her car, then took her keys, checked the trunk, and opened the driver's side door.

"Thank you," she said when he handed them back.

A grunt was his only response.

Right. Time to go.

She started to get in, thinking that now she was going to have nightmares about Caleb in the back of her car. So...*that* was a thing.

Go, her.

His hand dropped to her shoulder, squeezed lightly. "We'll make sure he can't hurt you again."

She glanced down, saw a strong hand, scars covering the back, faint traces of dark hair on his knuckles. Then up and noted the kindness in those stoic eyes, the warmth he didn't hide, exactly, but that he didn't broadcast either.

Another good man.

God, if she kept this up, she was going to have a stable of them in her life.

Though...she supposed she already did.

"Thank you," she repeated, covering his hand with her own.

Another grunt.

Then he squeezed lightly again, slipped his hand free, and...

Disappeared.

Straight up disappeared into the shadows.

She gasped, leaning up in her seat, wondering how in the hell he'd just *disappeared*. She searched for him, convinced she'd see a flicker of something.

Finally, after a few moments of seeing *nothing* and hearing nothing (except his disembodied chuckle—and great, another thing for the nightmares), she buckled up, closed her door, and drove back to Josh's place.

But not without stopping for a mint chocolate chip malt with brownie mix-ins and chocolate syrup first.

————

"And then he just disappeared," she said into FaceTime, scooping out the last of her malt and flopping back onto the mattress. "It was just like Sara said. He can just melt into the shadows."

Josh smiled. "Well, melting or not, I'm just glad he's there for you."

"I can take care of myself," she reminded him, just for posterity.

"Yes, I know." His voice was gentle. "So how about I say I'm glad he's there for you so I can concentrate on being here."

"Fair point." She set the cup aside. "So long as *you* remember that this isn't a permanent babysitter situation and that I'm a grown woman who doesn't need to be watched every second."

See?

She could be reasonable. Logical, even.

Especially when he agreed with her, smiling at her tart tone, and assuring, "Just until Pascal finds out about Caleb."

She tugged the blankets up to her chin. "How do you make it so easy?"

His brows drew together before he reclined on the pillows behind him, his bare chest on display. "What do you mean?"

"This. Us. It's—" A shake of her head. "I just feel like it should be harder, especially considering..."

"We fought for three years straight?"

Her lips tipped up. "Yeah. *That*."

"Well, I think we were fighting *us* for three years, and not that we've stopped, exactly." He rolled to his side. "But maybe there's nothing else for us to battle over."

She propped her phone up using the edge of the pillow then curled on her side and faced him. "That's a nice idea," she told him, "but I'm sure I can find *something* for us to fight over."

He grinned, did some propping of his own. "I'm sure you can." A wicked smile. "Now, do you think we should sexy Face-Time or find something to fight over?"

A finger tapping against her lips. "I think...hmm..." Another tap. "I think that we can accomplish both at the same time."

For the record...

She was right.

THIRTY-SIX

JOSH

"Joshie!"

He turned at the reproach.

(Though, it was paired with a small smile).

His mom came onto the porch to yell at him over the noise he was making, one arm in a sling, probably wondering what the heck was going on. And granted, it was early in the morning for his chosen activity, and he hadn't told them he was coming, but he'd made a pit stop on the road trip to come and visit his parents (he'd join back up with the team later that night since they didn't live far from the arena in Minnesota), seen the lawn was too long, and had decided to do something about it.

Less standing on the sidelines wishing things could be different.

More living in the present, showing his people he loved them with his actions.

And more...lawn mowing, apparently.

"What do you think you're doing?" she yelled, crossing her good arm over her chest as he started pushing the mower forward.

He glanced over his shoulder, raised a brow, but didn't dare to sass his mom further.

She rolled her eyes. "Besides the obvious. You shouldn't—"

He revved the motor, finished the last strip of the overgrown grass, and turned off the mower, wheeling it back to the shed where he'd taken it from.

His rental was in the driveway out front (he'd already cut that smaller lawn), and he closed the shed door, moved over to his mom, and bent to kiss her cheek.

She huffed. "You got grass all over your suit."

A shrug. "I don't care," he said. "I'm here."

"Joshie..." Her shoulders stiffened and her bottom lip wobbled, eyes going glassy. "I'm so—"

"No," he said before she lost it, squeezing her gently. "No apologies. I'm here now, and I'm not going to stay away, okay?"

A sniff. "I don't want you to."

He held on. "Good," he whispered, standing there, hugging her, her mom scent in his nose. Home. She felt like home, and God, he'd missed this.

"Ugh," she eventually said, pulling away and dashing her eyes. "Ignore your emotional mama and come inside. I'll make you my blueberry muffins."

They were from a box.

They didn't fit the meal plan.

But, as he walked into the house, listening to his mom chatter about what they'd been up to and how his sister had gone home the day before and about all the doctors and various appointments, as he moved into the kitchen and saw his dad sitting at the same table they'd had since they were kids, looking pale and thin but on the mend, Josh didn't give a shit about the meal plan.

At that moment, he didn't give a fuck about hockey.

He wasn't on the outside.

He was here.

He was going to keep it that way.

The pass came out of control and off-target, but he fought for it anyway, getting the tip of his stick on the puck, managing to redirect it enough so that it wouldn't be icing and end up with a face-off in their own zone.

"Fuck," he muttered, skating hard to chase it down, knowing he wouldn't beat the other team's defenseman there, but hauling ass anyway, making the other guy work for it.

No freebies.

No free passes, free pucks, free rushes.

The other guys wanted the win? They had to bring it, had to get it past him.

So, he skated hard, he didn't hesitate, and when he lost his breath for a second after getting checked into the boards, he kept moving.

The air in his lungs would come back.

They'd eventually inflate again, and in the meantime, he didn't need to breathe to shove off the fucker pinning him.

So, he did.

And then the tension on his torso eased, much-needed air entered his body, and he was able to rejoin the play.

Coop had picked up the puck behind the net and was cycling to the other side, chipping it up and off the boards so Logan could corral it at the blue line. A nice move from the defenseman to move around an opposing player.

Nice.

Josh whistled, calling for the puck as he hauled ass to the goal, sliding in behind the defensive just as Logan flicked a pass...

To.

The.

Exact.

Spot.

Josh.

Needed.

Grunting, he took the hit from the other team's center, glued his stick to the fucking ice, and—

Tipped the puck just as it flew in.

A sting in his palms. A heartbeat of holding his breath, waiting to see if...

Silence.

Then...

Cheers. Only a few of them, since they weren't on home ice. But they were quickly chased by groans, by the ref's whistle, by his teammates' yells as they swept in to celebrate.

Not much had gone right in the game that night, but he'd take that fucking goal.

Even if it came with a side of getting shoved to the ice by the other team's center and ended with him spitting out snow while his teammates aborted their celebratory bear hugs for him and transformed them into shoves for the other team (and the odd punch...and maybe a few face washes, just for good measure).

But eventually the linesmen came in to break things up, and Josh found his feet, stepped in between Logan and one of the other guys, stopping their interaction before it turned into a penalty for Logan and the team losing momentum after the goal. *Then* got his bear hugs from the guys.

After, he skated his ass to the bench.

Bernard gave him a look he couldn't decipher when he hopped through the door and scooted down to make room for Blue and Coop. But Calle nodded approvingly and clapped him on the shoulder.

He glanced up at the Jumbotron, watched the replay, wondered if Jess was tracking goals that night, and selfishly hoped she was.

Yeah, he wanted his girl to see.

Yeah, he was a show-off.

"That courtesy of the ball-tickler?" Blue asked lightly.

He sprayed his friend with the water bottle, listened to the guys bust up.

But all he could think was that he was *really* going to make Jess pay for that one.

———

"*Another* milkshake?" he teased later that night. "Now you're just trying to rub it in."

A beatific smile. "Maybe?" She lifted her thumb and forefinger. "Just a little bit?" Groaning, she set the cup down and rolled to her back. "Ugh," she muttered. "Okay, three malts three nights in a row is one too many."

"I consider the upset stomach as payback for tormenting me."

Now she scowled. "Meanie."

"I wish I was there to rub your back."

"I'd probably puke on you," she said. "So, it's better that you're not."

He sat up. "You're not feeling well?"

Jess shook her head. "It's not a big deal. Ever since I got food poisoning from that salad, my stomach has been touchy."

"Except for malts and mix-ins from the Dairy."

"Except for that," she agreed, propping the phone up and tucking her hand under her head. "Though apparently my streak has ended."

"Sorry, sweetcheeks."

"Meh." A wave of her hand. "Nothing for you to apologize for, but since I know you're about to say something sweet about caring for me—blegh—why don't we skip straight to the part where you tempt me into sexy FaceTime?"

"One," he said, ticking the items off on his fingers. "I *am* sorry you're not feeling well. Two, I'm not skipping to the sexy time FaceTime because we're not *having* sexy time FaceTime when you're not feeling well."

"But—"

"No buts," he said, "and that's not an order so much as a..."

Fuck. It kind of *was* an order—okay, no *kind of* about it. It *was* an order, and that order was intended as an order and...that was going to piss her off.

"As a what?" she asked archly.

"As a strong suggestion for us doing something that will make both of us feel good?" he attempted.

"Which is what?" Still asked archly.

"Planning what we'll do when I get home?"

Her expression softened. "Can we go see the lights again?"

He loved that she liked that spot as much as he did, so it was easy to agree. But he also asked, "Will you take me on a ride on your bike?"

Her brows dragged together. "I'd love to, except don't you have a clause in your contract about not doing dangerous things during the season?"

Shit.

He *did* have that.

And unfortunately, riding a motorcycle was specifically one of the things that was called out in that clause.

He also wasn't supposed to do them during the offseason either.

"Damn," he muttered. "You're right."

"Words I just love to hear," she sang.

Words he didn't mind saying, even *if* it was unusual for him to forget any part of his contract, especially important things like tasks he wasn't allowed to do. "That's noted." He rolled to his side, studied her face, the dark circles beneath her eyes, the creases on the edges of her mouth, her eyes. "Okay, so how's this? We take a drive—in a perfectly safe vehicle that my contract allows—and you show me where you go when you head over the Golden Gate?"

Her cheeks went a little pink. "It's not nearly as cool as the light exhibit."

"It's a piece of you."

Explanation enough. In his mind, anyway.

But also, an explanation she seemed to understand, even without expounding on it.

"And you want to know every part of me?" A soft question.

"Ding. Ding. Ding," he said gently, quieting the volume even further when she yawned, eyes fluttering closed.

Damn, he hated that she was so tired.

Hated that part of that was probably because of Caleb, and Pascal not being able to track him down.

Hated that another part might come from her not sleeping in her own bed.

Didn't hate that some of it might have come from missing him.

Hello, Ego. Meet Reality.

Grinning when her eyes didn't open back up, when her face relaxed and she fell asleep while still on the call, he did the creepy thing and watched her for a few moments.

Only when his own eyes grew heavy did he hit the button to end the call, not wanting to waste her battery if she didn't have her phone plugged in.

One more game.

One more night.

And tomorrow he could slip into bed after his flight, could wrap his arms around her, pull her close, and...

Be whole again.

THIRTY-SEVEN

JESS

"The guys in the control truck think you're hilarious," she muttered, glaring at him through her phone's camera.

"I thought you liked the celebrity Chrises," he said innocently as he sat down in his seat on the plane.

She *did* like celebrity Chrises.

They were pretty and talented and...yeah, circling back to pretty.

She did not, *however*, appreciate leaving to use the restroom, being delayed by an intern in on the prank, and then returning to find the entire video suite covered with pictures of the hunky Chrises.

It was...

In poor taste.

Hell, who was she kidding?

It was freaking hilarious.

But she wasn't going to admit that. Not right then, anyway. Not when he was on the team plane and was flying home...and had that damn sexy smirk on his face.

Speaking of pretty and talented men.

"Nice goal tonight, by the way," she murmured.

A shrug. "It was okay, but it was a point which led to us getting two points." Another lift and drop of his shoulders. "So, I can't complain."

His gaze darted away then back.

"You good?" she asked softly.

A nod. "But I should probably go, Bernard's giving me that look, and the rest of the guys will be getting on the plane soon."

She missed the booger, didn't want to get off with him, but... responsibilities and respect and all that nonsense.

"Okay," she whispered. "Safe flight, baby, and I'll see you soon."

His eyes went wide, and she froze.

"What?"

"That's the first time you've called me that."

She grinned, and though her heart skipped a beat, though it had been a long time since she'd used an endearment with someone who wasn't her friend, Jess stopped, breathed...

And embraced the good in front of her.

"Well," she whispered. "I hope you'll get used to it."

Warmth infused into brown eyes. "Yeah?"

"I've got all the endearments planned. Baby. Honey. Mr. McFluffertons." She laughed at his scowl and said innocently, "It's not my fault you started to grow a beard."

"You said that you liked the way it felt between your—" Another darting glance. A curse.

Laughter in the background.

"Right," she said. "Now, you *really* need to go."

"Unfortunately, yes. Before I give the guys any more material or get myself a fine for disrupting my teammates."

More laughter.

A balled-up paper hitting him in the side of the head.

The latter seemed unlikely.

But she was just a video coach. She didn't know what it took to corral rowdy hockey players. "See you in a few hours, baby."

His face gentled. "Bye, sweetcheeks."

"Bye."

They both reached for the button to disconnect, but before she could, another ball of paper tagged Josh in the temple. "You fuckers—"

She hit the button.

The call cut off.

And she fell asleep smiling.

———

The blankets pulled back.

An arm came around her waist.

She was instantly awake, fear pounding in her heart.

"It's Josh," he said, his voice careful, his arm light where it encircled her. "This okay?" His spicy scent in her nose, his stubble catching her hair. A kiss to the top of her ear.

His touch.

Josh.

The man she loved.

She went stiff.

Loved?

Fuck.

He sensed the taut muscles, started to pull away. "Jess, baby? Are you awake?"

A breath, forcing her body to soften. That was a stray thought. Just...that. A weird, stray thought that came from one too many romcoms while he was gone and being half asleep. And even if it *were* true, it would be a crazy notion, considering they'd been together for all of a couple of weeks. "Yes," she said and rolled toward him. "Sorry. I'm awake now."

He stroked a hand down her face. "No apologies, sweetcheeks. I wasn't sure if I should join you since Pascal hasn't..."

No sign of Caleb yet.

"I'm okay," she said. "When I heard your voice in my ear, felt your lips there, your arm go around my waist, I knew it was you."

"Good."

"Yeah."

They stared at each other, a note of awkward in the air.

But then he smiled.

And she settled.

"I missed you," he said.

"Well"—she snuggled into his arms—"I didn't miss you. Mostly," she added over the sound of his outraged gasp, "because I had my plethora of celebrity Chrises to keep me company."

He chuckled, but when that chuckle transformed into a yawn, she brushed a kiss to his lips. "Sleep, baby."

Those lips curved. "Still my favorite thing ever," he said drowsily.

"Even more than holding me like this?"

"Mmm," he said, totally noncommittal.

Well, it was *her* favorite.

Because this, just cuddling with him and talking about nothing, teasing each other, sleeping close, was the absolute best.

His arms tightened around her, and he pulled her closer until her face was pressed into his throat, until his chin rested on top of her head, warm breath puffing through her hair. But it was her heart that pulsed when he murmured, nearly asleep now, "Nothing better than this."

She couldn't agree more.

———

"I don't think they're going to wake up," the small voice intruding on the edges of her hearing whispered.

Or spoke.

It kind of sounded like a whisper.

But it was also loud.

Like *really* loud.

"Poke Uncle Josh harder."

"Okay."

Another loud voice, but this one came from behind her and was punctuated by the mattress shaking. Thinking this was a weird-ass dream, she sighed, rolled into Josh, and burrowed closer. More sleep.

She needed more sleep.

"Uncle *Josh!*"

Her eyes flashed open, blinking against the glare for a moment. At least until her eyes got used to the brightness enough to realize there was another person in bed with them.

"Uncle—"

That voice came from behind her.

Two someones in bed with her.

No. Not *someones.* Two *children* were in bed with them and—

She squeaked, started to sit up, remembered that the pajamas she was wearing barely covered all the pertinent bits.

Not to mention she was so close to Josh that she could feel all of *his* pertinent bits hard against her—

Right.

Enough talk of the pertinent bits.

Or thinking about them.

Or—

Whatever. *Right.*

More important things to worry about.

She focused on the voice behind Josh, saw a child of seven or eight with thick brown curls and the cutest frown of consternation on his face as he poked Josh. A glance over her shoulder showed her that his younger brother was doing the non-whispering behind her.

He waved. "Hi. Who are you?"

Oh fuck.

There were children in bed with her, and they didn't belong to her, and—

"Kids!" A voice echoed down the hallway. "Leave your uncle

alone. You know he sleeps like a log after a game day and—oh holy hell!"

Jess's gaze had gone to the door.

To the woman standing there, eyes going wide.

The little boy behind her giggled. "Mom. You said a bad word."

The mom's eyes stayed wide, flicking between her kids and Jess...and Josh. "Marcus. Samuel. Get your butts out of that bed," she said tersely, and when they didn't move quickly enough for her liking added, "Right *this* instant."

The boys moved, jostling the mattress as they climbed out.

Their feet echoing on the floor as they ran across it and into the hall.

"Oh, God. I'm Jordyn," the woman said. "Josh's sister, and"—her eyes closed—"I am so *freaking* sorry. I saw the truck in the driveway, but I didn't realize. I thought it was a teammate's car or—" A breath. Her lids peeling back. "I didn't realize he would be here with a..."

Jess tugged the blankets up to her chin. "It's okay. I'm—um... I'm sorry. I didn't know you were coming—"

God, this was fucking awkward, making introductions with a snoring Josh holding her tight and his sister—*sister!*—standing in the doorway like she'd popped over for a cup of sugar.

"I'm Jess. Josh and I are..."

Well, she didn't know exactly what they were.

"Dating," she finished somewhat lamely, because he was so much more important to her than that word implied.

Jordyn rubbed her forehead, averted her gaze. "It's nice to meet you, Jess. I—"

A crash.

"Hell," Jordyn said. "I'll wrangle them and get out of your hair. Will you tell Josh that we're in town?" A smile. "When you manage to wake him up, that is."

Jess opened her mouth—to say *something*—but then the door was closing, and the words never made it off her tongue and—

She finally pulled herself together, squirming out of Josh's arms and shaking him.

Roughly.

"Josh. *Josh!*"

His brows drew together, but she shook him again, not stopping until his lids peeled back and his sleepy eyes met hers. "Sweetcheeks," he murmured. "Is everything okay?"

"Is everything—?" Her mouth dropped open.

There'd been strange children in their bed.

Children who would be scarred for life and tell their therapists someday about this and—

"Okay?" she squeaked.

Another crash from downstairs.

Feet pounding on the floor.

His brows drawing tighter on his forehead. "What—?"

Suddenly, she swung from fear and shock to amusement, and truthfully, a bit of amazement. Josh had slept through *all* of that. The poking. The little feet making big noise on the hardwood floor. The apologies from his sister. The bouncing on the mattress.

How?

"Your nephews were in here," she said softly.

"My—" Surprise filled his expression. "They were here"—a wave of his hand toward the bed—"like right *here?*"

The chuckles were in her throat now, but she managed to swallow them back. "Yup."

"*In* bed?"

"Yup."

"And Jordyn?"

"Came right down the hall and carried on a conversation with me, like we were two old friends catching up." A giggle escaped. "Well, aside from the embarrassment of her finding her brother in bed with a woman she didn't know, and me dying inside because my boyfriend's family saw me in practically nothing."

He snorted.

Excited voices echoing through the floor.

Jess pressed a kiss to his cheek. "Apparently, she's going to get them out of our hair."

"Apparently, she's going to have to learn to fucking call before she shows up," he growled.

"Has this happened before?" she asked, sitting up.

"Her coming over without calling?" He sat up too. "Or the boys finding me in bed with a woman?"

"Either," she said, running her hand down his chest. "Both."

"Yes, to the first. No, to the second."

That pleased her. Not because she wanted to be the one to scar innocent children, but because she wanted Josh.

All to herself.

Her lips twitched. "Good."

He grinned. "Jealous?"

Yes.

Not that she'd admit it.

A casual—*not*—smirk. "Not my thing."

"Hmm," he murmured, pressing his lips to her jaw. "Well, Not Jealous, how about I go catch the crazy cakes downstairs before they leave, and I make us all pancakes?"

"Healthy pancakes?" she asked, wrinkling her nose.

He'd made some concoction with buckwheat the other day, and she was *not* a fan.

A kiss to the tip of her nose. "Cheat Day pancakes with fresh strawberries and homemade whipped cream."

Hell *yeah!*

Jess nodded. "Yes, please."

He leaned down to kiss her, but suddenly ravenous, she pushed him, accidentally almost sending him toppling from the bed. "Food. Cook. Now."

Because homemade whipped cream?

She needed. She wanted. She *needed.*

"Quick," she said, steadying him before he ate shit, stomach rumbling. "Catch them before they leave, otherwise I don't get pancakes, and that would be a crime against humanity."

His grin was quick and as wide as she'd ever seen it.

But he climbed out of bed and headed for the door, giving her a glimpse of that sexy as hell ass as he bent and tugged on a pair of sweats.

He paused in the door.

"You realize you just agreed to meet my family?" he pointed out.

Then disappeared into the hall.

And...fuck.

She *had* just agreed to meet his family.

That should be terrifying.

And maybe it *would* have been...if not for the nephew invasion and the sister-slash-bed-slash-hall conversation.

And the whipped cream.

Jess couldn't forget the homemade whipped cream.

That took the scary out of anything.

THIRTY-EIGHT

JOSH

He was still grinning when he hit the bottom step, saw his sister and nephews about to go out into the garage. No doubt to take advantage of his minivan.

"Breaking and entering again, J?" he called.

The boys whipped around. "Uncle Josh!"

"What am I missing?" he asked, tapping his finger to his chin. "*What* am I missing?"

That was all the encouragement they needed before barreling his way, two tiny tanks coming for him and all but checking him into the wall.

Future hockey players.

Or at least he hoped so.

He held his ground—barely—wrapped his arms around them and squeezed them tight. "You got plans?" he asked Jordyn, who was leaning against the closed door to the garage, arms crossed, smile curving her mouth.

"Surprising my brother, and apparently his girlfriend," she said dryly. "Of which none of his family knew about until about five minutes ago."

"We're new."

A lifted brow, saying that waking up together didn't exactly scream new, or at least not for him. He didn't really do casual.

"And serious."

Her expression relaxed. "She seemed nice."

"You'll like her," he said. "Her favorite pastime is busting my balls."

Samuel and Marcus giggled. His sister warned him about his "language."

"We're going to Disneyland tomorrow, Uncle Josh!" Marcus said—or rather yelled. "But Mom said that we get to see you first! And we got to take an Über from the airport and I got to get a sticker from the pilot and—"

"Let your uncle breathe," Jordyn said.

He ruffled Marcus's hair. "All of that sounds awesome, bud."

"And Mom said we could go on the new *Star Wars* ride first," Samuel declared.

Marcus scowled. "Did not!"

"Did so!" Samuel shot back.

"Did—"

"Boys," he said firmly. Quietly but firmly. A technique learned from his dad. He might have felt like an outsider always being away for hockey during his teenage years when he'd left home young to play juniors, but he'd still managed to pick up a few things from the family.

One of those being that sometimes quieter worked better than loud.

The boys looked at him.

He fixed them with a look. "How can I make pancakes with strawberries and homemade whipped cream if my nephews are fighting?"

Marcus stuck out his bottom lip.

"Can I have a *lot* of whipped cream if we stop fighting?" Samuel asked, always the pragmatic one.

"*I* get more whipped cream because I'm older."

"Do not—"

He shot Jordyn a pained look, and his sister only winced and shook her head in response. Early morning wake up, a plane ride, and a drive. Add in the excitement of an amusement park and siblings just being siblings and no wonder they were fighting. "Boys," he said again. They stopped and he asked, "How do we settle disputes in this house?"

Marcus glared. "But we won't be in this house when we ride the—"

Josh lifted a brow.

His nephew sighed, said begrudgingly. "We settle disputes with *UNO*."

"I'll get the cards!" Samuel ran into the hall.

"I—"

But before Marcus could get a true protest worked up, Samuel was back, passing over the deck to Marcus so that his big brother could shuffle and deal.

Then they'd plunked themselves down into chairs, were firmly entrenched in the game, and he turned to his sister, who was smiling fondly. *UNO* was serious business in the Webb household. "They off from school?"

He didn't know of any holidays coming up, and most of the guys with school-aged kids on the team hadn't mentioned the kids being off, but he wasn't a parent, and his sister was up in Oregon. Maybe they had a different schedule.

Unfortunately, he knew that wasn't the case the moment he finished asking the question.

Her face...

His gut twisted.

She shook her head and glanced down at her feet. "Uh, no," she said. "We're...um..." Her voice brightened. "Just playing hooky for a few days."

"Jordyn—"

Another shake. "It's—" A breath. "I'm not ready to talk about it, okay?"

Protectiveness welled up, but he swallowed it down, didn't push. He'd learned that from Jess, knew now that sometimes he just needed to be there. So he took a breath, crossed to his sister, and hugged her tight. "Okay," he agreed.

A shuddering breath, her little body relaxing under his. "Thanks," she whispered.

"But," he said, pulled back, "you'd better be ready soon."

A small laugh. "I'm sure I will be. You know Mom will pry it out of me in two seconds flat."

"Which is why you're here instead of home?"

Guilt in her eyes. "I'm sorry," she whispered.

He hugged her again then leaned back and tugged a strand of her hair. "No apologies for visiting," he said. "Not ever. I'm glad you and the boys came."

"Right," she said. "And you *so* love that I interrupted you in bed with your girlfriend."

"Okay, that part I could have lived without. Or Jess could have, anyway." He nudged her back. "And I would have loved for a touch more sleep. But"—he cupped her cheek—"anytime, yeah? You need a place for you and the boys, an ear to talk to who isn't Mom or Dad or one of your friends—"

That had her stiffening.

And had a sickening feeling settling into his stomach. "Really?"

"I don't want to talk about it." She sighed. "Except to say and Lori and Daniel are assholes."

Lori being her best friend.

Daniel her husband.

Fucking prick.

"As a reminder, I'm a big, badass hockey player now." He forced his words to be light and paired with a grin. "Which means I know people who might be able to—" He drew his finger across his throat.

That had her giggling and shoving him lightly. "You're terrible." A beat. "I just...need a little time to wrap my head around it so I can hold my head up."

He'd been joking about knowing people, but he'd bet Pascal would take Daniel down in a second.

"Well, just know that the offer still stands. Of"—that finger across his throat again—"or just of a place to stay. You know I bought this place so there would be plenty of space for all of you guys."

Their middle sibling, Jackson, had kids too, and Josh didn't want him having to fork out for a hotel every time they visited.

"I'm getting that," she said, tone more than a bit broken, and Josh fucking hated it. "And thanks, but I'm sure we'll be fine." And then her face went sad, and *he* felt like an asshole for continuing this conversation when she clearly didn't want to talk about it.

He opened his mouth, intending to apologize. "Jordyn—"

"Uno!" Samuel yelled.

His sister rearranged her face, the pain and sadness gone. "That'll be the end soon," she said. "You'd better get on that homemade whipped cream unless you want a revolt on your hands."

"I don't know who'd revolt more, you, Jess, or the kids."

Jordyn grinned and moved to the fridge, grabbing out a package of strawberries. "I like her."

"For the ten seconds you met her?"

"It was more like a good minute," Jordyn said. "And it says a lot about a woman how she handles getting woken up by two crazy kids she's never met."

"Don't forget their mother," he teased.

"Rude."

But at least she was smiling as she was slicing strawberries.

"I win!" Samuel yelled.

"No fair!" Marcus yelled back.

"We settle disputes"—and the way Samuel said *disputes* (pisdutes) was fucking cute as hell—"with *UNO* in this house."

Marcus growled. "That's *not* fair—"

"They're feral," Jordyn said, putting down the knife and turning to intervene. "I swear to God—"

"Wait," he said.

Because miracle of miracles, the kids decided to settle *that* dispute (pisdute) with another round.

He grinned.

She rolled her eyes. "Okay, parenting guru, you've had them for all of ten minutes."

"Not an expert here," he admitted, mixing flour, salt, and baking soda in a bowl then adding some milk, oil, and eggs. "Totally stole it from Dad, and I know the over-under on it working all the time is slim."

"Can I play?"

He turned, saw that Jess had slipped into a pair of leggings and one of his sweatshirts. She'd piled her hair on top of her head and was sliding into the chair next to Samuel.

Who frowned. "Do you even know how to play?"

She laughed, her eyes coming to his over Sam's head. "How about you bring it, little man?"

His chin lifted, glower forming. "I'm not little, and my name's not *man*."

He and Jordyn started laughing. Jess held it together a bit better. "I'm sorry," she said, and her tone said she meant it. "I know you're not little, but I also don't know your name. I'm Jess." She stuck out her hand.

"My name is Samuel." His annoyance had cleared with her apology. "Your eyes are very pretty," he said, and his expression and tone were so serious when he shook Jess's hand that Josh had to bite back another laugh. Kid was a straight-up baller. Not that he didn't agree with the sentiment.

Jess's eyes were fucking beautiful.

"I'm Marcus, and I'm older."

Josh bit his lip. *Hard.*

Then harder when Marcus cocked his head to the side and said, "Your hair looks like a spider like that."

Jess choked.

Josh lost his grip on his amusement.

Jordyn, meanwhile, gasped in horror. "Marcus—"

But then Jess was giggling, leaning in, and tickling his nephew. "Well, spider hair or not," she said. "Can I play? I'm really good at shuffling," she added, picking up the deck and shifting the cards. "*And* I can throw down a mean Skip card."

His nephews exchanged a look.

Then Samuel said. "You shuffle the cards first."

Marcus nodded, in agreement with his brother for once. "And *then* we'll decide."

THIRTY-NINE

JESS

She hadn't wanted to eavesdrop on what was obviously a private conversation, but she also hadn't wanted to interrupt and stop Jordyn from getting it off her chest.

So, she'd stood in the hall, shifting from foot to foot, eavesdropping...until the conversation had changed, and she'd managed to sneak in.

Four rounds of UNO later, whatever argument between the brothers had been settled (probably because they'd both decimated her in the game despite her mad Skip skills), and they'd all had pancakes in front of them (with whipped cream that was delicious and went perfectly with the sliced strawberries).

She and Josh had spent the day with Jordyn and the boys, taking them to the Exploratorium and to the waterfront, and even though it wasn't the day off she'd imagined, she'd had a lot of fun hanging with Samuel and Marcus and getting to know Jordyn a little bit.

Then they'd gotten clam chowder and sourdough bread bowls and walked Pier 39 and eaten fresh crab cakes from a little stand down the road.

And, of course, scarfed down ice cream sundaes as big as their heads from Ghirardelli's—well, for all of them except Josh, who'd stuck with his vanilla cone.

It had been one hell of a Cheat Day for him, for her. For *all* of them.

Which was probably why she was ready for bed. All those empty calories and the sugar and...oh, right, there was the whole being dragged around by a six- and an eight-year-old who seemingly never ran out of energy.

Because they didn't *stop*.

Until they *stopped*.

Which had been about ten minutes ago when one minute they'd been awake, talking to her about a video game and the next, they'd quite literally passed out on the couch. She hadn't been counting then...or not counting on anything but a glass of wine in her hand and one for Jordyn, because the woman was a superhero who deserved it. Which was why she'd gone for wine while Josh had carried the boys up to the room they shared when they stayed here.

And yup.

They had a room at their uncle's place.

Which was so freaking sweet that her heart didn't even know what to do with it.

Okay, her heart *knew*.

Which was why she was only *semi*-freaking out.

Because her heart was going full-on *I want to squeeze and love and hug him, and I shall call him Squishy and Joshie shall be mine.*

He *was* hers.

"For a second there," Jordyn said, taking a sip from her glass of wine, her legs tucked up beneath her on the couch, and her gaze on Jess's. "I was actually worried I might be pregnant with a cheater for a husband. But it was just stress, apparently. Because I swear, the moment I walked in the door to Josh's place, my uterus was like *huzzah, bitch!* Here I come!"

Jess hated that Jordyn's husband and best friend were assholes.

Yeah, she didn't know the whole story and had just overheard a bit of what Jordyn and Josh had been discussing before she'd gone into the kitchen, but anyone who could cheat on Jordyn, especially with a friend, was an asshole.

Jess took a sip from her own glass. "Yeah, I know the feeling," she said, glancing at Josh to see if the period talk had put him off. But he appeared nonplussed as he loaded up a hockey game on the TV. "A little stress at work, and my cycle is *all* messed up."

And speaking of messed up...

Had she?

Wait...*had* she?

She pulled out her phone, creeped casually on the health app, began silently counting as Jordyn talked.

And *counting*.

And...oh holy fuck.

How many days had it been?

She'd said she was on her period the night of Peace Offering Gate, and she'd been a few days late even then.

But...she hadn't gotten it between then and now...had she?

A lot had happened. Her bike. Caleb. The calls. Her actually in a relationship with someone. Work and the season starting.

But not her period.

No, that hadn't started yet.

"I can't believe I was so stupid and didn't pick them up when I was out." Jordyn sighed heavily, and Jess stopped focusing on her phone for a moment, turning her attention to Josh's sister. "I guess with everything happening, my brain isn't working. *Ugh*." She rubbed her forehead. "So anyway, I'm sorry to ask something else of you after this morning and hijacking your day with Josh" —Jess had tried to bow out, to give them family time, but they'd all insisted she join them—"but do you think I can borrow some tampons or pads or whatever you have?"

Jess took a breath.

She'd freak out later.

It was probably fine. She'd taken the Plan B, and her periods were finicky like she'd told Jordyn. With the stress of everything with Josh and Caleb, no *wonder* she was late. Any day now the pipes would open, and the Red Sea would flow, and she'd be bloated, cranky, and miserable.

Speaking of that, she *was* bloated. And her boobs hurt.

So yeah, her period was a coming.

Totally nothing to worry about.

Just a few days—*cough*—weeks late.

"I can pick some up when the boys and I leave in the morning," Jordyn said. "Drop them back at the house to replenish your supply."

"No," Jess said quickly, realizing that Jordyn was mistaking her mental soliloquy with reluctance. She shook her head. "No need. I —this is probably TMI, but I use period cups, so I don't have any tampons or pads. But I do have a brand new, unopened one I'm happy to give you," she hurried to add. "I actually bought it to keep here at Josh's as a backup, and I have another stash at home, so you're more than welcome to have it."

"Oh, that's amazing. I actually use a cup, too—which of course, I forgot to pack *and* why I've already used up my meager emergency stash of tampons." Jordyn smiled as she smacked herself on the forehead. "I'll pay you back for it."

Gah. She was so sweet. A good mom. Smart, funny, gorgeous.

And married to an asshole, apparently.

"Why don't I just go grab it, so you have it when you need it? Especially since you guys are leaving so early in the morning."

"Thanks," Jordyn said, smiling at her over her glass of wine.

Jess smiled back, but the freaking out was closing in because if her counting turned out to reveal...

Fuck.

Fuck.

But the Plan B. It was supposedly like really effective. If taken in the first twenty-four hours. But...she *hadn't* taken it until the next evening, and—

Oh shit. What if he thought she'd meant to get pregnant?

No.

He wouldn't.

He was logical and calm, and they'd figure it out. But—*shit*—her panic slid up her throat. What was there to figure out? If she was pregnant, pregnant by Josh, it wasn't even a question. She would have it. A hundred times over.

She set her wine aside.

Because her boobs hurting and the "food poisoning" and the fatigue and...the *no freaking period.* How could she be so stupid?

Oh God.

Stop.

A breath as her glass hit the coaster, and she hightailed it up to Josh's bathroom, snagging the spare cup out of the drawer he'd given her.

Drawer.

No *drawers.*

Two in here.

Four in his closet.

Along with hanging space.

And seriously, how in the fuck had she gone from single and locked down to in love with the man who'd given her *drawers?* And she'd been seeing the guy for all of how long?

Yeah, *that* one had the nerves roiling right along with the panic. Because they *hadn't* been seeing each other long, and if she was—*cough*—he might—

He would—

"Enough," she breathed, gripping the counter and staring at herself hard in the mirror.

This was fine.

It would all be fine.

She knew Josh. Knew the kind of man he was and wasn't. And anyway, there was no point in worrying because she didn't have any answers at that moment. She needed to go to the store, get a test, and take it.

Then she would deal with whatever the result was.

An inhale. Hold.

An exhale.

See? She had a plan. It would all be okay.

But as she turned from the sink, started to pick up the box with the cup again, bile rose in her throat, and...

She barely made it to the toilet before losing the crab cakes and the ice cream and the sourdough...and the half a glass of wine she drank before she'd begun counting.

"Fuck," she whispered after she'd finished. "Fucking *hell.*"

Then she tucked that away—because there was still nothing she could do about it at the moment—went downstairs, gave Jordyn the menstrual cup.

"I'm going to go up to bed," she murmured to Josh. He'd finished putting on a game featuring the team the Gold would be playing the following night, and she knew it was less for entertainment and more for research.

Fuck, she loved him.

Fuck, she might be carrying his baby.

Fuck, she needed to go to bed and deal with this in the morning. Either that or sneak out and get a pregnancy test like a teenager.

Which was seeming like the more viable alternative.

Because it wasn't like she was going to be able to sleep.

Not with all her Count from *Sesame Street* intoning—one, two, three days late, ah-ah-ah, four, five, six days late, ah-ah-ah—

"You okay?" he asked, frowning.

Probably because she was slowly going insane and turning into a vampiric puppet.

Oh, and maybe because he'd asked her a question and she was just staring at him.

Right.

"I'm fine." She forced a smile. "Just tired."

"I'm sorry we crashed your day off," Jordyn said softly, and the guilt in her expression killed Jess.

Hurrying over, she took Jordyn's hands in her own. "Don't apologize," she said quickly. "I'm so glad to have met you guys. Though next time, I'll take it without the bedside talk." This time her smile wasn't forced, especially when Jordyn giggled. "But honestly, I haven't been sleeping well and we played tourist all day. I'd forgotten how exhausting that is."

"Exhausting *they* are, you mean," Jordyn said softly.

"Also honestly."

Her eyes danced. "Well, if nothing else, my boys have energy."

"That they do." Jess squeezed her hand. "And I'm not gonna lie. I'm glad you're the one taking them to Disneyland and not me."

More laughter.

Less guilt.

Thank God.

Then Jordyn leaned forward and hugged Jess, her words soothing the panic, at least for the moment. "I like you," she said before she pulled back. "I like you for you, *and* I like you for my brother."

Jess had once been made of paper and paste, so many layers slathered together that it was both mask and shield.

But the Gold had been slowly peeling away at those layers over the years.

Josh had sliced right through them, reduced them to dust.

And Jordyn? Marcus and Samuel? They'd swept that dust right into the trash.

Jess was exposed and vulnerable...and okay.

She was *okay*.

Josh insisted on walking her up to bed, waiting while she changed into her pjs then tucked the covers over her, kissing her on the forehead before going back downstairs to finish the game and spend time with his sister.

And she knew that she wasn't just okay. She was...protected.

Safe.

Strong.

Valued.

She'd promised herself to never get deeply involved with a man again, because they would only tear her down, dismantle what she'd worked so hard to build.

But Josh built her up.

Had spent years doing it, all while fighting with her and getting along and with everything in between.

She only hoped that her counting—and its results—weren't about to blow all that to pieces.

FORTY

JOSH

He rolled over, expecting to find a woman beside him.

But when his eyes opened, it was to see that the bed was empty.

He'd peeled himself out of bed that morning to drop Jordyn and the boys at the airport, and when he'd stumbled back in, Jess had still been asleep.

So, he'd joined her.

Expecting to wake up with her next to him.

But all he found was a note.

I have a bunch of errands to run.
I'll see you at the game tonight.
-J

Scowling, he rolled back over and stretched.

Maybe he should be happy to have his bed to himself, especially since he and Jess had gone zero to one hundred, and Jordyn and the boys had shown up, and the likelihood of him having much alone time in the future wasn't very high.

Between games and practices and travel, he'd be surrounded by people.

And Jess.

All of which he liked, which was why rolling over on the mattress just felt wrong. Empty.

They'd been apart a week, hadn't had their day yesterday.

And today—tonight—work.

Sigh.

"It's one morning," he muttered. "Get it together, man."

Plus, when he grabbed his phone to start clearing off notifications, he saw it was almost noon. So, it wasn't even an *entire* morning. It would be more like a couple of hours.

Then he'd roll into the rink, do all his prep, stretching, and PT, and before he knew it—Game Time.

But after the game, the rest of Jess's night was his.

Muhaha.

He texted his woman, letting her know he was thinking of her, then put on a podcast—random nerddom stuff—and hopped in the shower. After he'd scrubbed, buffed, and rubbed (himself with a towel, not his dick, for the dirty-minded folk), he checked his phone.

No text back.

Maybe she'd gone out on her bike and couldn't respond at the moment.

He missed her, but she was busy, and he needed to stop being co-dependent and get on with his shit. He had bills to pay, groceries to pick up, a life to live.

A woman to fuck...but—

Yeah, that could wait until tonight.

Unfortunately.

Scowling, he oiled his beard—gotta keep that baby soft—got dressed, and left the house. And if when he drove to the grocery store he went a bit out of his way to see if Jess was home...then call him co-dependent.

Alone and co-dependent though.

Because Jess wasn't home.

———

"Seventeen." Brit tossed the hacky sack to Logan.

"Eighteen." Logan to Ben.

"Nineteen." Ben lofted it up.

But *too* up.

It hit the ceiling and even though Blue dove for it, the ball dropped. (And wouldn't *that* be a fun thing to explain to Mandy? *How did Blue break his ass? Oh, only because we were playing our dumbass game of hacky sack and he decided to leave it all on the line just so we could get our twenty touches).*

Groans echoed around them, but they were good-natured.

By this point, everyone had taken a turn fucking up on the later touches and knew their competitive asses hated to be the one doing the fucking-up. So, there were groans and a few teasing remarks, but just as quickly Ethan shagged down the ball again, touches were being countered, and Ben was back in the game.

Ben's head wasn't, though.

Not even when Brit sent it to him, and he got the thirteenth touch.

Nor when the team got to twenty.

Something had triggered him.

Right. Okay. The point was to get everyone loose and comfortable, not tense and pissed because they'd fucked up a stupid game.

Plenty of other stuff got fucked day-to-day, play-to-play.

The point was regrouping and battling back.

"Ben," he said, moving after his teammate when they'd gotten their twenty touches and everyone began breaking off to get ready for the game. "What's the matter?"

Ben shook his head. "I'm fine, man."

He wasn't fine.

Not in the fucking least.

Anyone with eyes could see that.

Dark circles. Lines etched into the corners of his mouth. Shadows and pain and something like worry grounding into his expression.

"Hey." Josh snagged his shoulder when Ben started to take off again. "Wait—"

"I'm not a fucking charity case."

Josh's fingers tightened. "I know, I just—"

Ben shoved him.

That was so shocking and out of character that Josh's hand dropped, but before he managed to say anything, or pin Ben's ass to the wall and demand that his teammate tell him what the fuck was going on, Ben shoved him again, making him drop the hacky sack and stumble back a step, and by the time Josh regained his balance, Ben was disappearing down the hall.

What the fuck was that?

Josh had no clue, but he was going to find out.

Later.

After Ben had a chance to cool down.

Sighing, he collected the ball, started toward the training suite. He needed some tape for his wrists—something Mandy told him did absolutely nothing, but something he did anyway because he was a superstitious hockey player and had done it for years. Plus, it would give him an excuse to see Jess.

She hadn't texted him back before he'd gotten to the rink, and since his phone was in his locker, he couldn't call her.

At this point in the pregame prep, they weren't supposed to have any distractions...no phones, no curvy brunettes who fucking *owned* him.

But just happening to run into her wouldn't be a distraction.

Right?

Grinning, he popped his head into the training suite, swiped the roll of tape under Mandy's watchful—and rolling—eyes then continued down the hall to the former conference room, now kitted out video room.

TVs all over.

Desks and computers (and a few interns manning them).

Dani, headphones on, fingers flying on the keyboard.

And...his heart rolled over in his chest, exposed its vulnerable underbelly, his woman at her desk, pulling out her laptop.

She looked...tired.

Worried. More than a little on edge.

Striding over to her only took a couple of seconds. "What is it, sweetcheeks? Did that asshole call you again?" He reached into his pocket, prepared to call Pascal and forgetting for a moment about not having his cell. When all he pulled out was material, he remembered, and then, anyway, Jess was talking.

"Not Caleb," she said. "I haven't heard anything about him."

Her tone was off.

Shit.

"Was it yesterday?" he asked. "Was meeting them this soon too much?"

Her face gentled. "No, baby," she whispered, stroking his jaw. "It was fine. Great, actually. I...I hadn't ever had *that*. Enjoying hanging out with my family, not getting yelled at. I know you say that you missed out on a lot by playing hockey, but they *love* you, Josh. They know and are attached to you in a way that tells me you've put the effort in."

"I've spent most of my life states away from them."

"And *I* spent most of my life in my family's house, and don't have the relationship you do." She smiled. "Don't make me admit that I spied on you during Family Day and saw that the rest of them act the same with you. Oh, Uncle Josh, tell me about that goal. Oh, Uncle Josh, that time you got the game-winner was awesome! Oh, Uncle Josh, will you sign my jersey? Oh—"

He clamped his hand over her mouth. "You've made your point. Plus, I've already decided—thanks to you—that I'm going to be there whether they like it or—*ew!*"

She'd licked his palm.

"And *that* right there, folks, is what I learned from *my* family," she said, reaching over and high-fiving Dani, telling him that she'd no doubt learned that from one of the guys. "Trickery and..."

"Licking?" he asked dryly, wiping his hand on his sweats.

A grin. "Something like that."

"Well," he said, tucking a strand of her hair behind her ear. "Now that you've both made fun of me *and* licked me—"

"You know I'm just teasing," she said, expression solemn, "and it's only because your family so obviously adores you." Her fingers brushed through his beard. "It's just a little funny you had a hard time seeing it."

He *hadn't* seen it.

He hadn't understood.

Not until his mom had clued him in.

Now that mix of guilt and distance, having missed birthdays and holidays and inside jokes alike and the guilt that came with that was subsiding.

He was going to be there.

No matter what.

Just...like how he felt joining this team.

Not quite part of the inner circle. On the outside looking in, not being able to fill those shoes and live up to the expectations. But he'd pushed beyond that without even realizing. He'd been present with the rookies and he'd brought a piece of himself with the pregame rituals, had taken the teasing and shit-giving, lobbed it back. He'd chased Brit's ass around the arena.

His family had been one circle. His team the other.

He'd been smack between the two, but *in* them.

Or so he'd thought.

Until Jess had made him see different, made him understand that he could make the circles wider, make them one, make himself a place in it.

"And it's all because of you," he murmured, pressing a kiss to her forehead.

Her brows furrowed. "What?" A beat. "Is this something to do with the licking?"

A chuckle. "No, sweetcheeks. I just...realized that I made the inner circle of my family wider, found my spot in it, and"—he stroked her cheek—"that's all thanks to you."

Jess's face softened. "That was all you." Her expression sobered. "And seriously, baby, I won't tease you about your family if it bothers you."

"I like your teasing." He tugged her ponytail. "As long as it comes with a side of licking."

"Ew."

They both swiveled, saw Dani and Ethan were shamelessly listening in—the former pounding Hot Tamales like it was her life's calling, the latter probably taking mental notes to share in the locker room.

Ask Josh if he gave a fuck.

That would be *no*.

"Go on," Ethan said, pretending to be writing things down. "Please, share some more inner secrets."

Josh launched the roll of tape at him. "You're an asshole." He turned to Jess. "And *you're* the love of my life." Her eyes went wide. "Something"—he winced as he lightly cupped her cheek— "I should probably have told you in a much more private and romantic setting, but it's the truth, sweetcheeks." His lips tipped up, voice dropping. "I fell for you when you yelled at me."

Silence.

Wide eyes.

Lips parting and no words emerging.

Then she whispered, "Which time?" and he knew that he would never, *ever* regret loving her.

He grinned. "*Every* time."

"Man must be in deep," Ethan said.

Josh glared, but Jess's giggle drew his focus back to her. "I do yell at you a lot."

"Did," he corrected. "You *did* yell. But now that we're together, I can just orgasm you into submission."

Another *ew* from Ethan.

Josh ignored him.

"So long as that orgasming doesn't happen in this room then I'm good with it," Dani quipped.

He ignored her, too.

"No promises," Jess said, reaching for Josh and pulling him close. "Because I'm going to kiss him, and the man is an excellent kisser and—"

A knock on the door had them all glancing up, seeing Ben in the doorway.

"Sorry," he said. "Bernard wanted me to let you guys know that there's a team meeting in ten minutes."

Dani glanced at Ethan. "About the captaincy, you think? I can't believe you guys haven't voted yet."

"Not sure." Ethan's eyes hit Josh's. "I don't think we've done anything to get yelled at. Not yet anyway."

"Well, you'd better get to that meeting," Jess said, shoving him lightly. "I don't want to be responsible for any yelling besides my own."

Warmth in his heart expanding out. "I love you," he whispered.

She opened her mouth—

He placed a finger over her lips. "Tell me later." A brush of his lips over her forehead. "When I can't get in trouble for excellent kisses leading to orgasms."

A flick of her tongue (which was dangerous because it would eventually lead to *his* orgasms). "Okay," she whispered. "Go kick some ass out there." A nod toward her monitor. "I'll be watching."

"Creepy *and* beautiful," he said, leaning in to press a kiss across her lips. Then another, just for good measure, running his thumb under each eye, grazing the dark circles there. "Are you sure you're good?"

"Fine." Something flashed within those blue depths. "We'll talk later, I promise. Now *go*," she ordered, pushing him back.

Grinning, he turned from her, saw Ethan rubbing Dani's stomach.

Lucky bastard.

He'd love to have kids one day, to build his own family, his own inner circle.

To build it with Jess.

Because he knew as he walked toward the door, clapping Ben on the shoulder and thanking him for tracking them down, he and Jess would both make damn sure that their circle would always have room for more.

FORTY-ONE

JESS

Dani was grinning.

But she didn't say anything until she'd asked the interns to go and retrieve some cables (which they absolutely did not need).

The moment the door closed behind them, she swiveled in her seat and squealed.

"I have *never* been part of a patented Gold Happily Ever After. Until tonight that is," she added, scooting her chair toward Jess. "He loooooooves you," she sang.

A roll of her eyes. "Never been a part of one, except for your own, that is."

Dani waved a hand, as if to say, *Pish-posh, that doesn't matter.* "Being part of one is something, *witnessing* it is a whole other. No wonder Mandy, Brit, and Rebecca are so obsessed with matchmaking. It's a freaking *high.*"

Dani turned and began tapping merrily on her keyboard.

"I think that baby has gone to your head."

Dani shrugged. "Probably." Then tossed a grin over her shoulder. "I know that Josh has gone to *yours.*"

Good God.

It wasn't like she hadn't gleefully watched several happen over the years, but Jess finally knew why people were obsessed with everyone else's happy endings, it got the focus off of everyone having their noses in *their* business.

Maybe she should take up matchmaking herself.

Jordyn could use a man that wouldn't fuck around on her.

Then everyone else would be focused on *that* instead of Jess and Josh. Though, of course, that would mean setting Josh's sister up with someone on the team.

And there weren't too many single guys on the team.

Hmm.

Something to ponder.

Especially since the gleam in Dani's eyes told Jess that her friend wasn't going to give up on crowing about her matchmaking any time soon.

"How's the baby?" she asked, both because she wanted to know, and also because it was a much-needed distraction.

Dani's smile was a thing of beauty. "Our little nugget is doing good. Fourteen weeks next Monday. Of course, our timing wasn't quite right because if he or she comes early, the team will—hopefully—be in the middle of playoffs. But that's a worry for another day." A few clicks. "Now dish, honey. How's *your* baby?"

Jess had started to turn back to her desk.

It was getting near puck drop, and she had lots to do.

Dani's question had her freezing.

"What are you talking about?" Jess asked as she turned back, going for innocent.

"Um"—a wave toward Jess, a no-nonsense expression on her face—"your hand on your stomach, you sneaking off to puke after Ethan brought me in that pasta I've been craving—"

Jess shuddered, her hand indeed on her stomach.

But mostly because the memory of the way that sauce had smelled...bleh.

"You," Dani said, nibbling on her bottom lip, "can hate me

for this later, but I knocked over your purse earlier. I saw the positive test."

Oh.

Oh.

She didn't know why she'd brought it with her. She'd just taken it—and six others—earlier, and instead of throwing it away like she'd done the others, she'd put it in her purse.

To show Josh.

But not before the game, and now especially not with that curveball he'd just thrown her.

She needed to make it special.

She needed...to do something besides shoving something she'd peed on in his face and announcing that she was freaking the fuck out.

Oh.

And excited too.

It was too soon. But...she already loved the little peanut.

Would she or he have Josh's deep brown eyes? Or his black hair? Maybe her nose or lips or—

"I hope you washed your hands," she said quietly, fingers toying with the strap of her purse.

Dani chuckled. "No hiding—behind sarcasm or snark or otherwise."

"You like my sarcasm and snark."

"Damn right, I do, but Jess, honey." Her voice went careful. "It's a lot and really fast and...I just...are you happy?"

"I love you."

It was a total blurt and the first time she'd said that seriously (meaning not to a person who'd brought her a malt from the Dairy) in years.

But it was the truth, and she was wide open and vulnerable and sharing all sorts of shit.

But she'd been doing a lot of that lately.

And she hadn't spontaneously combusted.

"And I'm happy," she added while Dani gaped at her. "Very

happy. Happy in a way I'd always thought was impossible. Is it too soon and bad timing and unexpected and from a time when I didn't use my brain? Yes, to all."

"But?" Dani asked.

Because her friend knew there was a *but.*

"But I think it's going to be okay. Or at least I know *we're*"—there her hand went again, resting on her belly—"going to be okay."

Dani's expression was soft.

And then her eyes went damp.

And, hell, *Jess's* eyes went damp.

Dani sniffed.

Jess sniffed.

"Shit," Dani whispered.

She'd second that. "We're screwed, aren't we?"

"You mean because the Gold have just signed up for nine months of two watering pots in the video booth?"

Jess nodded. "Precisely."

"Well, watering pots or not, who are we going to fix up next?"

Now her lips curved up. "I have an idea about that."

Just like she now had an idea about telling Josh...

And it wasn't going to involve shoving the pee stick in his face.

Forty-Two

JOSH

The meeting ended up just being a chalk talk, but before he got suited up, Bernard's eyes caught his, and he inclined his head toward the hall.

He'd be lying if he said he was totally comfortable being pulled into a meeting with the head coach.

After he'd been pulled into a meeting with the team.

But this was professional hockey, and if he was going to get reamed for some indiscretion or another, at least it was going to happen in private. So he didn't delay, just walked into Bernard's office and took the seat that his coach indicated.

Then he braced.

Because that was the moment Bernard dropped a giant bomb on him.

———

His head was still spinning three hours later when he stepped off the ice.

Still spinning when he finished his post-game cooldown (running the stairs after Brit, stretching, a little bike).

Rotating as he showered.

Wobbling as he walked down the hall and into the video suite...

To find it empty.

The lights were out, and there was a distinct absence of two lovely, talented women, one of whom was *his.*

He pulled out his phone to call her, saw that there was a text on his screen.

Meet you at my place.

Disappointment coiled through him, a sharp shove of emotions that sent him spinning faster.

"Damn," he muttered, adjusting his bag, and turning for the hall, for the exit to the arena, and for his car.

Fatigue dragged at him, clawing through his quads, lying heavy on his biceps, but he pushed through it and stopped at the Dairy, getting nothing for himself but picking up a mint chocolate chip shake for Jess.

Torture.

His mouth actually watered, especially since he couldn't even have his vanilla cone since it wasn't a Cheat Day.

But he loved her, and she loved the shakes, and...he wanted to spoil her a bit.

He did steal a brownie piece off the top, because he wasn't made of stone, for fuck's sake. It was there and tempting, and hell if that one bite nearly undid him.

Thankfully, just as he was contemplating throwing his diet out the window and downing that shake, he pulled up to Jess's house.

It was dark, which was weird.

But he'd taken a little longer than normal with the stop at the Dairy.

Maybe she'd gone to lie down or was in the shower?

"Right," he muttered, snagging the cup. If it was the first, she was about to find herself on her feet—or at least on her back. He needed her. If it was the second, well then, he supposed it would be more time on her feet, only this time with the special addition of water.

Grinning, he got out of the car—and good God, his *legs*—then walked (hobbled, *thanks, Brit*) up to the front door, digging out the key she'd given him a few days back.

But as he went to put it in the lock, the door slid inward.

Not locked.

Not even latched.

What the fuck?

He pushed the door wider, flicked on the hall light. "Jess?" he called, moving into the kitchen, turning on more lights as he went. But it was empty, along with the family room and her office, the bathroom, her bedroom.

"What the fuck?" he said, out loud this time, checking the final room, the guest bedroom, and finding it empty.

He pulled out his phone to check her message. Maybe she'd meant his place?

But as he started to unlock it, a call came through.

"Hello?" he answered, expecting Jess's voice, expecting her to tell him that she'd messed up and was currently in his bed and that she would make it up to him with copious orgasms, lots of oral sex, and then extra regular sex for the inconvenience.

Not that there was anything *regular* about Jess, sex or otherwise.

But the voice that replied wasn't Jess's.

The voice didn't even belong to a woman.

It—

"Josh, it's Pascal."

"It's about Caleb."

Not a question. The truth in Josh's gut spoken aloud.

Gut churning, he looked around the empty house, remembered the front door, the lock not used, the latch not engaged, and he knew.

Knew.

"Yes."

The cup dropped out of his hand, splattering his pants, the floor, the wall of the hallway with green and black.

FORTY-THREE

JESS

It had taken a long time at the store to figure out the best way to tell Josh that she was pregnant.

A long time because even though she'd had an idea of the words she wanted to use, she still needed to figure out the execution. And for that, she'd been stuck with a twenty-four-hour grocery store and the selections *there* were limited to Halloween candy (not on the diet plan), a card (could definitely be cute), flowers (he didn't really seem like a flower kind of guy), and the item she'd eventually settled on.

The bag crinkled as she slung it onto her arm, tucking her purse on her other one, and squeezing past Josh's car.

He'd taken up most of the driveway, probably thinking that she was already inside.

Of course, she hadn't realized it would take so long to find the perfect vessel to reveal something like this.

Something that told him she paid attention and loved him back.

Something that said she was excited and scared but wanted this and hoped he did, too.

Something that...

"Isn't going to get said at all if you keep standing in the drive-way, Jessica White," she muttered.

Right.

Into the house she needed to go.

The lights were blazing. Her *nerves* were firing on all cylinders.

And—

"Just go."

She moved around his car, up the stairs to the porch, in through the wide-open door, and...the scene inside didn't make any sense.

A Dairy cup on the floor.

Mint chocolate shake splattered in all directions.

Brownie bits on her wall.

And Josh, on his knees, phone glued to his ear, the other grip-ping his hair.

Holy fuck, what had happened?

She dropped her bag, her purse onto the floor, ran over to him. "Josh. Josh!" She grabbed at his face, tried to turn him toward her. "What's the matter? What's happened?"

Slow motion.

His neck rotated.

His eyes came to hers, held for one, two, *three.*

Then they went wide, and he shuddered, hard enough to nearly knock her hands off, but she held fast. "Josh, baby. What's going on?"

Carefully, he peeled one hand free from his face then shifted, placing his phone between them and hitting the button for the call to go on speaker. Nothing for a moment, and then Pascal's voice came on. "He's in county jail. Picked up just after that second call a couple of weeks ago and booked under a fake ID. That, along with the harassing calls, the pound of cocaine in his car, and the unregistered gun, means that he did my job for me." A rough chuckle. "He's going away and going to be away for a good long while."

The puddle of milkshake was crawling toward her knee.

But the only thing she could process was that Caleb was locked up.

The last piece of her was free.

He. Was. Locked. Up.

"Wow," she whispered.

"Jess?" Pascal said. "You're there?"

"I'm here."

"You heard?"

She nodded even though he couldn't see her. "I heard," she said quickly when she realized.

A beat then a gruff reply. "Left the same in a message on your cell, just in case you missed anything."

"Okay. I—I don't know what to say, except thank you."

"No thanks necessary," was his only response, and when she said goodbye a few minutes later, he didn't reply.

Okay, well, he *grunted* in reply, but that was it before he ended the call and left her and Josh in the milkshake-covered hall.

Her man—her big, broad, hockey-playing *man*—was shaking.

Positively rattling in the hallway, fingers trembling as he reached for his cell.

"I got it," she said, snagging it and locking the screen. "Now, baby." She ignored the growing puddle soaking into her pants, took his hands in her own. "What happened?"

"I—*you*—"

He slipped his hands free, dropped his head into them.

A breath, his words slightly muffled. "I got here, and you weren't and the door wasn't locked or latched and then you hadn't waited for me, just sent that text and—" His head lifted, eyes locking with hers. "I thought Caleb—I thought you might be, that I wasn't here to help you and—" Another breath, voice cracking, and she got it, finally understood.

"I'm here," she told him. "I'm safe."

And she kept telling him, kept repeating it.

Until the trembling ceased.

Until the terror in his eyes cleared.

Until he wrapped his arms around her and held her tight. "I'm so sorry about the door," she whispered. "I was frazzled this afternoon, and I must not have shut it all the way and I mean, I can't believe I didn't lock it, but..."

He leaned back, his gaze focused solely on her. "But you were frazzled?"

She nodded.

A brush of his lips on her cheek, sounding much more like himself when he asked, "Why were you frazzled, sweetcheeks?"

She was sitting in a puddle of milkshake, after her ex had intruded on her life again—though this time it thankfully had a happy fucking ending, one that she hoped would mean that he'd never be intruding again—and the entirety of her cute plan to tell Josh the life-changing news had just been dropped on the floor.

Literally.

The bag going one way. Her purse with the pee stick the other.

Neither of them were where she wanted them.

Which was in Josh's hands so that he could—hopefully—be as happy as she was.

"Hmm?"

"Why were you frazzled?" he asked.

"I—" She scrambled to her feet. "Hold that thought." Then she was down the hall, tracking footprints of milkshake but unable to really care. Maybe she should hold off on the news-telling, just put it off until their emotions weren't so all over the place. Probably she should stop grinding milkshake into her hardwood floor.

But...she didn't do any of that.

She ground that milkshake right in as she grabbed her purse and the plastic bag and brought them both back to Josh. "I—" A breath. "This is probably the wrong time for this, but—"

She shoved the plastic grocery bag at him.

Brows drawn together, he peeked inside. "Um," he said, pulling out the carton of vanilla ice cream she'd bought for him. "Thank you." The V didn't disappear. "I do like—"

"Open it."

His mouth opened, closed, but then he shrugged, tugged off the lid, and...

The ice cream was mush, melting on the edges, and the underside of the lid was covered with thick white goop.

Right.

This was not going to plan.

Think, White.

She grabbed the carton, set it to the side and then took the lid, using a finger to slop the goop off and revealed...

But will you share?

The V deepened. "I—"

She reached into her purse and pulled out the test.

"I..." she began as his face went pale, her words tumbling out. "Turns out the Plan B didn't work. And I realized last night when Jordyn and I were talking that I'd never actually gotten my period after I'd lied about it. Which could have been stress, but then I remembered I'd gotten that food poisoning and my boobs hurt and I started counting and when I got to weeks late instead of days..." She cleared her throat.

"Jess."

"I can be late sometimes," she hurried to say. "But not *weeks* late. And then I puked up all the food from yesterday and still no period and—"

"*Jess.*"

"And I didn't plan this, I swear. Well, I mean, I planned *this*— the whole wanting to tell you in a cute way because I'm fucking terrified, but I love you and I want this baby and—"

He kissed her, swallowing the rest of her words, kissing her until her brain was fuzzy and her heart thudded, and she wasn't blurting out an entire monologue and not letting him get a word in edgewise.

"You're pregnant?" he asked when they broke apart.

She nodded.

He grinned, a huge, bright smile that pierced her straight through the heart and filled her with sunshine.

"I know we're new and this is a lot and—"

His thumb dragging over her bottom lip. "You know what I was thinking tonight when I saw Dani with Ethan?"

She shook her head.

"I was jealous as hell because I wanted *that*." He cupped her jaw. "I want you. *All* of you. Every part and parcel and memory and life stage that comes our way. Is a baby a lot? Yeah. Is it faster than most people might advise? Of *fucking* course. But have I spent the last three years hoping for a chance with you? Yes." His hand slid into her hair. "And I'm not going to squander that chance, my future, the woman of my fucking dreams just because this happened. No fucking way."

Tap-dancing.

Her heart. Her pulse through her veins.

"Josh," she whispered.

"Are *you* happy?"

"Yes."

"Do *you* want the baby?"

"Yes."

His face was so fucking gentle that she felt like she was being wrapped in cotton candy. "Then we expand our circle to welcome one more in."

"Just like that?" she asked.

Fingertips massaging her scalp. "A really smart woman once convinced me that it was just *that* easy."

"I think I'd like that really smart woman."

"Probably"—he tugged her closer, making her squeak in surprise—"but she's mine and she's carrying my baby and she's going to—"

Amusement sliding through her. "Oh God, here we go with the orders."

"—she's going to come on my fingers and my tongue and my cock," he finished without missing a beat.

A wave of heat covering her from head to toe. "Oh?"

"Yup. *Oh*."

Nuzzling her throat, he pulled her a little closer, and she wrapped her arms around him, holding him as tight as she could manage, and no lie, she teared up a little bit when he gently ran his hand over her stomach.

But then something else occurred to her.

"Did we just both show our love with ice cream?"

A grin as he coaxed her back onto the mint-splattered rug and dropped a kiss to her belly. "I think we did."

She giggled. "So, our combined love language is ice cream."

Brown eyes on hers, so much love and joy in their depths that she knew she'd never again need to protect herself with paste and paper and layers of masks.

Her.

She could be just *her*.

And that was enough.

Would always be enough.

He dipped his finger into the carton of vanilla, reached up and smoothed it over her lips, his mouth curved up into a wicked smile. "Yup."

He kissed her, licking the ice cream off.

"It's not a Cheat Day," she protested.

A nip to the corner of her mouth. "It's not cheating if *you're* the one eating it."

"Oh," she asked lightly. "Is *that* how it works?"

He bent, kissed her until she'd forgotten what question she asked, so that it took a minute after him saying, "Yup," to connect with the query and have it make sense in her muddled mind.

Then she grinned, pushed him over onto his back and clambered on top of him. She dipped *her* finger into the ice cream and smoothed it along the skin of his throat, licking it up as it dribbled down, keeping her hands free so she could unbutton his shirt, revealing that gorgeous chest, the squeezable pecs, the flat, hard plane of his stomach.

"Well then," she said, scooping up some more of the treat. "I guess I found a whole new appreciation for vanilla."

In fact, she gained an entire carton's worth.

Laughter joined the love in his eyes.

And, funny story, it turned out that vanilla paired perfectly with mint chocolate chip.

Epilogue

Josh

"So," she asked, tracing a finger down his chest, "when were you going to tell me?"

He captured her fingers, lacing them with his own as they walked out of the arena. Jess had traveled with the team for this trip, and he had *plans*.

Plans that didn't involve him stopping and finding a supply closet.

Mostly because this wasn't the Gold Mine, and he didn't have any knowledge of the inner workings of its closet system.

A pinch to the skin on the back of his hand.

"What?" he asked innocently.

"When were you going to tell me?"

"About my wishing there was a supply closet nearby?"

Laughter in her eyes, her side pressing into his. "Really?" she asked. "A supply closet is what got us into this mess in the first place."

"No." He kissed the top of her head. "*That* was my romantic talk of wet dreams."

"Yup." A grin. "Just melted my heart."

Fingers in her hair, tilting her head back. A brush of his mouth over hers. "I think it melted something else."

She'd gone soft in his arms, just like she did every time he touched her, kissed her. But his words—even though they took a minute to process—earned him a swat. "You're terrible."

"I love you."

Soft again. "Thank you for the ginger ale," she whispered, smoothing her hand over his cheek.

He'd had a can brought to her because he'd seen the sheen on her skin, the paleness of her cheeks before they'd split up to prep for the game. She'd said she was fine, and his woman was a badass who'd escaped her past, was tough as nails, rode a motorcycle (though she'd put that on hold the moment she'd gotten the positive test), and as thus, she was determined to deal with the nausea on her own.

Mostly through a series of *I'm fine*s and *I'm okay*s.

Which he'd ignored.

His woman. His baby. His inner circle.

He was going to take care of her.

Which was why even though it had been seventy-two entire hours since he'd found out about the pregnancy, he'd spent most of that time reading. Learning.

If only he had some tape to study—though he supposed there probably *was* tape out there, but not of the variety he'd like to view.

Birth videos?

Too soon.

"You're feeling better," he said, and it wasn't a question. Her complexion had evened out and fatigue wasn't pinching at the edges of her mouth and eyes.

"I am." A faint smile. "Though I'm craving vanilla ice cream."

He chuckled. "You'd better stop right there because I *will* find a supply closet."

"Threats by orgasm," she murmured. "My favorite."

"*You're* my favorite."

Pink on her cheeks. "And the cheese has arrived," she murmured. "Just when I thought I'd gotten away with having a big, sexy hockey player who *wasn't* a cheeseball, the cheese shows up anyway."

A kiss to the tip of her nose. "I only speak the truth."

"Ugh. More cheese."

"Would it help if I told you that the cheese is accompanied with more orgasms?"

"In supply closets?" she asked archly.

"Maybe." He tugged her forward. "Though most of them involve our hotel room and the king-sized bed inside it."

Of course, they still had a flight to catch between now and then, but since his woman would be on the plane with him, he was going to see about sneaking up into the front and sitting with her instead of the guys in the back. On the way over to Colorado, she'd refused to move to the back, since that was where the players sat, and they were new and she was hormonal and she'd said she loved him, so he'd let that slide.

This plane ride he wasn't going to.

"Okay. That *might* be acceptable." She leaned forward, pushed open the door that led to the parking lot and the team's bus. "*If* you tell me why you *didn't* mention that C was going to be sewn on your jersey."

The guys had voted.

Apparently in some top-secret Gold voting ceremony that he hadn't been privy to because he'd been the only nominee.

The only player the guys thought would fit the role of captain.

Him.

It blew his fucking mind and it felt right and...he was going to give every bit of himself that he could to the team.

The conversation that Bernard had wanted to have wasn't because he was fucking up or needed to improve something, but because he was quote, "showing leadership, the guys looked up to him, and management thought that the future of the organization lay with him."

With. *Him.*

So, he'd been named captain.

Of the San Francisco Fucking Gold.

"It's not a big deal," he said.

Which was a total lie.

Jess dug her heels in, dragging him to a stop. "Baby," she whispered, smoothing her hand over his cheek again, and fuck if his heart didn't roll right over in his chest. Her voice went stern. "You are *so* full of shit." Fingers on his jaw, his lips. "It's a *big* fucking deal. They made you captain, baby. That's amazing."

"I still feel...I don't know, strange about it, I guess," he murmured. "It feels unreal, because I don't do what I do because I'm trying to fill a role. I just care about the guys and the team and—"

"Which is why you are the *perfect* choice."

His heart skittered.

"The *perfect* choice," she repeated. "You broke through my walls with sparkles and wet dreams." Light words, but seriousness in her brown eyes. "And by figuring out what I needed and giving it to me. Trust. Love. Respect. The occasional order." She grinned. "But seriously, I've known you for three years. I've watched you with the team and with me. I've fought with you. I've *loved* you. I've seen you, even when I didn't want to."

"Jess," he whispered.

"And God knows, if there is one person on this planet who is perfect for the position, it's you." She smiled. "Mostly because you can't see it."

"Sweetcheeks."

"You," she said and lightly tugged his beard. "I've watched you. I've seen it on the screen and off the ice—"

Blue came up beside them, punching him on the shoulder as he moved on by.

"Good game tonight, man," Blue said.

"That was your effort off the puck, bud," Josh replied, tugging Jess a little closer.

Who grinned, rose on tiptoe, lips hitting his ear. "And *that* is why they made the right choice," she whispered. "Mostly because they know that you'll rise to the role." A tap to his chest, to the spot over his heart. "Because of *this*. Because you have it in here. Because you love them. Because...it's instinct for you, baby."

Fuck, he loved this woman.

"Do you get me?" she asked, words still spoken directly into his ear. "Because no more self-doubt. No thinking you don't deserve this. You are an incredible—"

He turned his head, slanted his mouth across hers, tongue sliding between her lips, drawing her body flush against his, kissing her with every ounce of love he felt in his heart until his lungs threatened to explode.

Only then did he pull back.

Hear the bus-full of catcalls...saw his woman with bright pink cheeks.

"Rise to the role?" he asked, brows waggling once her eyes had cleared.

A glare.

Then a shake of her head, her giggles filling the air.

And a smile.

A real one. Not a mask. Not armor.

Just Jess.

"Come on," she murmured, taking his hand and drawing him forward.

Toward the bus and the team. Toward his future—*their* future. Toward a circle that wasn't ever going to be closed. Because he was going to make certain of that. Because he had Jess and he had hockey. He had his family by both blood and sweat— and sometimes a little extra blood, depending on where the pucks and sticks and skates hit.

All he ever wanted, all he'd dreamed.

No.

More.

"Um, Josh?"

They'd reached the door to the bus, but he turned back, seeing that Ben had stopped him.

"Got a second?" Ben asked.

With everything going on, Josh hadn't had a chance to circle back to him yet.

But he'd hadn't forgotten the interaction in the hall.

Because based on the ever-present dark circles beneath Ben's eyes, the lines that seemed permanently etched around the corners of his mouth, the hint of pain that never appeared to fully dissipate, Ben was wrestling with something big and fucked up and... he was asking Josh for a second.

Jess's face went soft.

She kissed his cheek, released his hand, and whispered, "Time to rise, baby."

———

JESS, SIX MONTHS LATER

Jordyn was...broken.

There was no other way to describe it.

The light that had been in her chocolate eyes, so similar to Josh's, was gone.

"I tried," she whispered, staring up at Jess, tears glistening and hopelessness etched into the lines of her face. "I always promised myself that I would never, *ever* tolerate cheating. But—" A sharp exhale. "If he'd wanted it, I would have taken him back. I *would* have."

A tear slid free, and Jess surreptitiously passed over a tissue, trying to hold it together herself while Josh and the boys messed around in the pool.

"You can stay here," she whispered. "For as long as you need."

"No."

Jess watched her wipe her eyes, pull some strength from somewhere, and compose herself.

"No," she said again. "I need to figure it out by myself."

"Bullshit."

Jordyn blinked.

"You're not alone," Jess said firmly. "And you're not doing this by yourself. First, you're family. Second"—here she allowed her lips to twitch slightly—"do you honestly think that *that man* is going to let you go it alone?"

Her hand rubbed the curve of her stomach.

"Spoiler alert. I tried that and got here."

Jordyn went still. Then blew out a breath, a quiet chuckle filling the air and a small smile on her face. "Yeah. That's a good point."

"I know."

That smile widened slightly at Jess's know-it-all tone.

"So, you and the boys are going to stay here until you get your feet under you and—"

"No."

Jess shot her a glare.

"You guys are starting your life together." And now it was Jordyn's turn to dish a little firmness back. "The boys and I will not intrude on that." Her chin lifted, shoulders straightening. "I have savings. We'll stay until I get us a place to rent nearby."

"I'm sure Josh can help you."

"Not with this," she said softly. "I know he would in an instant, and if things get really bad, I'll...you know." She sighed. "But I need to do this for them." A jerk of her chin to the pool. "And for me. I need to know that I can help us, that I can be there for them like they need."

Jess sniffed. "Sorry," she whispered when Jordyn glanced over. "Hormones."

Jordyn squeezed her hand. "Let's change the subject," she said. "The weather is nice and the boys are on spring break and I want to know all the things you're craving."

Jess laced their fingers together, allowed the diversion, mostly because an idea about where they would stay had begun to form in Jess's mind. "Besides boring vanilla?"

A flash of white teeth. "Yeah, besides Joshie's favorite. Which"—a nod to her belly—"tells us that you not finding out the baby's gender means nothing. That kid has *got* to be a boy."

"Maybe."

"No, maybes"—Jordyn took a sip of her wine—"it's—"

"Hey, Jor?" Jess interrupted, probably rudely.

But...ideas.

She'd moved in with Josh a couple of months back.

Her house was just sitting there empty, waiting on some repairs so she could rent it out, and her family needed a place to stay, one that was affordable (because Jess would offer it up for free, but she knew damn well that free and Jordyn weren't going to mix). They needed someplace that could be their own.

Totally their own.

And Jess's was empty and boring and beige.

They could do *anything*.

They could make it home.

"Jess?" Jordyn said when pregnancy brain had her not responding for long moments. "Are you okay? Is the baby—"

Jess spun in her chair.

"How do you feel about a small, but mostly-updated two-bedroom cottage in a nice neighborhood that's only about fifteen minutes from this one?"

Jordyn blinked.

And then...she smiled.

———

JORDYN, SIX MONTHS LATER

She sighed, brushing the hair off her forehead and reaching into the van for a box.

Not hers.

None of what was in front of her was hers.

It was Jess's—her future sister-in-law's—house, and her brother Josh's van. They weren't even her boxes. Not her house. Not her money because Josh had set up an account for her and the boys. Barely even her clothes, since she'd sold most of her belongings.

The boys' stuff was theirs, would *always* be theirs. She'd make certain of that.

They were going through enough, what with their father fucking their godmother, the person Jordyn had considered her best friend in the entire world. So yeah, fuck it. She would never *ever* make them give up anything, not so long as it was in her power to give it to them.

Which was why the minivan had been packed to the fucking brim with their stuff, so much so that she hadn't been able to see out the rearview on the drive down.

Her belongings? Gone for the most part.

The memories given away and sold and boxed away so that she didn't have think about them, deal with them.

A few outfits, clothes she'd need to find a job when she hadn't worked in a decade, wasn't even sure what skills she might have to offer.

Not as a wife. Or as a partner in bed. Or one outside of it.

She sucked at all of those roles apparently.

All of it.

In bed. In conversations. In—

"Everything," she whispered. "I suck at everything." A breath, or more accurately, a long, drawn-out sigh that attempted to expulse all the dark shit inside her head...and didn't make the least bit of difference in excising any of it.

Nope.

It was there, floating around, jabbing at her, reminding her how much of a failure she was.

Fun times.

"Beat yourself up later," she muttered. "Now is the time to get our stuff in the free house with the fridge stocked with free food with the free utilities and"—a grunt as she hefted—"free furniture and free pool and—"

Books.

Why did it have to be books?

Why did Marcus's prized possessions have to be books?

Probably for the same reason that Samuel's had to be Legos. Heavy, cumbersome belongings meet breakable mementos made of teeny tiny pieces that were impossible to keep together and then even more impossible to track down the evil, miniature pieces that always went missing.

And she had about eight more boxes of books to bring in.

Then at least as many of Legos.

Suitcases shoved and stacked and crammed onto the floor and passenger's seat. A cooler that was mostly empty of the sandwiches and drinks and snacks she'd packed for the boys. Of course, it had fueled the frequent bathroom stops, made the drive even longer.

Jess had been here to let them into her place, but then she'd needed to go to work.

So, Jordyn had been on her own.

Something she was used to.

Of course, she'd also promised to leave the boxes in the car because the team was coming over tomorrow and would help get her moved in.

She'd agreed because Jess had needed to go and, uh, do her freaking job.

But there was no way in hell that she was going to let Josh and his hockey team move her into the house he was letting her live in for pennies on the dollar (and not free only because Jordyn had demanded to pay at least *some* rent). The boys were asleep, their bellies full, having finally crashed after the long drive, watching the Gold and their uncle crush their opponents on TV, after the excitement of staying at Auntie Jess's house had faded.

There was no point in sitting in a quiet, mostly-empty house.

No point in sitting in the dark of the guest bedroom (because fuck all if she'd take the master from Josh, even if he was technically living with Jess now) wondering how a year ago, hell, six months ago, she'd thought her life was together and now it had all fallen apart.

A fucking mirage in the desert.

Gone like it had never been there in the first place.

"Books," she muttered. "I'm focusing on books. And starting over. And it will all be fine, and the boys will be fine, and *I'll* be—"

The bottom tore out on the box.

Books hit the ground, scattering like confetti, bouncing off her feet and hurting like hell (*unlike* confetti). They bounced along the sidewalk, disappearing beneath the car, bouncing into the bushes, dropping onto the damp grass.

Christ.

She dropped the box and then fell onto her knees, grabbing the books off the wet grass as fast as she could. "Fuck," she whispered, wiping Marcus's signed copy of *Captain Underpants* on her shirt. That was his favorite and now the cover was wet and a little wrinkly. It'd dry, but it wouldn't ever be the same as it was before.

It would function.

It would be fine.

But it wouldn't be the same.

A breath. Another. But, fuck, her eyes were stinging, her throat had closed up, and fucking tears, tears she hadn't let fall through the entire process of moving, of getting a lawyer, of finding her fucking best friend and husband in bed together, of trying to figure out the way forward began to fall.

Then her lungs began to hitch.

Sobs rose up and instead of swallowing them down like she had managed in the past couple of months, they escaped.

And she sat there in the driveway, forehead on her knees, clutching that damned book, crying her fucking eyes out.

Until a pair of arms wrapped around her, tugging her close to a hard male body.

She fought at first.

Then figured that her brother was as stubborn as she was, and anyway, her brother gave good hugs, and she was too tired to fight him and so she slumped over, rested her head on his chest, and just...gave in.

To the strong arms.

The warm hold.

The gentle hand sliding down her head.

But then he spoke.

And...

He wasn't Josh.

Scrambling, she jumped out of the hold, pushing back, lurching to her feet. "What the fuck?" she gasped. "Don't *touch* me—"

The man was tall and big. Much taller than her when he pushed up to standing, so much so that he practically towered over her. He studied her for a second, biceps pushing at the sleeves of his T-shirt, strong legs on display in his sweats.

A hockey player.

If his body hadn't given it away, the tattoos and beard would have.

And now that she got a closer look, Jordyn recognized him.

One of Josh's teammates.

B-something.

Barry? No.

Bartholomew? Nope. And her even considering that for a millisecond proved she was losing her mind.

Ben?

Better. And also correct.

This beautiful, *huge* man with the shadows in his eyes, shadows that called to the ones she carried was named *Ben*.

But she didn't know him, not really.

So when he reached in, reached for *her,* she jerked, started to back away, but instead of touching her or taking her into his arms, he only handed her a small stack of books. Books that would have been soaking in the grass the entire time she'd spent crying if he hadn't picked them up, she realized.

Marcus's treasures getting ruined.

Because *she'd* been crying.

Mutely, she took them, held them tight to her chest.

Then he turned away, and instead of leaving as she'd expected, he went to the back of the van, grabbed a box...

And walked right into the house like he owned the place.

————

Thank you for reading! I hope you loved meeting Jess and Josh as much as I did! The next book in the Gold Hockey series is COVERED. **She's his best friend's sister. He's going to keep her anyway.**

CLICK HERE TO GET COVERED NOW>

And if you enjoyed CAP, you'll love the bad boys of the Rush! This brand new hockey series begins with BIG PUCK ENERGY. *I played hard, and lived even harder...*

CLICK HERE TO PREORDER BIG PUCK
ENERGY NOW>

———

Big Puck Energy

AXEL

I groaned and tried valiantly to open my eyes, but my head was pounding, so the moment light passed my lids, I slammed them closed again.

"Fuck," I muttered, running a hand over my face—

Or trying to.

Because it was impossible.

No, not *impossible*. I frowned, forced my lids open, ignoring the sunlight stabbing at my brain.

Only *one* was impossible because...it was handcuffed to some sort of rail above my head. The other hand was at my side, pinned half under my ass. *That* one was just numb, and I moved it carefully, nerves prickling, tingles shooting up my arm.

What kind of freaky shit had I gotten into last night?

I squinted, trying to remember, but not able to recall anything more than swatches of noise and things breaking and booze going down smoother and smoother.

Until it had tasted like water.

That's probably why it hurt so much to open my eyes today.

A foot kicked mine, and not lightly either.

"Ow," I muttered, glancing up and squinting at the sun. Someone was standing there, not that I could see more than a wavering black silhouette.

"Whatcha doing down there?"

Female.

My mind perked up. My brain focused enough for the wavering shadow to steady, to turn into something...delicious.

Small. Curvy. *Delicious.*

"Depends." I said, curving my lips into the smile that had gotten me pussy from the time I was fifteen. "You coming down here to experience it?"

Silence.

Long and quiet enough that I could hear the birds chirping and the insects buzzing, and seriously, what the fuck time of the day was it?

I hadn't been up this early in...

I couldn't remember. Or maybe I *could* have remembered if the woman standing over me hadn't started laughing. Not a gentle, quiet, tinkling laugh like so many of the puck bunnies that hung at the rink and wanted a piece of me before I hit it big, but a loud and hearty guffaw that shouldn't have been sexy and yet somehow was.

Roughened velvet.

I wanted to fuck her, and I hadn't even seen her face.

But hell, the way the shadows had coalesced into something curvy and petite paired with that sexy unhindered laugh, and I was hard.

"Baby—" I began.

The *click* of a shotgun cocking had my mind rocketing well away from my dick.

Okay, this wasn't nearly as amusing.

Or sexy.

"Hold on a—" I tried.

The laugh had disappeared, taut intensity had surrounded him. "I'm going to talk." Deadly words. "And you're going to speak when I give you permission to do so."

Ice. Orders.

They both began prickling down my nape, curling in my stomach like a poisonous snake prepared to strike.

Meh.

Just call me Steve Irwin.

Of course...there was also that sting ray.

And I had a shotgun pointed at my head.

So...right. I kept my snark locked (albeit loaded, *heh*). The sun, on the other hand, was a total bitch, and since I was tired of squinting against it, I dropped my gaze to my feet.

The woman nudged me with her foot again—this time hard enough to hurt. "I'd advise that you keep your eyes on mine."

"I would," I said, getting frustrated now, that snake darting forward and baring its fangs as I stupidly reached out to grab it, "if I could fucking see you instead of burning my fucking irises by staring into the *sun!*"

Silence.

Shit.

I clenched my teeth against an apology and waited, trying to hold back a wince, expecting the shotgun to go off.

Instead, she surprised me by stepping to the side so that I could look up at her and see something besides blinding white light.

Blinking a few times to steady my vision, I felt my cock get even harder.

Fuck.

She was a porn film come to life.

A cowboy hat on her head, a low-cut white tank covered by a flannel only halfway buttoned up, skintight jeans, and boots.

Not cowboy boots, but sturdy, brown leather boots with bright red laces.

They were well-worn. They were dirty.

They did *not* fit with the curvy little woman in front of me.

"Baby—"

The gun leveled at my chest.

"I don't believe I gave you permission to speak," she gritted out.

Probably, I should shut up, but I'd never been great with authority or people telling me what to do. "I don't believe I asked *you* to wake me up and point a shotgun at me," I snapped.

Slowly, she lifted one hand and tilted back her hat.

That snake coiled again.

Only this time, I could admit it was coiled in the corner in fear, hoping to not be provoked, because it wasn't sure it would survive if it struck again.

"Well," she said lightly, "I normally point shotguns at people who show up unwelcome on my porch, but I *especially* point shotguns at those who show up unwelcome *and* spend their free time tearing up my town." The gun didn't waver, not in the least. "So, what the fuck are you doing here, Axel Finnigan?"

Come to think of it, I didn't *know* what I was doing here.

Last I remembered, I'd been cuddled up to a rather tall blonde and her hands had been sliding beneath the waistband of my jeans.

Had I fucked her?

I couldn't remember.

And it hurt too much when I tried to, so I just let it go. The blonde wouldn't be the first girl I didn't remember sleeping with. If I was being truthful—something I despised—she also probably wouldn't be the last.

"I don't know," I said, squinting against the sun and trying to actually see where I was. I should also probably be sorting out how I'd become handcuffed to the railing, but...meh.

I'd been in stranger scenarios.

One time I'd woken up floating in a pool, naked, sunburned to hell and precariously perched on one of those inflatable rafts shaped like a giant pineapple. Another time, I'd woken up naked and with half a watermelon (half-eaten to go with the theme) over my junk. Still once more, I'd peeled back my lids and woken up between three nude people—*people* because only two of them female.

The common theme was nakedness.

Yeah, yeah I liked to take off my clothes.

But I had a nice body, and *people* didn't seem to mind.

Not to mention, I grew up in locker rooms, grew up with stall showers where shyness and covering my junk wasn't necessary. I'd seen more dick than most porn stars, but it was part of the game—well, not the game so much as the cleaning up process afterward.

As was the partying and the waking up naked—and sometimes still drunk.

Not much fazed me. Not the dicks or the nakedness or the women and booze. Every time I'd ever woken up in a pesky scenario, I'd just shrugged, dragged my sorry ass out of there and stumbled home.

Sometimes remembering (the watermelon had been a joke by my linemate). Sometimes not (like not remembering if I fucked the blonde from last night).

But I'd never woken up like this.

First, I wasn't clothed.

Second, I was handcuffed.

Third, I was staring down the barrel of gun, the other side held by a gorgeous woman who appeared to be looking for any excuse to pull the trigger.

"You don't know," she said slowly, as though I were an idiot.

And maybe I was. I hadn't gone to college. I'd barely graduated high school. I was good at exactly three things—hockey, fucking, and drinking.

The middle skill was what prompted my next reply.

"Do you have a bondage fantasy?" I asked, rattling the cuff. "Because I'd be happy to oblige."

The gun dropped further...pointing at my dick.

I watched her finger tighten on the trigger, and I felt fear—*real fear*—for the first time in a long, *long* time.

But I couldn't even push out the request to ask her not to shoot me.

All I *could* do was stand there and watch and cringe and . . . *wait.*

Just when I thought she was definitely going to fire, she spun on her heel, stomped back across the porch, and disappeared into the house.

The door slammed.

And silence descended again.

CLICK HERE TO PREORDER BIG PUCK
ENERGY NOW>

———

And don't forget to dive into the the sexy, sweet, and close-knit Breakers Hockey crew. The first book in the series, BROKEN, is now live!
It is sexy, hot, adorable and such a fun read. You will not be able to put this down!" —Amazon Reviewer

———

I so appreciate your help in spreading the word about my books, including sharing with friends! Please leave a review on your favorite book site!

You can also join my Facebook group, the Fabinators, for exclusive giveaways and sneak peeks of future books.

SIGN UP FOR ELISE FABER'S NEWSLETTER HERE: https://www.elisefaber.com/newsletter

———

Hate missing Elise's new releases? Love contests, exclusive excerpts and giveaways?

Then signup for Elise's newsletter here!

http://eepurl.com/bJnmEj

———

And join Elise's fan group, the Fabinators (https://www.facebook.com/groups/fabinators) for insider information, sneak peaks at new releases, and fun freebies! Hope to see you there!

———

GOLD HOCKEY SERIES

ALSO BY ELISE FABER

Coasting

Centered

Charging

Caged

Crashed

A Gold Christmas

Cycled

Caught

Cap

Covered

Breakers Hockey (all stand alone)

Broken

Boldly

Breathless

Ballsy

Rush Hockey

Big Puck Energy

Filthy Puckboy

So Pucking Over It

Love, Action, Camera (all stand alone)

Dotted Line

Action Shot

Close-Up

End Scene

Meet Cute

Love After Midnight (all stand alone)

Rum And Notes

Virgin Daiquiri

On The Rocks

Sex On The Seats

Life Sucks Series **(all stand alone)**

Train Wreck

Hot Mess

Dumpster Fire

Clusterf*@k

FUBAR

Roosevelt Ranch Series **(all stand alone, series complete)**

Disaster at Roosevelt Ranch

Heartbreak at Roosevelt Ranch

Collision at Roosevelt Ranch

Regret at Roosevelt Ranch

Desire at Roosevelt Ranch

Phoenix Series **(read in order)**

Phoenix Rising

Dark Phoenix

Phoenix Freed

Phoenix: LexTal Chronicles **(rereleasing soon, stand alone, Phoenix world)**

From Ashes

In Flames

To Smoke

KTS Series (all stand alone, series complete)

Riding The Edge

Crossing The Line

Leveling The Field

Scorching The Earth

Cocky Heroes World

Tattooed Troublemaker

ABOUT THE AUTHOR

USA Today bestselling author, Elise Faber, loves chocolate, Star Wars, Harry Potter, and hockey (the order depending on the day and how well her team -- the Sharks! -- are playing). She and her husband also play as much hockey as they can squeeze into their schedules, so much so that their typical date night is spent on the ice. Elise is the mom to two exuberant boys and lives in Northern California. Connect with her in her Facebook group, the Fabinators or find more information about her books at www.elise-faber.com.

facebook.com/elisefaberauthor

amazon.com/author/elisefaber

bookbub.com/profile/elise-faber

instagram.com/elisefaber

tiktok.com/@elisefaberauthor

goodreads.com/elisefaber

www.ingramcontent.com/pod-product-compliance
Lightning Source LLC
Chambersburg PA
CBHW061918130726
47908CB00017B/1853